HOLLYWOOD MAD DOGS

WITTLIFF COLLECTIONS LITERARY SERIES

Steven L. Davis, General Editor

HOLLYWOOD
MAD DOGS

A Novel

Edwin "Bud" Shrake

Foreword by
Steven L. Davis

Afterword by
Alan and Ben Shrake

TEXAS A&M UNIVERSITY PRESS
COLLEGE STATION

This paper meets the requirements of ANSI/NISO Z39.48–1992
(Permanence of Paper).
Binding materials have been chosen for durability.
Manufactured in the United States of America

Library of Congress Cataloging-in-Publication Data

Names: Shrake, Edwin, author. | Davis, Steven L., writer of foreword.
Title: Hollywood mad dogs: a novel / Edwin "Bud" Shrake; foreword by
    Steven L. Davis; afterword by Alan and Ben Shrake.
Other titles: Wittliff Collections literary series.
Description: First edition. | College Station: Texas A&M University Press,
    [2020] | Series: Wittliff Collections literary series | Summary: "Before
    his death in 2009, legendary Texas author Edwin "Bud" Shrake completed a
    final novel based on his real-life adventures as a Hollywood
    screenwriter in the 1970s and '80s. This rollicking new novel,
    discovered among Shrake's literary papers at the Wittliff Collections,
    provides a hilarious and insightful look at the Hollywood meat
    grinder"—Provided by publisher.
Identifiers: LCCN 2020022393 (print) | LCCN 2020022394 (ebook) | ISBN
    9781623498825 (paperback) | ISBN 9781623498832 (ebook)
Subjects: LCSH: Screenwriters—California—Los Angeles—Fiction. | Motion
    picture authorship—California—Los Angeles—Fiction. | Motion picture
    industry—California—Los Angeles—Fiction. | Hollywood (Los Angeles,
    Calif.)—Fiction. | LCGFT: Novels. | Autobiographical fiction.
Classification: LCC PS3569.H735 H65 2020 (print) | LCC PS3569.H735
    (ebook) | DDC 813/.54—dc23
LC record available at https://lccn.loc.gov/2020022393
LC ebook record available at https://lccn.loc.gov/2020022394

Foreword

A Note on *Hollywood Mad Dogs*

Edwin "Bud" Shrake vividly recalled watching Paul Newman and Robert Redford clown their way through *Butch Cassidy and the Sundance Kid*. As a novelist who paid his bills by writing for *Sports Illustrated*, the only thing Shrake knew about movies was how to order popcorn at the counter. But as he watched this film he noticed how simple the dialogue and plot seemed to be.

"Hell," he said, "I can do that." He went home and immediately began writing a screenplay. He had no idea how to format one, but paperback copies of William Goldman's script for *Butch Cassidy* were available at the bookstore, so Shrake bought the book and copied Goldman's template.

He was soon finished. "I was amazed at how easy it was," he told me later. "Writing a script was a lot more fun and so much easier than writing a novel. Writing a novel's the hardest thing I've ever done in my life."

He sent the script to his agent, who sold it to a Hollywood studio within hours. Then Shrake got the biggest, fattest paycheck he'd ever seen—all for a few weeks' work. It was as though he'd pulled off his own heist worthy of Butch Cassidy and the Sundance Kid.

That first script was eventually filmed as *Kid Blue*, starring Dennis Hopper. Shrake made his film acting debut in *Kid Blue* playing "Town Drunk." More importantly, he soon left behind *Sports Illustrated*—and novels—to become a screenwriter. He wrote dozens more scripts and saw seven of them produced as films, a very respectable batting average in Hollywood.

The times were wild and the money was good, but he eventually drifted away. With newfound financial security, he returned to his great love: writing novels. He resurrected his literary career and remained incredibly prolific. In the last decade of his life he published three novels—*The Borderland, Billy Boy*, and *Custer's Brother's Horse*—all of which were well received.

He also began writing his long-anticipated Hollywood novel, one based on his often-outrageous real-life experiences with the actor Steve McQueen. In 1979, McQueen hired Shrake to write the script for *Tom Horn*. The actor was often erratic and seemed to have a death wish. Unknown to nearly everyone, McQueen was suffering from terminal lung cancer and would die soon after the film was released.

Shrake finished his Hollywood novel in 2008, just a few months before he, too, was diagnosed with the terminal lung cancer that would claim his life. The book never made it to a publisher. The manuscript came to the Wittliff Collections, where it resides among Shrake's literary papers.

Before long, word began circulating among Shrake aficionados about this final novel. His family granted a few of us permission to view the manuscript. Like others who've read this book, I was dazzled by the story, which, I believe, reads nearly as a sequel to Shrake's classic novel *Strange Peaches*. If you're familiar with that excellent book, then you can consider this a "John Lee Wallace Goes to Hollywood" kind of story.

For years I worried that few others would get a chance to enjoy this fine, final novel from Bud Shrake. But thanks to Bud's caring and thoughtful sons, Ben and Alan, and to our publishing partners at Texas A&M University Press, we are so pleased to be able to present *Hollywood Mad Dogs* as part of our Wittliff Collections Literary Series.

Unbuckle your seat belt and get ready for a wild ride.

Steven L. Davis
Series Editor and Literary Curator,
The Wittliff Collections

HOLLYWOOD MAD DOGS

One

When I was a little boy my father told me the way to assure myself of an interesting life was to become fluent in a foreign language, learn to play the piano reasonably well, and take golf lessons at an early age.

The day this story begins, I criticized the Dodgers in Spanish to the parking valet at the Westwood Marquis, played golf with a movie star at the Riviera, and sat down at the piano at a party that evening in Malibu where I was an invited guest but had yet to learn whose house it was.

I don't care how many stars are in the room, when you slide onto the piano bench and start into Duke Ellington's "It's Kind of Lonesome out Tonight," you quickly become some kind of hero. There are a lot of lonely people at parties, and they like to gather around the piano.

"I want someone to hug me; I want someone to kiss me." I sort of halfway sang the lyric. I'm no Bobby Short or Michael Feinstein, but they look like cabaret piano players and I look like a guy you might sit next to ringside.

"Now who are you again?" asked a blonde woman as she put her wet glass down on top of the Steinway where it would leave a white circle for the host's household staff to scrub and polish away. You could tell she didn't mind leaving messes for other people to clean up. Her hair was pulled back and bound by a diamond clip. Her ears were like antique china pitcher handles. "Oh, wait, never mind, I don't care who you are," she said. "Do you have any blow on you?"

I kept playing.

A man in a pink shirt reached into the inner pocket of his blue cashmere jacket and pulled out a silver bullet, then tossed it to the woman. She unscrewed the top, inserted the bullet into one nostril, and did a mighty snort. Her blue eyes widened. She cleared her throat. Then she stuck the bullet into her other nostril and took a whiff that sounded like a tire going flat.

"I'll remember you fondly, if I remember you at all," the blonde said, lobbing the silver bullet back to the man who stood three lonely people and one gloomy drunk apart from her around the piano.

"Anything for you, Queen Bee," grinned the man. He tucked the silver bullet back into his coat pocket. I recognized him as an agent from ICM. I had seen him in the bar at the Westwood Marquis having a drink with Dustin Hoffman, who lived in the neighborhood. Luis the bartender had told me in Spanish that the star took a lot of meetings on the big couches in the bar where he could listen to Gertrude playing the harp.

I swung into "My story is much too sad to be told, but practically everything leaves me totally cold." The Cole Porter songbook has kept cabaret piano players in material for sixty years. But when I reached the lyric about how I get no kick from cocaine, Queen Bee began loudly humming "Don't Cry for Me, Argentina."

Since I don't play the piano for a living, I rested my fingers on the keys for a moment and then stood up and smiled at Queen Bee and the agent and the others who were standing around the piano, blocking what would otherwise have been my view of the beach and the ocean just after the sun has gone down and left a yellow smear on the waves.

"Sit back down," said Queen Bee.

"Sorry," I said.

As I walked away from the piano I heard her yell, "Hey, fuck you, buddy boy!"

I stopped at the bar for a Black Label and water with one ice cube, then walked out onto the terrace. I could hear the ocean sloshing onto the beach and see lights far out on the dark water. There was a lot of chatter around me, some laughter. I saw a number of faces I recognized from movies or television or photos in the trades, but nobody I knew personally.

Jack had invited me to this party while we were playing golf this afternoon. He wrote down the address and said he'd meet me here. But Jack has a way of getting involved. With him life is moment-to-moment reality. I began to think about leaving.

"The Queen Bee is not accustomed to anyone telling her to shove it," a voice said.

I turned and saw the agent in the pink shirt had come onto the terrace and was lighting a filter Winston with a gold Dunhill.

"Did I say that out loud?" I asked.

He dropped the lighter into a coat pocket, shifted his vodka on the rocks into his left hand, and stuck out his right.

"Max Bloom," he said.

"I'm Richard Swift," I said.

We shook hands. He had an enthusiastic grip, as if this handshake really meant something to him.

"I know who you are," he said. "You were pointed out to me the other day in the bar at the Westwood Marquis. You're writing the new Jack Roach picture at Fox."

"Yeah. I'm supposed to meet Jack here. Whose house is this?"

"You're kidding. You don't know?"

I got a whiff of his cigarette smoke. It smelled so good that I lit one of my own. I was trying to hold myself to ten cigarettes a day, but so far it wasn't working. I inhaled deeply and blew out a satisfying trail of smoke, rattled my ice cube, and looked at Max Bloom. He was built like a second baseman who had packed on about fifteen pounds too much. His skin was coffee-with-cream dark—I was guessing maybe three weeks in Hawaii—and his black hair was glistening with testosterone.

"You've heard of the Malibu Zulu?" he said.

"Not really."

"Adam Wachinski."

"Oh." Adam Wachinski had produced three monster hits in a row. He was bigger than *Jaws* or *Beverly Hills Cop* or any of them. "I always thought he was white."

Max smiled. "It's just a nickname. Adam can be pretty fierce sometimes. He scares people. He yells and screams and waves his arms. He throws staplers. He acts like a fucking Zulu on the warpath. This I know. He's my client."

"You speak well of him," I said.

"It's nothing I wouldn't say to his face. He's proud of his moods. He thrives on them." Max sipped his drink. "I hear you're a pretty good golfer.

I'm a twelve at Riviera. Should we have a game, say, Sunday morning at nine thirty?"

"Look, Max, I've already got an agent. It's Louie Lester in New York, and his wife, Lillian Newport."

"Hey, man, I'm not hustling you. I wouldn't poach on Louie and Lillian —they're dear old folks. I liked the way you dealt with the Queen Bee just now, and I thought you might be a good guy to play golf with."

"Who the hell is the Queen Bee?" I asked.

"She's Adam's mother."

"Excuse me? I'd pictured Adam Wachinski as a grown man."

"Adam is thirty-six. The Queen Bee is in her fifties, could pass for forty, and would claim to be thirty except it's awkward to be younger than your own natural son."

We heard a boat's horn out in the dark fog that was rolling in across the water. I decided to have one more drink while waiting for Jack. If he didn't show up by the finish of the next scotch—I should make it a double, then—I would claim my rented Mercedes from the parking valet, in Spanish of course, and be off down the Pacific Coast Highway. I saw myself taking a left on Sunset and winding my way back to the Westwood Marquis to call room service. I was tired. I had been in Los Angeles for two weeks of days that turned into nights and back again into days that seemed stuck in a perpetual loop. That's how it was, hanging out with Jack Roach.

"So, how about Sunday morning? Balls in the air at nine thirty?" Max said.

"I don't know. I might have to work."

"Hey, bring Jack with you. I heard he broke eighty out there with you today."

I walked across the terrace back to the bar. Glasses filled with sand held candles that flickered in the cool breeze off the ocean. Max followed me. I heard the piano through the open door and saw that it was being played by a black guy in a red dinner jacket. The professional had arrived. The Queen Bee sat on a high stool beside the piano, her legs crossed.

"I don't know, Max. If you want to meet Jack, maybe you should just give him a call."

"I know Jack already. I took a shower with him last month," Max said.

The bartender was a stout man with a black bow tie and a pale yellow

4

buzz cut. He looked like a middle-aged German surfer. He poured me a tall Black Label and water and dropped in two ice cubes. I put a five-dollar bill in his palm.

"At Riviera, I mean," Max said. "In the locker room."

I watched a young woman wearing a short white dress with bare shoulders stroll across the terrace to join a group of people who had gathered in a small circle and seemed to be smoking a joint.

"Got a wife?" Max asked.

"Not any more."

"Want to meet Katie Wynne?"

I realized Katie Wynne was the woman I had been staring at. She had starred in a couple of movies I had never seen, but *People* magazine had done a layout on her recently. My ex-wife was an editor at *People*. There were always copies of the magazine around the apartment in Gotham. Even though my ex-wife had moved out of our place at 86th and Madison and had moved in with her lover on Riverside Drive, she hadn't been gone all that long and I'd just let the *People* magazines stack up.

"Maybe later," I said. "I'll wait and see what Jack wants to do."

"Jack will scoop Katie right out of your arms, you know. He's like a wolf that's lost any fear of humans. He'll come right into the glow of the campfire and have his johnson inside your girl before you can say 'down, boy.'"

"You sound bitter, like it might've happened to you," I said.

"He snaked my wife—soon to be my ex-wife—out of a cocktail reception fundraiser for animal rights at the Beverly Wilshire last year and screwed her behind a potted fern."

"I don't think I'll bring him to your golf game, then," I said.

"Hey, there are no hard feelings on my part. Jack can't help it. The women can't help it. It's something primal. Jack projects penis extension. It's made him a star."

"Jack is a good actor," I said.

"This town is full of good actors. The waiter who brought you your breakfast this morning is a good actor. The guy who parked your car is a good actor."

"The guy who parked my car is a writer."

Max pulled the silver bullet out of his coat pocket then lifted it to his nose. He took a sniff in each nostril and offered the silver bullet to me.

5

I shook my head. He didn't try to force it on me. At a hundred and fifty dollars a gram, you had to be very generous or pretty drunk to insist people share your load, unless of course they were the mother of your biggest client.

"I hear Katie Wynne's hot tub is a scene out of a Caligula fantasy," Max said.

"Why don't you go after her yourself?"

"Violation of protocol," he said. "She's represented by Buzzy Klein at William Morris. If I try to fuck her, he'll think I'm poaching and he'll do something terrible back to me and then I'll key his Ferrari and then God knows what'd happen."

I glanced at my drink. The scotch was half gone, but the ice cubes were holding up well in the cool evening. I thought about the ocean breeze touching Katie Wynne's bare shoulders.

"I'm about to head back to the hotel," I said.

"You shouldn't leave without meeting Adam," Max said.

"Is he as much fun as his mother?"

"Adam is one of a kind. Well, out here there are more than one of his kind, and plenty more in training, but Adam is very near the top of the heap right now. He's got the jungle fever. He pounds his chest and King Kong runs away."

Katie Wynne broke away from the smokers on the terrace. Someone reached for her, but she laughed and pushed the hand away, stumbling a bit. She was wearing white high-heeled sandals that caught on the flagstones.

"Hey, Katie," Max called.

She turned to us with a vague smile. She had dimples and the kind of short brown hair that looked like she just ran her fingers through it and was good to go.

"There's a big fan of yours here who wants to meet you," Max said.

"Is that you, Max? I don't have my contacts in," she said, coming toward us.

I frowned at Max, but a mere facial expression didn't have any effect on him.

Her eyes brightened when she was closer and was sure it was him. She looked at me and smiled warmly, as if she had always hoped for this pleasure. Max kissed her on the cheek, but she kept her eyes on me. I could almost see the pages turn in her mind as she flipped through her recognition data.

"This is Richard Swift, the great writer," Max said.

"Glad to know you, Richard," she said, holding out her hand. I took it and her fingers gave me two little squeezes. You know how sometimes somebody can touch you, and everything around you sort of changes? There's a shift of your personality to accommodate something new and nice. Katie looked me in the eyes. "Are you new in town?"

"I live in New York," I said.

"I've got an idea," Max said. "Let's go see Adam, the three of us."

"Really? Where is he?" said Katie.

Max went around behind the bar to a panel with about twenty buttons on it. He ran his fingers over the labels, selected a button, and pushed it. Katie let go of my hand, but she stood close to me as she smiled expectantly and leaned forward to try to hear what Max was saying into the microphone in the wall. She smelled a little gamey.

"Bruno says he will let us enter at our own risk," Max said, turning to be sure Katie and I knew we were included.

"I think I'll pass," I said.

"What kind of writer are you to turn down the chance to get blasted with Adam Wachinski?" Max asked. He called to the bartender, "Refills all around and give me a bottle of Stoli for Adam."

"Oh, come on, Richard," Katie said, and gave me another little squeeze.

So Katie Wynne and I stepped hand-in-hand into the rabbit hole.

TWO

We followed Max along a hallway, weaving through people who stepped out of rooms with drinks in their hands, or people who ducked into those rooms, where I could see gatherings of two or three huddled together looking suspicious. I recognized a few of the famous faces, but none of them were Jack Roach.

At the end of the hall was a solid oak door with black iron hinges and a door handle that looked like a murder weapon. Max punched five numbers into the security box beside the door, turning so that Katie and I couldn't see the combination. She rolled her eyes at the back of Max's head and smiled at me, then took my hand again and squeezed to remind me we were in for an adventure.

Max got the door open. Inside was a large bedroom with floor-to-ceiling windows looking out at the Pacific. Max locked the door behind us then led us into a walk-in closet the size of an ordinary living room. Racks of Armani and Brioni hung on both sides of the closet. There were tilted shelves that probably held forty pairs of shoes. Beyond the suits, I saw on wooden hangers what I would guess to be a hundred dress shirts, most of them white and shining with the pure glow of cloth that costs so much you would never see it in a store with a price tag on it.

We could see ourselves in the mirrored wall at the back of the closet. Katie's bare shoulders looked brown against her white dress. She tugged up the top of her dress, and I saw her looking at her ankles and high-heeled sandals, just checking them out. With her free hand, she lightly mussed her hair. She caught me looking at her in the mirror. She didn't care. She leaned close to the glass and inspected her teeth.

"Stand back, Katie," Max said.

Max pushed what looked like a light switch, and the mirror swung open like a door. Max led us through the mirror, which shut behind us with the click of a lock. In front of us was what appeared to be a tunnel. It was well lit, but I couldn't see where the light was coming from. I couldn't see the end of the tunnel, either. This was not a rough tunnel like you would find in a coal mine. This was more like that famously long hallway at the Turnberry Hotel in Scotland, where I took Paula on our honeymoon, which was a mistake. Turnberry is for golf.

"Just a brisk walk and we'll be there," Max said.

"Be where?" I said.

"At Adam's house."

"I thought we were at Adam's house already," I said.

"No, we've been at Adam's fake house. We just left his fake bedroom. Queen Bee lives in the fake house. Adam lives next door in his own house at the end of the tunnel. Not many people know it. Dope dealers don't even know it. Hah!"

He thought that was funny. Katie smiled, too. As we walked along the tunnel, I saw a painting on the wall, a Modigliani, covered with clear plastic, a print, I assumed.

Max said, "Adam needs privacy. He does much of his work at home. When he's reworking a script, he'll hole up here for days, totally incommunicado except for Bruno, who is his man for all seasons. Wait, that sounds gay, doesn't it? Bruno is his servant, not his lover."

Max set a rapid pace along the tunnel. A lot of the movie guys would rather be jocks. In their dreams they score thirty points against the Knicks. They run in the mornings no matter how late they were up. They play softball on Sunday afternoons. They work out at the health club. Gold's Gym is full of them. I could picture Max hanging his cashmere jacket with the silver bullet in the inside pocket to join a pickup game in the park, any game in any sport.

I found myself wanting to turn back and go find my car and head for Hilgard Avenue, which I would have done if I thought Katie would go with me. But she was matching strides with Max, and of course I was keeping up with her, now realizing that she also had been some kind of athlete.

Ahead of us glowed the flames of two tiki torches, one on either side of a curtain of beads that hung across a door with a scimitar-shaped viewing port cut into it but no doorknob on this side. A dank odor came through the wall of the tunnel to our left. It smelled like an overflowed pissoir. I realized it was the smell of the ocean seeping through the concrete.

I looked higher up the wall and at the ceiling to reassure myself that it wasn't dripping. I saw two cameras up there looking at us from different angles, no doubt recording our images and printing the date and time of day on the tape.

The viewing port slid open. Two eyeballs peered at us. I heard a grunt. Max jingled the coins in his pocket. He was nervous, or in a hurry to get inside and dig out his silver bullet.

"Come on, Bruno, for God's sake. I've gotta use the toilet," Max said.

The eyeballs turned toward me.

"Who's the guy?" Bruno asked. His voice sounded like it had been through a hamburger grinder set on coarse.

"This is Richard Swift, the great writer," Max said.

Katie squeezed my fingertips. "Max really likes you," she whispered.

The viewing port shut as Bruno went to ask if a great writer should be admitted into Adam Wachinski's lair, where scripts underwent major surgery and many didn't survive.

"Is that the ocean I can feel hitting the wall?" I asked.

"Don't worry. Adam hired the people who built the Pyramids to construct this tunnel. They're the best," Max said.

Max looked at Katie with a sudden longing in his eyes.

"You're gorgeous, babe," he said. "You and I should slip off to Maui and start breeding the perfect race."

"Buzzy will be thrilled to hear of our plan," Katie said with a smile that would have been heartbreakingly attractive in a close-up, the way Ingrid Bergman could do it. I knew Katie didn't mean it, but I would have believed it if she had aimed it at me.

The door swung inward silently. Max entered first, then Katie. Bruno was holding the door. I had figured Bruno would look like an overgrown gymnast who had become a trainer at a gym, but instead he looked like his name sounded: like a gangster. He wore a white tee shirt, white cotton trousers, and white sneakers. Bruno's large nose had been broken more than once. His hair was a brown thatch with some gray in it, unparted and unbrushed. He looked to be about fifty years old..

"The boss is in the big bedroom," Bruno said.

"Is he alone?" asked Max

"Not exactly," Bruno said.

Bruno had stuck a finger between the pages of a book to keep his place. He clutched a pair of horn-rimmed reading glasses, the small professorial ones, in the hand that held the door. I bent my head to see what he was reading. The book was *The Stranger* by Camus. Bruno noted the surprise in my eyes.

"Who's in there with him?" asked Max.

"I'd rather not say," Bruno said. "Hello, Miss Wynne."

"How are you, Bruno?" she said.

"Just taking it easy tonight," he said.

Ocean spray spattered the dark plate glass walls. It sounded like sporadic bursts of rain. The area where we stood had the feeling of a carpeted guardhouse. There was a leather couch with a reading lamp, a chair and table with a telephone on it, and a panel of TV monitors showing views of the tunnel and the interiors of both Adam's real house and his fake house.

"What should we do?" asked Max.

"Just stand here," Bruno said.

A figure appeared in the doorway of what seemed to be a sort of vestibule that probably led into what Bruno was calling the big bedroom. I would have laughed at this guy, but something told me to shut up, because this must be our host.

He wore a a pair of white Jockey shorts and green flip-flops. Two bullet belts crossed his chest, like you see in photographs of Pancho Villa. His chest was white and hairless and trending toward pudginess. His hippy hair hung to his shoulders. Max had already told me that Adam was thirty-six. I would have guessed much younger. Queen Bee had passed him the look-young genes.

He was grinning like a maniac who has suddenly escaped from the nuthouse and realizes the world is spread out before him, ready to be raped or eaten. His eyes looked like strawberries. In his right hand he waved an old

Winchester Model '73 carbine like the one James Stewart went after in the movie named after it.

"Think this fucker won't shoot a hole in their ass" he yelled. "Tell me it won't!"

"Adam, please," said Bruno.

"No son of a bitch is gonna take my stuff away! Not to-fucking-day while I've got my Winchester and my bullets."

I couldn't smell booze on our host, but it might have been vodka that had him twisted, and beneath one nostril was a smudge of white powder that a sinus drip was carrying down to his lip. It also occurred to me that he might have nipped a tab of acid. Whatever it was, Adam Wachinski was at this moment a loon with every possibility of becoming dangerous.

"Adam, you better let me have that," Bruno said.

"Out of my cold dead hands," said Adam.

"Not the rifle," Bruno said. "You better let me have that check."

With a left hand fast enough to impress Sugar Ray Robinson, Bruno snatched a piece of paper sticking out of the elastic waistband of Adam's shorts, right at the navel.

"Give me back my fucking check, Bruno," Adam said.

"You'll jump in the hot tub and ruin it," said Bruno.

Adam reached for the check, but Bruno put a hand in his chest and pushed him away. The check fluttered to the floor at my feet. I picked it up and glanced at it as I was giving it back to Bruno.

The check was made out to Adam Wachinski for thirteen million dollars.

Adam frowned, but he watched Bruno tuck the check into *The Stranger* to keep it safe. Then Adam looked at Katie and Max for the first time.

"Welcome, babe," he said to Katie. "Haven't seen you in a while."

"It's been too long," she said.

Adam's eyes fastened on me. "Hey, you," he said. "Come in here and tell us which one is the real fucking Zulu."

Adam gestured with the rifle to point my way into the big bedroom. Not since I was in basic training in the infantry many years ago had anyone addressed me as "hey you." I didn't move or answer. Adam kept staring at me.

Max stepped into what was becoming an awkward moment.

"Let me roll the credits here," Max said. "This is Richard Swift. He wrote that Fox movie a few years ago that you liked, with Dennis Hopper, about the dope heads in Mexico. He's got his name on that bomb at Columbia about the vampire bats that attack the Hopi Indians. He's writing Jack Roach's new picture about the guy who shoots rustlers and gets hanged for it. He's written two or three novels—."

Some of the lunacy was fading from Adam's expression as he concentrated on listening to Max. His brow wrinkled. His red lips rubbed together. The Winchester was pointing dangerously down at his toes.

His eyes lit up. He had hit a connection.

"Hey, Richard, I was just having fun with ya!" he screamed.

We all took a step backward at his outburst. Water flew off of him—it was sweat, saliva, snot, who knows what else.

Adam lowered his voice to a mere shout, waving the rifle.

"Forget those piece of shit movies," he yelled. "Forget the fucking novels! I've been reading your stuff in *SI* ever since you did that cover story on number thirty-two when he won the Heisman!"

Number thirty-two would have been O. J. Simpson, who won the Heisman Trophy about fifteen years ago.

"The Juice and I were at USC together. Juice and I were just people in those days," Adam said, much calmer, as if the wave were passing. "Well, The Juice was never just people. He was always The Juice. Always special. You ever see his dick?"

He waited for me to answer.

"Yeah," I said.

"What the fuck brings you to my house, Richard?" he asked.

"I'm supposed to meet Jack Roach here."

"Ditch that asshole," Adam said.

"I may already have done so," I said.

"You'll be better off! Jack Roach is big trouble," Adam said. He rapped on the doorframe with the barrel of his Winchester. "Let me restate my request, Richard. Please come in and do me a favor and settle this real fucking discussion."

Somewhere in his voice and manner, the personality that had produced all those blockbuster movies came to the fore, and we did as he asked.

Adam pressed against the wall in the vestibule to make room for us to pass him, but close enough that he brushed each of us with some body part or other. I went first, holding Katie's hand, naively imagining that I might shield her from Adam or that she would want to be shielded from him.

We entered an area the size of half a tennis court. Off to the right sat a bed that was about ten feet by eight feet and covered with a white, wooly spread that I supposed was llama because it reminded me of the photograph in *Sports Illustrated* of the llama spread that Joe Namath had in his apartment in Gotham. There were two couches, two easy chairs, a writing desk made out of a slab of wood that looked like a church door, and a tall bar stool. On the writing desk stood a black Smith-Corona typewriter with a stack of white paper beside it, next to a jar of pencils and pens and paper clips. Paintings hung haphazardly all around the room. I saw Modigliani again, and Miró and Cézanne. I saw a Magritte of a man in a bowler hat. These paintings looked like the real thing. I thought about the humidity. To the far right was an open door that we could see led to an enormous mirrored bathroom with huge towels hanging on chrome pipes.

Max jumped in front of me and steered us to the left, where a wall of glass was slid open across the middle of an indoor-outdoor pool and Jacuzzi. I could hear the surf and the wind, but they were blocked by a seven-foot wall that hid Adam's pool from the beach.

Even though the night was foggy and growing chilly, I realized that I could see dots of light moving along the beach and figures leaping in the surf. Adam's wall was made out of a substance that looked like gray wood from the outside but on the inside was a tinted window. Adam could see the figures on the beach, but they couldn't see him.

"Now, Richard, let me make my case!" Adam yelled and switched on lights that shone down onto the pool and also lit up the water from underneath.

I saw there were two people already in the water. One was a tall black man with very wide shoulders soaking in the hot tub. The other I recognized as Sugar Delaney, the fourteen-year-old child star that everybody in the country knew from her soft drink commercials on television. She was drifting in the pool beside the windowed wall, her blonde ringlets soaked against her head. She was naked.

"You tell this fool how it is, Richard," the tall man said, rising up in the hot tub. He took a while to stand all the way up, because he was six feet, nine and a half inches tall. When I knew him, he was a power forward for the Knicks. He was never quite good enough to be a regular starter, but he was good enough to make a living at it.

His name then was Erazmo Jones, and he was from Brooklyn.

His name now was ErazmoX, and he was working in action movies, where he was a superhero. I saw that since leaving the Knicks, Erazmo had picked up three scars on each cheek that looked like tribal markings.

He still had what looked like the same two gold earrings he'd worn as a Knick.

The jock strap he was wearing had writing on it that might have said "KNICKS" if you wanted to stare at it.

"There is only one real Zulu in Malibu." Adam said.

"You are never close to being a Zulu, man. There is a color barrier, for one thing," said Erazmo.

"How you been, Erazmo?" I asked.

"I'm X now, Richard."

Erazmo had signed with the Knicks straight out of high school, but he was a smart kid and he got a good education in the NBA, what with the travel to the big cities and the people he met—and he had the money to take a long look at things. I think Erazmo finished his career playing in Spain and Italy before he found his role in Hollywood.

"I know you are, X," I said.

"I at least have been in Africa, where Adam has never been," Erazmo said.

I was trying to guess how serious Erazmo was about the question being considered.

"Do I have to call you 'X'?" I asked.

"No, man. I don't care. You're from my past. I'm almost the same person as 'Jones,' just better."

Erazmo smiled at Katie. He looked at Max with vague recognition.

"You're the champ, X," Max said.

"And what about me?" piped up a childish voice. Sugar kicked her legs and floated toward us. "I'm getting hungry," she said.

Adam flicked the switch three times in rapid order, blinking the lights off and then on, creating a halo that drew attention to himself.

"Look at him," Erazmo said and pointed at Adam. "If you wanted to hire a Zulu, would you go to a fat white man, or would you come to me?"

15

"Hey, listen, everybody, let's take five on this and have a cocktail," Max said. He'd heard in X's voice a hint of physical danger. Erazmo was never violent, but he weighed two hundred and fifty pounds and had the competitive pride of a big-league professional athlete. He also seemed a little drunk and on edge.

"There's only one real Zulu in Malibu, and everybody knows it," Adam insisted.

"I never claimed to be a Zulu. You started this argument," said Erazmo.

I was torn between heading for the bar with Max, and heading for the door. Looking at the naked fourteen-year-old girl in the pool, I was trying to remember what the law said about this situation when combined with guns, dope, and booze.

"You're the fucking Zulu, Adam," Max said. "Everybody knows it! You're the only actual village-burning, cattle-stealing, fear-arousing Zulu warrior that actually lives in Malibu."

"I am the King of the Imbeciles," Adam said, dropping his Winchester. The rifle clattered on the tiles. His mouth opened in a sort of eureka way. He brushed his hair out of his eyes with his fingers. Inspiration had struck him. He clawed at his chest, reaching for a pen in a pocket that wasn't there. He had to get this down, whatever idea he was having. I recognized the need. Anybody who writes for a living finds that you should write down the ideas that suddenly rattle into your head, especially if it's four o'clock in the morning in a barroom.

Erazmo stepped out of the hot tub and stood shedding water on the deck. He was a splendid specimen of man. There were a great many splendid specimens in show business, but X was unique in being the only movie superhero with tribal markings on his face.

"Are you calling me an imbecile?" Erazmo asked.

But Adam had abandoned their confrontation. He turned and ran into the bedroom. Through the door I saw him climb onto the barstool at his writing desk. He rolled a sheet of paper into the Underwood typewriter and called out, "Bruno!"

Bruno stepped out from behind the blackout curtain that had been drawn back from the door. I realized Bruno had been there all the time, watching the whole scene. Bruno went to the cabinet beneath the Miró and opened the ice bucket. He poured vodka over rocks into a glass and took it to Adam, who lit a cigarette and began typing rapidly.

"He didn't mean you're an imbecile, big man," Max said.

"Who did he mean then?" said Erazmo.

"He meant everybody in Malibu except you and him," Max said.

"Did he mean me?" asked Sugar, crawling out of the pool and reaching for a towel on the deck.

"Please put on your clothes, Sugar," Bruno said. "Your driver is waiting at the gate. You're already late to dinner."

"Are we through with our meeting?" Sugar asked. She stepped into a pair of shorts and pulled a tee shirt over her golden head. "I didn't get to say my ideas yet."

"There will be another meeting soon," Bruno said.

Sugar scampered ahead of him toward the house. Bruno looked at me as if he regretted letting me in. He followed Sugar into the house, steering her away from Adam, who was crouched over the typewriter, his butt barely on the stool, a cigarette hanging from his lips, and then he guided her toward her waiting limo.

"Shit, these movie meetings are as dumb as listening to Red Holzman," Erazmo said.

"You're doing a picture with Adam?" I said.

"Yeah. Me and the little girl are."

I must have looked relieved.

"Oh, hey, man, what did you think was going on?" Erazmo asked.

"Sorry, X."

Katie hadn't said a word all this time as we stood by the pool, but I could feel her presence near me. Certain people project their essence out from their bodies in electrical waves that make others always aware of them. Some turn this charisma to movie stardom, some to political office, and some become swindlers. There are some who have it and never do anything but surf.

When Katie did speak at last, it sounded like poetry to me. She said, "Would you please give me a ride home?"

Three

Young Latino men dressed like tennis pros were running the valet parking in front of Adam Wachinski's fake house. Dashing back and forth through the traffic in the dark to wherever they had parked the cars was a dangerous job. My red Mercedes was up front. A moment of chatting in Spanish followed by two twenty-dollar bills when I arrived had earned me a spot near the door.

Katie looked impressed. She hopped over a flagstone that threatened her high-heeled sandals. Max Bloom came out behind us and frowned when he saw a Guatemalan open my Mercedes door for Katie.

"Here's the creep with the black Porsche," one valet said in Spanish, glancing back at Max. Actually, he said *pendejo*,; "creep" is a generous translation.

"Hey, boys, watch your tongue," the valet I had gotten friendly with said in Spanish.

"No problem," I replied in Spanish. "You probably know him better than I do."

The valets laughed. Katie looked at me as if she had begun to think she was riding with Einstein. Being fluent in a foreign language is unexpected in the US. My father is a wise man, down on his goat ranch in the hills west of Austin.

"Be careful with my girl," Max said.

"Always with respect," I said.

"How about the golf on Sunday? Nine thirty at Riv. Forget about bringing Jack Roach. I'll round up a couple of guys you'll enjoy playing with."

Max pulled a notepad out of his cashmere jacket and wrote a number on it.

"Here's my really private line, not my fake private line," he said, and smiled. His thick, black hair caught a yellow glow from the lamps above the gate. Max had what I thought of as rich, European hair. He could be charming when he cranked up the wattage on his smile.

"I'll have to see how it's going with Jack," I said.

"Call me by Saturday night and let me know one way or the other," Max said.

"I'll try to remember," I said.

It was reassuring to slide into the Mercedes's leather seat with the new-car smell and look at the dashboard lit up in green with the speedometer that went to 140. I pulled onto the highway, headed south. I hadn't asked Katie if she might live to the north, somewhere like San Francisco. I would have driven her there. I hadn't even bothered to look for Jack Roach when we came back through the crowd in the fake house.

"What did the valet say about Max?" she asked.

"How'd you know he was talking about Max?"

"I saw the look he gave him," she said.

"He said Max had a black Porsche."

"I got that part of it," she said. "It was the insult I missed."

She opened her purse, took out a red and white package and shook a Winston out of it. She offered me one. I nodded. She pushed in the dashboard lighter.

"Very cool of you to talk Spanish," she said.

"One of these days you'll need to speak Spanish just to buy a taco in LA."

"Pretty soon, too. I agree," she said.

Katie lit the two cigarettes, taking a drag from each. The smell of cigarette smoke tapped a pleasure button in my brain. I could taste the tobacco even before she put one cigarette between my lips. The cork tip was sticky from her lipstick.

"What's this with you and Queen Bee? What was she yelling at you for when we were leaving the house?" she asked.

"Her theme was that I'll never work in this town again"

"What have you done to her?"

"I walked away while she was talking to me."

"She's a dangerous person," said Katie.

"You know Queen Bee very well?"

I swerved around a biker and back into the right lane. The headlights refracted in the mist blowing in from the ocean.

"Adam brings her to parties sometimes. I saw her last week in a candy-striped circus tent pitched over Marty Ransohoff's tennis court in Holmby Hills. She was backstage at the Oscars when Adam got his. We had a chat. She enjoys being mean, I think."

I was trying to remember if Katie had been nominated. She read my face.

"I was a presenter," she added.

"How do you know Adam? Did you ever work for him?"

"Adam has never offered me a job. I would love a gig in one of his blockbusters. But he doesn't even tease me about it. I was having lunch at Spago two or three years ago, and Adam came over to the table and introduced himself to me. Since then, he's invited me to all of his parties and screenings and he's always very sweet to me, but he doesn't mention hiring me. Not even an audition."

She touched a button on the door to lower her window a few inches to let the smoke out. The wind ruffled her hair.

I get the strange feeling that Adam is in love with me," she said. "I'm sure that couldn't be true. But he gets tongue-tied when he talks to me. He sneaks peeks at me, then he looks away when I catch him."

"I'm sure you've had lots of experience with boys being in love with you," I said. "You would be hard to fool."

"I'm sorry. I shouldn't have said that about Adam. I don't even know you, really."

"Why don't you have a car?" I asked.

"The people I came with had to leave early. I chose to stay and go to Adam's real house. Do you mind giving me a ride?"

"I am very pleased to give you a ride. I was just figuring somebody like you always had somebody around to drive them and do everything they want. It now occurs to me that the somebody I am talking about is me."

She laughed.

"Take Sunset," she said.

The numbers on the dashboard said it was eight twenty and the temperature was sixty-eight as the Mercedes hummed through the turn off the Pacific Coast Highway.

"Are you hungry?" I asked.

"I need to go home. I'm working tomorrow and there are lines to learn. Why don't you come in? We'll have sandwiches, open a bottle of wine."

"Sounds like a great plan," I said.

"I'd better not have another drink. I'm from the 'three martinis is not enough' school. I had two at Adam's party. Two is too many," she said.

"Have one glass of wine. I'll run lines with you if you want."

"Maybe one, but no more than that," she said.

She mashed out her cigarette in the ashtray. It was a major sin to throw a cigarette out the window of a car here. We were on Sunset Boulevard, not in the canyons, but you could still burn down a city that way.

"You must promise to leave by midnight," she said. "I have a nine o'clock call at Paramount. The car is picking me up at six thirty."

"I promise," I said. "But you haven't told me where you live."

"Head for the Beverly Hills Hotel. I'll guide you from there."

Fly, swift arrow, in thy flight. I'd heard Warren Oates say that in a movie at the New York Film Festival about ten years ago. He meant something poetic, and so did I in urging the red Mercedes to greater speed. We went under the 405. I pushed a cassette tape into the dashboard, and Jerry Jeff Walker began singing from eight speakers. Palm trees appeared along Sunset. We passed the Bel Air gates.

"What does Max want from you?" she asked.

"A golf game," I said.

"Oh, please."

"That's probably all there is to it. Somebody may have told him I'm better than he is. Max seems like the kind of guy who would have to see for himself."

"Are you better than he is?"

"Yeah."

Katie dug the Winstons out of her purse again and offered me another one, but I shook my head. I was over the limit already. Katie lit a cigarette and lay back with a shoulder against the door and eased her feet out of the high-heeled sandals. She sighed and rubbed her feet together. It was a relief to get the sandals off.

"What was Adam saying about *Sports Illustrated*?" she said.

"I used to work there. I quit."

"To write movies?"

"Yeah."

"You gave up a good job writing about sports for a famous magazine to get into this meat grinder at the age of, what? You must be about forty," she said.

"Just about," I said.

We were coming up on the Beverly Hills Hotel, which always makes me think of a huge pink birthday cake. "Which way?" I asked.

"Forty is old age out here," she said. "You must not be as smart as I was thinking you are."

"Forty's not old for guys," I said. "Guys don't get old and stupid out here until they're fifty."

"Like Jack Roach?" she said. She was smiling, but I wondered at the sublayer of malice in her tone.

"Jack is a very bright guy, and he is forty-eight."

"So says his bio."

"I've got to turn one way or another, or do I go on past the hotel?"

"Take Benedict Canyon Drive. I live in an old house up behind the hotel."

I turned left at Will Rogers Park. We were in old Beverly Hills. The houses were covered with vines and roses and flowers that I have never known the names of. A few years ago while in LA to write about a Muhammad Ali fight, I had been to a party on Summit Drive at Pickfair, the mansion where Douglas Fairbanks Jr. and Mary Pickford had invited Charlie Chaplin over to dinner and created the United Artists studio. Pia Zadora lived in the mansion now. The neighborhood had an air of lush, quiet elegance. Walls hid the houses and the residents and their Rottweilers and poodles and such children as might be home for the holidays.

Katie guided us onto Summit Drive. This area was heavily marked on the maps of the stars' homes. Jimmy Stewart, Dinah Shore, and Lucille Ball lived around here. I knew they did because Pia Zadora had told me at that party. That meant Katie Wynne was scoring major paydays. Or maybe she was sleeping with somebody who was into big money.

"It's the gate right there in the hedges," Katie said.

"This is like *The Secret Garden*," I said.

"I love it here," she said. "This house used to be Tom Mix's stable."

She told me her code number to punch into the box. The gate swung inward. The Mercedes cruised silently onto a red brick driveway. The gate closed behind us. The driveway led past the blue glow of a swimming pool and a small pool house. The air smelled of gardenias. A black BMW sedan glistened in lights that shone from the hedges. Also parked in front of the two-story brick house was a pale blue Ford pickup truck. One of the three garage doors was open, and I could see another car inside. It was an old Cadillac with fins on the rear fenders.

"Well, are you coming in? What's the matter?" Katie said.

"I'm fine," I said.

What Katie had said about being forty had let the air out of me for a minute. It wasn't the fear of age so much as it was the anxieties that go with flying blind. I had quit the magazine and left New York at the height of a very dramatic domestic turmoil. In sober moments, inner voices nagged at me that I had done the wrong thing.

"I like the truck," I said.

"That's Ava, the balky beauty," Katie said.

She found her key and unlocked a tall oak door.

"You drive Ava yourself?" I asked.

"Sure. I've had a pickup since I was a kid. Everybody in my hometown had a pickup. Weatherford, Texas, had a big sign at the city limits that said 'The Pickup Capitol.' Soldiers used to come up from Fort Hood to see if it was true."

"You're from Weatherford?" I said.

Katie took a step back and looked at me with a strange little smile.

"You don't really know who I am, do you?" she asked.

"I have a fair idea, but I'm a little out of touch," I said.

"Actually, I suppose this is refreshing," she said. "Come on into the kitchen."

She led me through the house. The walls were white stucco, the paintings were western landscapes in handsome frames, the chairs and couches were leather, two of them draped with brown-and-white cowhides. There was a large fireplace with piñon wood stacked beside it, Santa Fe–style. The long dining table with seats for eight gleamed with polish.

"I was born in Texas," I said, following her, trying for a comeback. "My father was a lawyer in Austin. My mother left him when I was twelve and took me with her to Long Island. But down deep, I am Texas to the bone."

Katie laughed. "No need to impress me by bragging."

The kitchen wall was hung with serious-looking pots and pans, and the chrome on the oven and the refrigerator doors was glowing. Katie tossed her purse onto the kitchen table. This table had four chairs.

"Sit down," she said. She opened a refrigerator door and took out a covered dish and a bottle of white wine that had been recorked. Then she took out a second bottle and brought the whole armload to the table. I poured two glasses of wine while she went to the wall and pushed an intercom buzzer. She pushed it twice, waited, pushed it hard, waited, pushed it hard again for maybe five seconds.

A woman's voice said, "What the fuck is it that you can't wait a minute?"

"Dolly, bring me that script off my bed. I'm in the kitchen," Katie said.

"Sorry," said Dolly's voice. "I didn't know you were back yet."

"Who'd you think it was?" Katie asked into the intercom.

"I wasn't thinking. I was in the bathroom."

Katie sat down at the table. She took the lid off the dish to reveal a stack of tuna fish salad sandwiches surrounding a mound of deviled eggs. Despite knowing that I shouldn't, I had been falling in love with Katie even before that moment. My heart had started pounding. I felt a little crazy. It was totally ridiculous to fall in love with a movie star, even if you had the excuse of not seeing any of her movies. Falling in love with movie stars was for other movie stars to do, an arrangement that provided both of them many fire escapes to freedom when things didn't work out. Or falling in love with movie stars was for those sad, desperate fans who crowded against the ropes and wept with hopeless longing as their fantasies paraded past. This was stupid. Falling in love with a movie star certainly wasn't anything for a smart guy like me to be doing. That's what stars like Katie Wynn did for a living—make you buy a ticket to fall in love with them.

But it just so happens that since I was a kid, tuna fish sandwiches and deviled eggs are two of my favorite things to eat. I would choose them over anything on the menu at the 21 Club.

"Sorry to reach, but I just love deviled eggs," Katie said, picking up two halves and getting the stuffing on her fingers as she popped them into her mouth in one smooth, erotic motion. "I stuffed these eggs and made the sandwiches before I went to Adam's fake house, and they have been calling to me all night, saying, 'Come and take me, Katie.'"

My heart flew out of my chest. I had met the woman meant for me.

Four

"I feel like I've lost you or something," Katie said. "What are you thinking about?"

"Nothing. I hadn't realized how hungry I am."

I drank half a glass of wine and stuffed a tuna fish sandwich into my mouth to keep from blurting out the truth.

"Who is Dolly?" I asked.

The picture of how beautiful Katie looked to me at that moment should have been painted on the Great Wall of China, as I once heard Rip Torn say in a movie. It wasn't that I never went to movies. But the movies Katie Wynne had starred in came from novels by writers like Jane Austen and were not at the top of my viewing list. When I was married you might have found me slumped in an aisle seat beside Paula, eating popcorn and hissing at Darcy, but now that Paula was gone the only costume dramas I went to see had cowboys in them.

"Are you sure you're all right?" Katie asked.

"I'm fine," I said. To prove it, I ate two deviled eggs.

"Dolly is my assistant. She lives here. That's her BMW you saw in the driveway," Katie said.

"You drive the pickup and the old Cadillac?" I asked.

"The Cadillac belongs to Mrs. Garcia, my housekeeper and cook. She lives here, too, with her dog, Bananas."

I found myself staring dreamily into Katie's brown eyes and wondering how much of my romantic rush had come out of Adam's scotch bottle, when a voice intruded on my thoughts.

"I couldn't find the fucking thing at first. You put it under the pillow," the voice said.

A tall woman about thirty, wearing a flowered robe and pink fuzzy slippers, appeared in the doorway. She had dark, shoulder-length hair and wore reading glasses down low on her nose. In her right hand was a script with a red cover. She held a cigarette in her other hand. Two puffs of smoke spurted out of her nose when she saw me.

"Sorry. I didn't realize you have a gentleman caller," said Dolly.

"This is Richard Swift. He gave me a ride home from the Queen Bee's party."

"Hello, Dolly," I said.

No matter how you say it, "Hello, Dolly" sounds theatrical. She scowled at me.

"You can be leaving now, Richard," Dolly said. "Katie has work to do."

"Richard is going to run lines with me," Katie said. "It's all right. He's in the business."

Dolly dumped the red script on the table and ate half a deviled egg, never taking her eyes off me. I appreciated that she was protecting her boss and her livelihood, but I felt like an encyclopedia salesman with my foot in the door.

"Really, Dolly, it's all right. Richard is a writer," Katie said.

"Lester won't like another writer fooling with his lines," said Dolly.

I glanced at the script and saw it was by writer-director-producer Lester Ferry. I knew Lester from the Crosby pro-am tournament at Pebble Beach. I had played in the Crosby three times before my angel on the committee had a heart attack and my pro tore a rotator cuff. Lester played in the Crosby every year and was a champion consumer of cocktails in the lodge. He loved to sing while I played the piano. "You Do Something to Me," was a favorite of his.

"Lester is a friend of mine. He won't mind," I said.

"Lester Ferry is a friend of yours?" Dolly asked, lifting a brow as if I had asked her to believe I was the Prince of Wales disguised in a navy cashmere blazer and a pair of Gucci loafers..

"I play golf with him," I said.

"Richard is quite a golfer," Katie said.

This news thrilled Dolly as much as any traffic report or chemistry lecture. "Really," she said, but not as a question that might require an answer with details.

"You can go back to whatever you were doing, Dolly. I'll be running lines for another hour with Richard," Katie said.

We heard a loud crash from down the hall, then a woman cursing and screaming in Spanish. She was screaming, "Motherfucker, get away from that window! I will shoot your ugly head off! Go away, go away!"

A white lattice door swung open and a short, stout señora wearing a yellow housecoat with her hair in curlers burst into the kitchen. She held a 12-gauge double-barrel shotgun in her hands, cracked open, barrels empty. Behind her the dog yapped furiously.

"Where did we put the fucking shells for this shotgun?" she yelled in Spanish. Then in English she asked again, "The shells? Where are the shells?"

"I put them away," Dolly said. "What the hell are you yelling about?"

"A prowler is looking in the window! I want to shoot him!"

I jumped up from the table manly habits taking over, and spoke in Spanish to the woman I took to be the housekeeper, Mrs. Garcia. "Show me where you saw him."

Realizing I had understood her cursing, Mrs. Garcia blushed and crossed herself. "At the back. He was standing in the rose bushes looking in my window," she said.

All four of us hurried through the swinging door, down a hall past the pantry and the laundry room, and into Mrs. Garcia's bedroom, where her fluffy white poodle jumped onto an armchair and clawed at the window. All I could see in the window was the poodle's reflection.

"How do I get outside?" I asked.

"Don't go out there, Richard," Katie said.

"We have to check it out," said Dolly.

"Come this way," Mrs. Garcia said in Spanish.

She and the poodle and I ran into the hall and through a door onto the back porch. The dog barked madly and dashed across the lawn to paw at the hedges covering the back wall. Suddenly the whole yard lit up—Dolly had switched on the floodlights—and I hurried toward the window where I guessed Mrs. Garcia's room to be. Mrs. Garcia scurried behind me with the empty shotgun clutched against her bosom.

"Next time I will shoot him!" she said in Spanish. "He's starting to scare me."

"He's been here before?" I asked.

"Somebody has been haunting us for weeks," she said in Spanish. She glanced toward the porch as Dolly came out to pull Katie back inside. "I'm tired of it."

Mrs. Garcia pointed to the ground below the window. A rose bush grew up to the height of the sill. I could see a disturbance in the dirt that might be a footprint. "He was standing here looking in the window at me when Bananas started barking," she said in Spanish.

"So you truly saw him?" I asked.

"I didn't see his face. I just saw a shape. I think I saw his eyes." She rested the shotgun against her knee. "We've never seen him. We just know he's around. A gate will be open, or there's a movement in the dark, or once the doorbell rang and nobody was there."

"Don't you have a security service?"

"Yes. They call us up and say they got an alarm or they heard a suspicious person was in the alley, but they never find anybody. I think it's a pervert who gets his sex fun spying on Miss Wynne."

Katie came onto the porch again and was trying to listen. Dolly had gone back into the house.

"What do the police say?" I asked.

"We haven't told the police. Dolly says if we report this pervert, it will be on the front page of all the magazines at the grocery store."

"Hey, speak English," Katie said.

Dolly appeared at the door. "The security guys called and said there's a prowler in the alley," Dolly said. "The Beverly Hills cops are sending a car because Harold Lloyd complained he nearly ran over a stranger in front of his house."

"Why didn't your alarm go off in your house?" I asked.

I turned if off when you and I were at the door, and I forgot to turn it back on," Katie said

"Turned it off?" Dolly said. "What on earth for?"

"I don't know. I just flipped the switch.".

"Wait a minute," I said. "Harold Lloyd has been dead for ten or twelve years. This is a surprisingly creepy neighborhood."

"I don't mean Harold Lloyd in person. It was somebody at the Harold Lloyd house," said Dolly. "It's a block away. Katie, don't ever turn the alarm off at night."

"All right, all right," Katie said."

Bananas had given up barking and peeing on the bushes. The poodle nudged against Mrs. Garcia's leg and got a pat on the head. Apparently the intrusion was over. We filed back into the kitchen as the telephone started ringing. The buttons lit up on all three lines.

Dolly punched two of them immediately onto hold and answered the third.

"No need to send a car, thanks," she said. "No, really, we've had a look around and everything is in good shape. I appreciate that a car is near our gate, but Miss Wynne is hard at work memorizing a script and wouldn't really have time for that. Yes, tomorrow would be good. Yes, please circle the block and keep a look out. Thank you, officer."

She answered the second line. "We had a little mixup with the alarm, that's all. No, it's not your fault. Yes, we are fine. No, nobody is holding a gun at my head. Yes, I would tell you if they were, even if they warned me not to. Now, good night."

She hung up and said, "That fat guy at the security office thinks he's funny."

Dolly lit a cigarette and looked at the third blinking light.

"This is your private line," Dolly said and blew smoke in my direction, but she was looking at Katie.

Katie picked up the phone. "Hello?"

Her eyes widened as she listened. She reached out toward Dolly and made a wagging gesture with two fingers. Dolly put her own cigarette between Katie's fingers. Katie took a deep drag and kept listening.

"I didn't know that," Katie said.

Mrs. Garcia was spooning Columbian coffee into the coffee machine. She had propped the shotgun against the drain board. Bananas chomped a gingerbread man dog biscuit, scattering crumbs on the polished wooden floor. Mrs. Garcia swept the crumbs into a pan.

I stood awkwardly and tried to appear not to be listening to Katie's conversation. Dolly poured herself a glass of V8 juice. Mrs. Garcia turned on a small TV on the counter and cranked the volume down low.

"I'd like a cup of coffee, too," I said in Spanish. I needed an eye-opener for the drive back to the Westwood Marquis, which I had decided to make the moment Katie hung up and I could tell her goodbye and somehow arrange to see her again.

"She speaks English," Dolly said. She sat down at the table and began flipping through the script by Lester Ferry.

"You really know this guy?" Dolly asked.

"I really do," I said.

"Is he having a problem with the bottle?"

"I don't know. I haven't seen him in a couple of years."

Katie laughed into the phone. We looked at her. The evening had gotten chilly, even inside the house. Katie still wore the white dress with her shoulders bare. Her shoulders were wide and square—strong and athletic. In photographs, she looked smaller and more vulnerable. Maybe that was because in the pictures I remembered, she was dressed like Louisa Mae Alcott. With shoulders like she had, she ought to be in a ball gown, waltzing with the prince.

The coffee machine started sputtering.

With the phone at her ear, the cord over one shoulder, Katie mashed out her cigarette in a silver ashtray. She was listening intently. Whoever was on the other end had a lot to say.

"They won't listen to reason?" Katie said into the phone.

I finished my cup of Columbian and a cigarette. Dolly was reading through the script. She took a Montblanc pen out of the pocket of her robe, unscrewed it, and wrote a note in the margin. I pushed back my chair. Katie had turned away from us while she listened to the phone. I looked at the back of her neck where it curved into her shoulders. Time to get out of here, I was thinking.

"This script is really good," Dolly said.

"What's it based on?" I asked.

"It's an original. Lester has done a ton of research on Victorian London. This script has the feeling of authenticity."

"Costumes, huh?" I said.

"Katie plays a whore who becomes a wealthy widow with a house in Mayfair and has a tragic love affair with an officer who gets killed in the Crimean War. It's a weeper at the end."

Anything critical I said would be exaggerated and repeated to Lester, and he's a nice guy. I kept my mouth shut and finished pushing back the chair and standing up. At the bars where I hang out in New York, at Elaine's or P. J. Clarke's, this was the point where I would say, "Where's my hat?"

"Tell Katie goodnight for me," I said.

"Thanks for bringing her home," said Dolly. "Listen, do me a favor? Don't be talking about us having a creeper. You know how they gossip out here."

"If you say so," I said.

"The police keep a close eye on this neighborhood, and our security system normally does work very well. I don't want to give this creeper the publicity. That's probably what he's after."

"I think he's after her underwear," Mrs. Garcia said in Spanish.

"Anyhow, I'll be going now," I said, "I enjoyed the deviled eggs."

"They're Mrs. Garcia's specialty. She has some Costa Rican recipe for the stuffing that's her family secret."

"Oh," I said. I looked at Mrs. Garcia and in Spanish said, "You're a genius. Thank you."

"Come see us again," Mrs. Garcia said in Spanish.

"Just a minute," I heard Katie say.

She covered the mouthpiece with one hand and smiled at me in her heart-melting way. "He wants to talk to you," Katie said.

"What?"

"On the telephone," she said. "It's Jack Roach."

Five

It's only a few minutes' drive from Katie Wynne's house to the Beverly Wilshire Hotel, where Jack Roach lived in a penthouse. Jack told me his next-door neighbor was Warren Beatty, but I hadn't encountered Beatty in the hall yet.

Katie buzzed me out of her gate and I made the swing down the hill around the Beverly Hills Hotel and curved onto Rodeo Drive. It's a straight shot on Rodeo between rows of palm trees to the Beverly Wilshire. All the way I was wondering what Jack had been talking to Katie about on the phone. I was surprised that Jack had Katie's private number. My impression when Jack's name came up at the Wachinski house had been that she hardly knew him. It made me a little angry. You might think I was jealous, but how ridiculous would that be?

On the way to meet Jack, I began rationalizing the deviled eggs. Maybe Katie used Mrs. Garcia's recipe but actually did mix the stuffing and stuff the eggs with her own slender hands. Maybe Mrs. Garcia did prepare the stuffing, but Katie boiled and peeled the eggs and filled the halves full of stuffing and then applied the paprika with her own fingers. Why would Katie have lied to me about fixing the eggs? Was she trying to impress me? That was the wildest rationalization of all.

Something was wrong about the mysterious prowler, too.

I wasn't so besotted that it didn't occur to me that Katie and Dolly might have a lesbian thing going. My world as a sports writer hadn't had a lot of personal assistants in it, but I felt it must be special to have your personal assistant actually live with you and run around in a robe and slippers.

But then there was the team of Adam Wachinski and his man Bruno.

From what I had seen tonight, I doubted Adam would survive for long without Bruno to protect him.

I wondered how many personal assistants were running the people who run Hollywood. But I didn't worry about it for very long.

There had been a tone in Jack's voice on the phone at Katie's that made me apprehensive. Since I had been involved with Jack, he was always standing with on one foot at the edge of some cliff or other just to prove he could do it.

All he had said to me on Katie's phone was, "We got work to do, buddy boy, and it can't wait. I'm at the bar downstairs at home. Look for the guy with the beard in the back booth."

There was tension in his voice I hadn't heard before. I had been with Jack in crazy situations in saloons and in meetings and on golf courses, but he had never for a moment seemed afraid that he might be overmatched.

Cruising along Rodeo in the Mercedes in the cool blue night with lights shining from the windows of elegant shops that were closed, almost no traffic, that sweet new-leather smell from the seats, and Bobby Short on my stereo, I had the sensation that I, too, was flush with money, and always had been. I felt that being well off was my natural state in life.

That's what hooks you out here, they say.

You never get over the good times, they say.

I waited for the light at Wilshire next to a silver Rolls Royce. The dog in the passenger seat stared back at me. I pulled into the entrance at the hotel and hopped out of the Mercedes and gave the valet ten bucks. Paula used to get annoyed at what she considered my over-tipping. I believe tipping is bread on the waters. It makes friends and saves lives.

There was no Spanish spoken with this valet. He was a tall Hungarian who wanted to be in the movies and let it be known that sex of any kind was no obstacle.

"Mr. Roach is waiting for you in the bar," the Hungarian said, slipping into the Mercedes. "He told me to tell you."

"Has he been here long?" I asked.

"I think about forty-five minutes. He looks all shook up."

"Really?"

"Please don't tell him I said that." He pulled the door shut and the car purred away with Bobby Short still pouring from the window.

My heart was beating faster as I walked up the red-carpeted stairs into the lobby. At the entrance to the bar the maître d', Fritzi, nodded and leaned close to me. He whispered, "Mr. Roach is in the far back booth on the right."

This was how, by keeping his life a secret, Jack had remained front-page material—everybody who knew where Jack was felt like they had to confide it to someone.

I went past the bar, where a dozen men who looked like hotel guests and two women who looked like one-nighters were having cocktails. A few of them were listening to Frankie Cocoa playing "They Can't Take That Away from Me" on the piano. I stuffed a twenty in Frankie's crystal tip jar on the piano as I went by. He glanced at me. Mine was the only bill in his jar, but he might have cleaned it out in the last few minutes. Most bar musicians keep bills showing in their tip jars on the theory that money breeds money. But some, like Frankie Cocoa, who played with the Philadelphia Orchestra before his hands became a little shaky, are embarrassed to be seen accepting tips.

A waiter in a black vest and a red bow tie approached as I was walking down the aisle between the booths.

"He's waiting in the back," the waiter whispered. Then out loud he said, "What may I bring you to drink, sir?"

I stopped and dug a cigarette out of my shirt pocket. The waiter lit it for me, and looked knowingly into my eyes. Now that he had shared with me the secret of Jack Roach's location, we were sort of brothers.

"What's he drinking?" I asked.

"Shots of Stoli with Carlsberg ale."

"I'll have the same. And bring us a plate of appetizers. Shrimp and crackers and antipasto stuff. Make up a big plate of food."

"A lovely idea," the waiter said.

I headed down the aisle to the right rear booth, where an old man with a gray beard was slouched against the far corner wearing a Ben Hogan–style white linen cap pulled down low on his forehead, like a Scottish caddie. His eyes, peering out from under the brim of the cap, were electric blue. A smoking cigarette hung from his lips. The beard covered most of the rest of his face. It wasn't even a high-class, glue-on beard—I could see a wire hooked over his right ear.

Jack had a shot glass in one hand and a glass of ale in the other.

"I'm here to meet Peer Gynt," I said. "Are you his father?"

"Do I look silly?" Jack Roach said.

I sat down opposite him. Jack nipped a sip of the vodka and swallowed a mouthful of ale. He was wearing the white golf shirt and khaki trousers he had worn this afternoon at Riviera. He had added a jean jacket with the cuffs turned up. The front of his jean jacket was embroidered with red roses and beaded stems.

"You look otherworldly," I said. "You could be on *Star Trek*."

"I was going for the Hemingway look," Jack said.

"You used too much club."

"I overshot it, huh?"

The waiter brought a tray to our booth. He unloaded a glass of ale and a shot of vodka for me. Then he put a large platter in the middle of the table. I saw hunks of lobster, shrimps, pieces of fish, lettuce, tomatoes, brown bread, coleslaw, cheese, pepperoni, a pot of mustard, and a pot of mayo.

"Will there be anything else?"

"Another round of drinks," said Jack.

When the waiter had gone, Jack said, "The thing is, I like this bar, I like hanging out here. But if I come in here without a disguise, people come rushing up and jump in the middle of my action."

"How did you find me?" I asked.

"I called Queen Bee's house. Somebody told me you drove off with Katie Wynne. You probably think you're a lucky guy to take Katie home, but let me warn you, buddy boy. If Katie picked you out of the crowd, you're in trouble. Run for it. Beware of that woman."

"Why?"

"She's a killer."

"What are you talking about?" I said.

"She broke my heart."

I downed my vodka, stacked some pepperoni on a piece of bread with a hunk of cheese, took a bite, and swallowed a long draught of ale to wash it all down. Jack was playing with his old silver Zippo on the table, spinning it back and forth while he watched me. The lighter had been a gift to Jack from an airborne unit in Vietnam. Jack had been too old for the war in Vietnam, but too young for the war in Korea. Fresh out of high school, he had done two years in the Navy in the Pacific. But the Screaming Eagles unit in Vietnam adopted him because he was their favorite movie star.

I picked up the Zippo and lit my cigarette.

"I see how that could happen," I said.

"It was twelve years ago," Jack said.

"Well, that's what you get for hanging around the school yard."

Jack chuckled. He stroked his beard.

"That's one thing I like about you, buddy boy. You don't know shit. How old do you think Katie is?"

"Twenty-five," I said.

"She's thirty-one, maybe thirty-two. I met her on location in Nevada. Twelve years ago I was a long way from being who I am today, and Katie was a nineteen- or twenty-year-old nobody."

"You were a star twelve years ago," I said. I remembered taking Paula to a Jack Roach picture the year we got married, which I mentally toted up as fourteen years ago.

"Yeah, I got the billing, but it wasn't like it is today. The fuckers are taking my breath away from me, Richard."

"What happened with you and Katie?" I asked.

"I fell in love with her on location. We were doing a picture in a small town. Katie had a few lines. She just knocked my socks off. But I was married to Angela. So I told Katie I would leave Angela for her, and I did, and then Katie dumped me."

I could have read about that in the gossip columns twelve years ago, but I was covering the Jets that fall, and I went to the four major professional golf tournaments that year for the magazine—plus I hid out in London for two months to finish writing a novel. Paula was an editor at *Time* magazine then, so there were not yet any issues of *People* magazine stacked around our apartment to tell me about the movie stars. Jack was right that there was quite a gap in my knowledge of show business, but I was working on it.

"But you still see her?" I said.

"Not in the same way, but we stay in touch. I like talking to her."

We sat and smoked for a minute and fiddled with our ale glasses, making wet circles on the table. Up front at the piano I could hear Frankie Cocoa singing, "I could write a book . . ."

"Jack, I've gotta ask you," I said. "I signed a contract to work for you for twelve weeks writing a movie script. Nearly three weeks are gone already, and I've got nothing on paper. Does this not bother you?"

"How much do I owe you from the golf?"

"From today, three hundred. All total, eleven-fifty."

"We'll play a $500 Nassau next time. Cash money. Pay up in the bar after the last putt. Give me five shots. Three on the back."

"All right," I said.

"I'm not worried about the script. You and I have talked the story over. We know how it starts, and the middle, and the end. When you get to the typewriter it will come flowing right out," Jack said.

"You sounded worried on the phone just now," I said.

"Did I? Well, maybe a little, very briefly. But I wasn't worried about the script. I sort of had a little dizzy spell a while ago. But I called Dr. Feelgood and he came over and checked me out. There's no problem, except I could use some sleep, he says."

"So could I."

"Sorry to drag you away from Katie's house."

"Comma, he lied," I said.

"She's got her hooks in you already, doesn't she?"

"Max Bloom told me tonight that she has outrageous scenes in her hot tub, but that wasn't the glimpse of her that I got," I said.

"Who told you that?"

"Max Bloom."

"Who is that?"

"You took a shower with him at Riviera the other day," I said.

"I never heard of him," said Jack. He pushed the plate of food away, put his elbows on the table, and lit a cigarette with the Zippo. He flipped the lid a couple of times.

"That's bullshit about Katie's hot tub scenes," he finally said.

"Actually, I'm glad to hear it," I said.

"People make up stuff like that. They act like they know something, but they really don't have a fucking clue."

The waiter brought two more rounds of vodka and ale. He tried to catch Jack's eye, but Jack wouldn't look at him. I looked at him so Jack wouldn't have to. I told him we were fine.

"You said you want to work tonight," I said to Jack. "Let's start with the ending. It's a bummer."

"Let's save this argument for way on down the road. Let's get to the ending before we fight about it. You can't win the fight, you know, so why would you want to have it so early?"

"Maybe you could get hanged off-stage after the movie is over, and we see a crawl on the screen that says Jack Roach does not really die at the end of this picture, even though his character may seem to."

"Weintraub told you to say that," Jack said.

Oliver Weintraub was the producer that Jack's independent film company had hired to oversee the movie. Oliver was about sixty. He had a background in New York nightclubs, and there were stories that he had been involved with shady elements, to which I would say, "Shady elements in New York nightclubs? Oh, no! I am shocked!" Oliver had made a fortune producing kung fu movies.

"He didn't need to tell me," I said.

Jack sighed. He reached up with both hands and unhooked the beard from his ears. The gray hair stuck to his cheeks. He peeled it off slowly, spluttering when a few stray hairs got in his mouth. The face he revealed was featured on millions of posters in millions of bedrooms. The mouth had a sly, tight grin as if he is about to tell you something that he knows you want to know, and maybe it has something to do with sex. He had a strong chin with a dimple in it. The nose was a little crooked. Shining out of this lean, determined-looking face were the famous electric-blue eyes.

He clawed gray hairs off his tongue.

"Did you happen to notice Claude Rimbaud in the coffee shop?" he asked.

"I came in the front door. I didn't look in the coffee shop."

"Do me a favor, buddy boy?" Jack asked.

He stuffed the gray beard under the table, lifted his cap, and brushed his fingers through his short, dirty-blond hair.

"It'll be a big help to me," he said.

"Yeah, sure I will," I said. "What do you want?"

"Go look in the coffee shop and come back and tell me if Claude Rimbaud is in there."

Jack looked at his watch.

"It's eleven o' clock," Jack said. "He's supposed to be there at eleven."

"I don't know what Claude Rimbaud looks like," I said.

"He's a short, furtive European who usually wears a fedora. He looks a little like Peter Lorre. He'll have on an expensive suit and a necktie. He'll be sitting in a booth alone."

"What should I say to him?" I asked.

"Nothing. Don't let him see you. Just come back and tell me if he's in there."

Jack lifted his briefcase off the seat, unzipped it, and took out a script, which he laid on the table. I looked at the cover page. The script was an adaptation of a best-seller about a US Navy gunboat in the South China Sea in the 1930s. I had read the novel. It was a good adventure story. The hero was a sailor who rescues a missionary's daughter from a warlord.

"Here's the thing," Jack said. "My price for reading a script is one million dollars."

"Just for reading it?" I asked.

"Claude paid me a million dollars to read this script," Jack said. "I cashed his check before I read a word."

"I didn't know anything like that was possible," I said.

"Like I keep saying, you don't know shit," said Jack, "So the deal is, if I say yes to making this movie I will deduct the million bucks from my fee, and Claude owes me five million more when we shoot it. If I say yes, he goes back to Europe and sells my name to raise the rest of the money for the production."

"But if you say no, you keep the million-dollar reading fee," I said.

"We need this million for our own movie," Jack said.

"What are you going to do?" I asked.

"I haven't decided yet."

"Why don't you go on in there if he's waiting for you?" I said.

"What if I walk in and Claude's not there? I'm left standing in the coffee shop with all those people looking at me and my ass is hanging out like some jilted asshole at a high school dance."

"You have his million bucks already," I said. "That's not exactly jilted."

"Listen, Richard, will you do it or not? I could send the waiter, but he'd try to slip Claude his audition tape."

"Claude looks like Peter Lorre?"

"You saw *The Maltese Falcon*? Claude looks like Peter Lorre in that one, but better dressed."

"Okay."

I slid out of the booth, walked along the aisle past the piano where Frankie Cocoa was playing and singing, "The sweetest sounds I ever heard . . ." He liked to mix Broadway tunes into his cabaret repertoire. Frankie had his eyes shut, a soft, tender look on his face. He was singing from his heart. The tip jar was empty.

I went through the lobby and stopped at the door that opened into the hotel's famous corner coffee shop. Many deals were closed late at night in that coffee shop. Some of them even had to do with show business.

I opened the door and peeked inside.

The counter and booths were full. Customers were waiting at the sidewalk entrance. One booth against the window was occupied only by a small, dark, bug-eyed man wearing a suit that I guessed to be Italian, maybe a Brioni. He wore a fedora hat at a sharp tilt, and his cufflinks glistened. His necktie was white silk, as was the handkerchief in his chest pocket. He was idly stirring a cup of coffee and glancing without the slightest show of remorse at the people waiting in line on the other side of his window.

I remembered a line from *People* magazine: "The fabulous international film mogul Claude Rimbaud . . ."

His dark eyes turned and gave me a quick scan. I was satisfied. I returned through the lobby and went back past the piano. Frankie was on break. The waiter fell in stride with me as if he were leading me back to the booth, where I saw Jack turning pages of the script. Surely, I thought, Jack wasn't just now reading it.

I took my seat in the booth.

"He's there," I said.

"Alone?"

"Yeah."

Jack closed the script and placed his right hand on it, palm down. I thought he was going to take an oath, and then I thought, no, he's getting

41

some kind of psychic revelation. With his left hand, Jack held out a key on a heavy gold medallion.

"This key is to my hooch," Jack said. "Make yourself at home up there."

"I was thinking about going home," I said.

"Please, buddy boy. I need you," Jack said.

I nodded and took the key from him. Jack stuffed the script back into his briefcase. "Take the case upstairs with you, too, if you will," he said. He pushed the briefcase across the table and stood up. He took off the Ben Hogan golf cap and tossed it on top of the briefcase. He combed his fingers through his hair, licked his lips, and brushed his hands down the twin roses embroidered on the front of his jean jacket.

"Are you a yes or a no?" I asked.

"I haven't decided yet," Jack said. "See you upstairs in a few minutes. Sign my name on the tab. Tip big. Ha ha." He seemed to find that funny.

Jack took a couple of steps. He stopped and turned back. "Hey, Richard, did you get Katie's phone number?"

"I forgot," I said.

"Sorry. I can't give it to you. It's private."

He smiled as if he were joking. Then he turned and I watched his back as he walked down the aisle between the booths, heads turning as he went past in his famous, ambling stride.

Upstairs in Jack's two-bedroom suite, I sat for a while on the terrace looking at the lights down Rodeo Drive and at the dark shapes of the mountains. It was an unusually clear night. Rain and wind off the ocean had driven away the day's smoke. I could see the stars in the sky.

I drank a beer and smoked a cigarette. I walked around the living room. Jack had thrown a western saddle into a corner along with a coil of rope. A Bowie knife was sticking out of a wall. The saddle was next to a closet door that was locked with a padlock. A hand-lettered sign said Keep Out of Here . . . JR. I watched television for a few minutes. The weather girl said it would rain tomorrow.

I went to the elevator. Once again I didn't see Warren Beatty in the hall. Downstairs I bypassed the coffee shop. The Hungarian valet fetched my Mercedes, and I drove through the dark neighborhoods to the Westwood Marquis. At the front desk I asked Mrs. Morton to hold my phone calls, please, until I signed into the world again.

Six

The next morning was the first day of April. I woke up to the sound of thunder and rain.

The red message light on the phone was blinking. I squinted at my watch. It was nearly ten o'clock. I had slept more than nine hours.

Last July in London I was talking to a glamorous Texas girl named Jerry Hall, who was living with Mick Jagger, and I mentioned that I had to get up at six to drive down to Sandwich where the British Open golf tournament was about to begin at Royal St. George's. I said five hours would be plenty of sleep. Jerry flashed her toothy smile and lectured me on the psychological and physiological need for sleep. She's a tall, high-IQ blonde who reads the science journals. Jerry told me she sleeps ten hours every night. I asked how she could do that and live the rock and roll life. She poked me in the chest with a long red fingernail and said, "I'm trying, Richard. Don't rub it in."

I lay in bed a few more minutes, remembering last summer's Open at Royal St. George's. Bill Rogers, a Texas boy from Waco, had won it. I remembered the house that Paula and I lived in for the week of the tournament. It was what the English call a "stately home." It was called Knowlton Court. There were so many rooms that five couples of us from the US—three television guys, another sports writer, three wives, and two girlfriends—had leased the house but saw each other only at dinner, which was served by staff at a long table in a dining room commanded by oil paintings of the sea. But even with such roomy privacy, one of the television guys told me that the others could hear Paula and me yelling at each other, and there was a betting pool every evening on whether both of us would come to dinner at the same time. That would've been the middle of July. In September, she filed for divorce.

I got up and went to the window and watched rain pour on the UCLA Medical Center across the street. A helicopter put down on the landing pad on the roof. A team unloaded a stretcher and carried a sad bundle inside. I couldn't see the mountains because of the rain, but I watched little rivers running along the curbs. No golf today. Today must be meant for me to sit down at the Smith-Corona portable typewriter that I had taken out of its case more than two weeks ago and placed on the desk beside the living room window. I could actually write a few pages today.

The Westwood Marquis was a dormitory for UCLA's women students in its original life, which is why it was all suites. When it was reborn as a hotel, they dressed up the place and put in a pool, a large restaurant, and a good bar with comfortable couches, tables, and a full harp. You were liable to see anybody in that bar. When I came through the lobby last night, Dolly Parton was standing in the doorway of the bar talking to a tall guy wearing a scarf, and Jackie Chan was just leaving.

I made a visit to the living room of my suite, looked at the typewriter, and then noticed several message envelopes had been slid under the living room door. I picked up the messages but didn't open the envelopes yet. Instead I called room service to order a ham omelet, hash browns, toast, grapefruit juice, and a pot of coffee. I opened the door and picked up the *Los Angeles Times* from the hallway. I went into the large bathroom that opened off the bedroom. I washed my face and decided not to shave yet.

I sat down on the bed and opened the newspaper. On the front page of the *Times* was a story about President Jimmy Carter's falling poll numbers. Personally, I had never forgiven him for pulling out of the 1980 Olympics. I voted for him and was rooting for him until that happened. The Russians blundered by invading Afghanistan and were getting their asses kicked daily by the Afghans. The battlefield was the place for violent political expression. The Olympics was the place for the human race to come together and show its finer qualities.

I looked through the sports section, read Jim Murray's column as always, read about the Yankees and the Dodgers. When I saw the photo of Jack Nicklaus, I realized with a sharp little stab of pain that the Masters golf tournament was coming up soon, but I wouldn't be there. I would be somewhere with Jack Roach.

When I heard a chime, I put on the hotel's terrycloth robe and went to the door to let Marian in with my breakfast. She was a cheery person. She chatted as she set up the table with linens and silverware and a rose in a tall, thin vase. Marian poured my first cup of coffee. The forecast was a Pacific front with rain, she said, and we need the rain. I signed the ticket with a nice tip for her.

In my opinion the civilized life begins with an hour at the breakfast table, reading at least one newspaper, drinking several cups of coffee, with very little conversation. Paula couldn't see it that way. Now, Paula was no longer on the other side of the table.

At eleven fifteen, with the rain still lashing at the windows, I felt sufficiently civilized to pick up the phone and punch the message desk. I liked talking to Ruthie. She made every message sound like something really interesting.

I opened the envelopes and read the written messages as Ruthie spoke to me, sort of double-checking like a good reporter should.

"My, my, Mr. Swift, you lead such a fascinating life," she said. "You have a call from Jack Roach, a call from Katie Wynne, a call from Max Bloom, a call from a man named Bruno, a call from a person named X, and here's one that says call Paula at her office in New York."

I didn't see the written message from Paula, but just then I heard a thump and an envelope slid under the living room door. That would be her.

"Is the call from Paula the most recent?" I asked.

"Paula was fifteen minutes ago," said Ruthie. "I took the call. Maybe I shouldn't say this, but she sounded furious."

I looked at the messages. Katie had phoned at twelve thirty last night, X had phoned at midnight, Max Bloom had called at nine this morning, and Bruno had called at seven this morning.

Jack Roach had phoned at three a.m.

I knew I had better call Paula first, because she was the only person on this list who could really shatter me. If she was too busy to shatter me, she could let her lawyer do it. We were divorced, but there were legal details yet unsettled. I took a shower, shaved, put on a clean white Brooks Brothers shirt with a button-down collar that stood up high on my neck the way I liked. The valet had left my dry cleaning in the closet. I found a pair of pleated cotton khaki slacks that looked nice with a thin alligator belt that had a silver tip and buckle. I pulled on tan cashmere socks and snuggled my feet into my Gucci loafers. I suddenly realized I was getting dressed up to talk to Paula, as if she could see me. So I slapped my cheeks with two palms of aftershave lotion Paula had bought for me at Truefitt & Hill in London, preparing my face for the proper stinging it was about to get, and then I phoned her.

She answered at her desk on the twenty-first floor of the Time-Life Building at 50th and 6th Avenue in New York City. Paula had a corner office with windows that looked down 6th and across to Rockefeller Center. She was an assistant managing editor of *People* magazine. Paula oversaw the longer feature pieces.

"Well, Benny, is there still time for you to make a game-saving tackle?" she said instead of hello.

"Benny" was what she called me when she was exasperated but wouldn't allow herself to call me a stupid asshole because she was above that sort of language most of the time. Benny Lom was the teammate who had tackled Roy "Wrong Way" Riegels on their own two-yard line after Roy's famous wrong-way run in the Rose Bowl. Paula said I was constantly letting my life run the wrong way and then rescuing myself with a desperate, last-second tackle. That didn't seem to be the truth at all from my point of view, but when she called me "Benny," I guessed what this call was about, and this time she might have a case.

"What is it now?" I said.

"I heard this morning that you quit *SI*. I thought you were on another leave of absence, but Elrod tells me you quit."

"Fuck Elrod," I said, and then wished I hadn't, because I had called up a picture of what she had been doing for about a year.

Elrod was her lover and now her housemate on the West Side. He was the head of the art department at *Sports Illustrated*. Elrod was a tall guy with wavy hair. He looked British, but he was from Connecticut and Harvard.

"Look, Richard, I am sorry that our breakup has caused you such emotional damage that you can't stand to see Elrod in the halls or in the meetings at *SI*. I had no idea it would go this far, that you would walk into Roy's office and tell him you are finished at the magazine. Roy is no fan of yours personally, you know, but he's a decent man and he likes your writing. If you phone him right this minute and apologize, he will take you back. Elrod is sure of it."

I propped the phone between my shoulder and my ear and was looking for my cigarettes. I was telling myself to stay Zen. Keep my mouth shut. I could gain nothing by being snippy or sarcastic with Paula.

"Fuck Elrod" I said again, and got a mental picture of Paula and Elrod on our big brown sofa at 86th and Madison.

"Could we discuss this intelligently?" Paula said. I heard her intake of breath as she lit a cigarette. I found my own pack on the counter of the kitchen area, but I couldn't find my lighter. "I can appreciate that you would be embarrassed by all of this. How do you think I feel when I can tell people are whispering about us?"

"Embarrassed is part of how I feel," I said carefully.

"And you're hurt. I can understand that. I'm sorry."

"But embarrassed is only part of it," I said. "Hurt is part of it, too. Pissed off is the rest of it—the major portion, I believe. I mean Elrod, for God's sake!" I was losing it again. "Elrod is such a jerk. To think my wife of however many years would run off with a total jerk, that's what eats me up. But that's not why I quit the magazine. Don't give yourself credit for that."

"I was giving myself blame rather than credit," she said.

"You don't deserve either one," I said. "I quit the magazine because it's time for me to move on with my life. I'm not running the wrong way. Hemingway said if you stay in journalism for too long it will ruin you as a writer."

"Oh, fuck Hemingway," she said. This was the Paula I had loved. "Hemingway is full of pretentious macho shit and so many pompous utterances about writing—wait a minute. You brought Hemingway into this to provoke me, didn't you?"

"Paula, the reason I quit the magazine is Louie Lester got me $250,000 to write a script for Jack Roach."

"But you've written two scripts before that got made into movies, and you didn't feel Hemingway was telling you to quit journalism and move off in the wrong direction," Paula said. "*SI* will let you stay on at the magazine and continue to write movies, as long as you do your assignments."

"This is different. This time I'm serious about Hollywood."

"What! I can't believe what I'm hearing!"

"I wrote those first two scripts on vacation and never thought of myself as a serious movie writer," I said.

"You're supposed to be a serious novelist, aren't you? The *New York Review of Books* said you are. You sit at the novelist table at Elaine's."

"Writing novels wouldn't pay the maintenance at 86th and Madison."

"I think we might do a paragraph on you with a photo in our "Faces" section next week. It'll say 'Richard Swift: He's serious about Hollywood.' I can hear the boys and girls laughing at the novelist table."

"How would it sound if you quote me saying film is our most popular art?" I said.

"It would sound like you're a fool who never heard of the Beatles."

"Is this what you called to tell me? That I'm ruining my life? I was afraid Elrod might have taken our dog to be put down, or something else important was going on."

"Richard, I want you to phone Roy the moment I hang up. Tell him you didn't intend to be rude to him in his office and that you are off in Hollywood having a brief adventure with Jack Roach, and you'll be back in time to go to the British Open at Royal Troon in July and you would love to have the assignment. Roy will probably vent on you on the speaker phone to save face, but you will be accepted back into the family."

"After I write this $250,000 script for Jack Roach, the next script I write will be $500,000," I said. "I'll take Roy to lunch the next time I have a movie on location in New York. I'll apologize to him then."

There was a silence. I found a book of Westwood Marquis matches and managed to light my cigarette. I could hear Paula breathing.

"I still care about you, Richard," she said finally.

"I care about you, too, Paula, but—"

"Don't you dare say 'a man's gotta do what a man's gotta do,'" she said.

"I was going to say I'm getting on the 3:10 to Yuma, and don't try to stop me if you know what's good for you."

"Goodbye, Richard," she said and hung up.

I sat on the bed, drinking a cup of lukewarm coffee and finishing my cigarette, the third of the day. I was feeling bummed out. Rain was smashing at the windows. The air in the room felt damp. I got up and turned on all the lights. I opened all the shutters, too, but that only made it darker.

Then I went back to the phone and started on the messages.

The number for Katie was her answering service. Of course, she wouldn't give her private number to a hotel switchboard. I told the girl who answered that I would try Katie again tonight around seven. I phoned X and got his answering machine. X's recorded voice said, "Don't bring that shit around me unless you can back it up. Leave a number." I left my number.

I looked at the message from Jack Roach and didn't recognize the number. At three o'clock in the morning, Jack was liable to be anyplace. I tossed the message onto the bed. I looked at the message from Max Bloom, looked at the rain pelting down, and put his message aside. I had said I would phone Max on Saturday night. That was tomorrow.

So who was left? Bruno? What could he want? Bruno was too spooky for comfort. Whatever he wanted with me could not be something I would enjoy. I crumpled his message and dumped it into the trash.

I sat down at my typewriter and rolled in a piece of paper. The typewriter had been set for double-spaced prose from the last time I had used it, doing an *SI* story on the National Finals Rodeo that Roy had wanted for a cover. I adjusted the margins for movie dialogue.

I sat and thought for a minute. I lit another cigarette. I sipped cold coffee. I called room service and ordered a fresh pot. I studied the stack of white typing paper on the desk. It looked like enough paper for a screenplay. Well, maybe not. A screenplay was about 120 pages. There were only about 80 pages in this stack. I should go to the store for more paper, but it was raining. Hey, I had an umbrella in the closet.

There was a knock at the door.

"Housekeeping," called a woman's voice with a Spanish accent. I yelled for her to come in. Behind the housekeeper came Marian with a tray bearing a pot of coffee, clean cups, cream, sugar, sweet rolls, and a copy of the new *Sports Illustrated* magazine that she had thought I would want to see. I tipped her nicely, gave five dollars to the housekeeper, and decided to get out of the suite during the cleaning.

I took the *Sports Illustrated* with me and got on the elevator down to the lobby. I was heading to the restaurant, which was serving a brunch buffet that was famous in Westwood, when someone spoke my name.

"Richard Swift."

Out from behind a potted tree stepped Bruno.

Seven

Bruno was wearing a cream-colored linen jacket with a pair of aviator sunglasses hanging from the breast pocket. Between his thatch of hair and his demeanor of a good German, he reminded me of the faithful servant in the movie *Sunset Boulevard*. Except Bruno's eyes held a mean, suspicious look.

"Richard Swift?" he asked.

"You don't remember for sure?"

"Forgive me for turning that into a question," Bruno replied. "The question is, 'Would you please join me for a cup of coffee in the restaurant?'"

"I'd be happy to, Bruno," I said.

We entered between potted palms and were escorted by an Asian hostess to a table with lime green wicker chairs that had soft white leather cushions. Half a dozen people were lingering at the buffet's mounds of shrimp on ice. I sat opposite Bruno, placing the *Sports Illustrated* on an empty chair. Bruno ordered coffee and orange juice and a toasted English muffin with butter and jam. I nodded to the waitress that I would have the same, and I lit cigarette number six.

"I have read one of your novels," Bruno announced.

"Yeah?"

"I saw the notice in the *New York Review of Books*, and I drove to a book store in Santa Monica. They didn't have it, but they phoned around and found me a copy of it at a shop in Beverly Hills. I should think an author would be upset to get a prestigious notice and then not have his book widely distributed."

"Did you like the novel?" I asked.

"Not so much. I prefer happy stories."

"You must be enjoying that Camus novel I saw you reading last night," I said.

"Camus was an intellectual. You are a sports writer. Those two facts temper my appreciation of the meaning of the way the writer ends his book."

"It's nice of you to drive all the way over here to tell me."

The waitress served the muffins and poured two cups of coffee. Bruno blinked at my cigarette, which was smoldering in a ceramic ashtray. The smoke was making his eyes water. Ordinarily I would have put out the cigarette, but something in the tenor of Bruno's conversation made me decide to keep it smoking.

"Sorry. I don't mean to offend. I admire the act of writing a novel, and my hat is off to anyone who can do it. I tried to write novels when I was young, but I didn't have the knack. You do have it. So I respect you."

Bruno reached over and mashed out my cigarette. "None of your three novels has been bought for a film," he said.

"Two were optioned, but the options expired."

"Why do you think that is?" said Bruno.

"I don't know."

"I can tell you that your agent placed them in the wrong hands."

"It wasn't my agent's fault. There was no bidding war." I said. "We took the first thing that sounded good. At that stage, they all sound good."

"If Adam Wachinski owned your books, at least one of them would be a film by now," Bruno said.

"They are available," I said.

"I am here to take you to see Adam," Bruno said. "He wants to talk about buying your books."

"He can call my agent. I'm not good at talking about money."

"Adam wants to see you face-to-face."

"Not today. I'm hard at work today. Maybe one day next week," I said.

Bruno smeared butter on his muffin and piled strawberry jam on it and bit the muffin in half with a loud crunch. "This is excellent," he said. He chewed. "Please don't be difficult, Richard."

"Sorry, Bruno. I'm on deadline and I've got to work. You must know how it is."

"It is important that Adam meets with you this morning. He has something to tell you about Jack Roach that you very much need to know."

"He can tell me on the phone," I said.

"This is not something he would say on the phone."

"Why not?"

"Adam will tell you."

The seven or eight cups of coffee were kicking in. I got a sudden urge to start moving.

"Wait here," I said. "Finish your muffin."

"I will be in the car," said Bruno.

I went to my suite and put on a navy blue waterproof jacket and a rain hat. I looked at my typewriter for a moment, lit another cigarette. On my way back from Adam's I figured I would stop at the stationery shop on the drag by UCLA and pick up a ream of typing paper.

Bruno was waiting at the curb in a black Rolls limo with a driver up front. The driver wore a gray uniform and a cap. He looked like one of those Samoans who played linebacker in college. The driver jumped out of the car and came around with an umbrella. The rain hammered on the hotel canopy and on the umbrella that he held over my head as I stepped over a puddle and ducked into the back seat with Bruno.

"We're going to the office," Bruno said to the driver and then he closed the sliding window between us and the driver.

"How much do you know about Adam Wachinski?" he asked.

"Practically nothing," I said.

"You have no doubt been told he can be a difficult person."

"Nobody needed to tell me, Bruno. I was there last night."

"He had an inspiration last night that saved a huge project from having its plug pulled," said Bruno.

"Who was going to pull the plug?"

"Adam was."

"On himself?"

"One of Adam's virtues is that he is ruthless if he needs to be. But he had an idea last night that made the picture clear in his mind, and he saw how to make it work. So five hundred people of various trades, skills, and crafts will be employed on this project for a year or more. If that idea had occurred to Adam next week instead of last night, it would have been too late."

I nodded and looked out the window at the rain washing Wilshire.

"I have been with Adam for twenty years. His father hired me to look after him when he was a teenage freshman prodigy at USC film school. Adam is good at heart. I know Adam better than anyone alive, except his mother. He is very close to his mother. You have met her?"

"We met last night," I said.

Bruno allowed himself to smile. "Adam's mother is the difficult Wachinski."

"Adam needed somebody to look after him when he was already in college?"

"Just to make sure he is all right."

"Where's the old man?"

"Twenty years ago he and two friends took the family boat out on a tuna run, and they never returned. They are presumed dead. Adam took it very hard. He has devoted himself to his work ever since. So this family tragedy has provided the world with a string of fantastically important films."

I glanced at Bruno, but if he was being ironic he hid it well.

"The fishing boat was never found?"

"No."

"No wreckage? No bodies?"

"Nothing."

"What kind of business was he in?" I asked.

"He owned fifty-seven Dairy Queens. He was very well off. This was no insurance scam. Ah, look. See the three prostitutes huddled in the doorway on Sunset?"

"I missed them," I said.

"They were soaked. Well now, here we are. Adam will be waiting."

The offices of the W Film Group were a block off of Sunset Boulevard, not far from the Chateau Marmont Hotel. The small, elegant sign simply featured a W on an iron post stood in a patch of green grass that was carefully tended but now flooded with rain. The building behind it looked like an old Spanish mission with a red tile roof. The driver wheeled the Rolls up a private drive and into an alley. He parked under a shed that had spaces for eight automobiles. The other spaces were filled—two Porsches, a Jaguar, a BMW, and the rest Toyotas.

We went in the back door, past a kitchen where three young men in shirt-sleeves and neckties were drinking coffee at a bar and talking vigorously. We passed offices with typewriters and women at desks before we came to the reception area in the living room of this former mansion. A motherly woman wearing reading glasses on a chain and a black pants suit sat behind a large, antique oak desk. She was hanging up a phone as we entered.

"Good morning, Bruno," she said.

"Mrs. Buckham, good morning to you," Bruno said.

I was looking around at the paintings on the walls. I didn't recognize all of the artists, but I did see a Goya. They were landscapes with animals, mostly horses. Two leather couches faced each other across a marble coffee table on an antique rug that looked North African to me. Off to the left of the reception desk I could see a room with a long table and eight chairs.

"Good morning, Mr. Swift," Mrs. Buckham said. "Mr. Wachinski is expecting you. Please follow me."

We went up a flight of carpeted stairs. A long hall led down a row of offices—four on each side—occupied by men and women talking on the telephone or typing or staring out the windows at the rain. In one office I saw a poster for one of Adam's movies, but that was the only outward sign that this was a show business factory. Otherwise it could as well have been an investment bank.

The hall ended at an eight-foot-tall door. Mrs. Buckham pushed a button beside it, leaned toward a wall fixture, and said, "Bruno and the gentleman are here."

The door silently swung open. Mrs. Buckham smiled and left us.

At first glance there were two things in the room that didn't fit—a blue surfboard leaning against the wall, and Adam Wachinski in and old-fashioned sleeveless undershirt, baggy knee-length shorts, and flip flops. No comb or brush had touched his long tangled hair since last night. He had a stubble of beard. Everything else in the room was elegant, tasteful, and very expensive. I noticed a large shaving mirror laying flat on Adam's desk, and he was licking his fingers when the door opened.

"Richard! I'm glad you could come!" he cried when he saw me and ran around his desk and shook my hand. "Look! Look at this!" he said.

In a dark, polished mahogany frame on the wall was a color photograph of number thirty-two wearing the uniform of the Buffalo Bills, a hand resting on the shoulder of a grinning Adam Wachinski. Written on the photograph was: "Love to my old buddy Adam from The Juice '73."

"You recognize the year?" Adam said. "He rushed for 2,003 yards in 1973. He was the first back in NFL history to rush for more than 2,000 yards in one season. You notice how he signed it? You notice the date? In 1973, I hadn't even had a number one movie yet or won an Oscar or anything. Did I say I knew The Juice way back at USC?"

"Yeah," I said. "You did mention it."

"You want a drink?" asked Adam. "Tall Black Label with one cube of ice?" He had done research on me.

"No thanks. It's a little early."

"Want to smoke a joint?"

"It's a little early for that, too. Thanks," I said.

"Do a couple of lines?"

I shook my head. If I needed a boost, I had some orange heart-shaped pills in a prescription bottle in my shaving kit. I would do a line of somebody else's coke now and then, but I never bought any, so to my mind I didn't do drugs. I had an ounce of weed in a baggie in a shoe in my closet in my bedroom at 86th and Madison, and I left home on trips with six joints rolled up and hidden in my socks, but I don't count weed as drugs any more than alcohol is.

"Well, then, would you like a cup of coffee?" Adam said.

"I'm fine, Adam. I don't need a thing."

"Sit down, Richard. Please," Adam said.

I lowered myself into a leather chair in front of his desk. Adam walked around behind the desk. He picked up a stack of 8×10 photos and showed me one of them.

"Look at the titties on this blonde pig," he said.

I looked at the photo of a young woman who wanted to be in the movies. She was standing naked in front of a white sheet tacked against a wall.

I looked back at Adam and nodded.

"Are you a sex man?" he asked.

I understood the words but not the question. I glanced at Bruno, who sat on the couch near the door.

"Meaning what?" I said.

"I don't mean are you gay. I mean are you crazy about sex?"

"About it or for it?"

"I mean are you obsessed with thinking about sex and doing sex?"

"I wouldn't call it obsessed, no. I suspect I'm somewhere in the normal range. Do you mind if I smoke?"

"Let me light that for you," Adam said.

He leaned across the desk and flicked a tall gold Ronson that he had been using as a paperweight. He watched me inhale. He put the lighter down and picked up another photo from the stack. He held up the photo for me to look at. She was a young woman, a little overweight, a sort of middle-European-looking woman. She was sitting on a kitchen chair in front of the same white sheet. She was facing the camera, naked and smiling, and her legs were spread wide.

"How can something like that drive men nuts?" Adam said. "Take a good look at what's going on between her legs. You've got Hitler's mustache sitting on top of a freshly opened oyster. Aesthetically, the whole arrangement is a flop. It's God's joke that men will give up their fortunes and their loved ones and even their lives to root around in that oyster for even a few minutes. Men will sacrifice their kingdoms, anything at all, to wade into that foul swamp of nookie."

"Are you a sex man?" I asked.

"No, I am a film-maker," he said.

He studied the rain on the windowpane.

He gestured toward a television screen built into a bookcase. On the shelf by the TV I saw two VHS tape cartons I recognized.

"I watched your two movies this morning," he said. "They're nice little pictures that should have been better. How many other writers worked on them beside you?"

"On the second one, they brought in a guy who changed a few lines and cut a few pages, but I think he didn't apply for credit. He was around for just about a week. On the first one I was the only writer."

"You know how phenomenal that is, Richard?"

"No."

"Well, if you stick around out here you will find out."

I could hear rain on the roof and see it sliding down the windows. The palm trees in the yard were nearly lost in the gloom. I started thinking I might take him up on the joint, though it was still too early for the scotch.

"Did you fuck Katie Wynne last night?" Adam asked.

"No."

"Don't worry, you will. She will fuck you twice to show that she can. After that, no more fucking, but you might stay friends with her or you might not."

"Are you speaking from experience?" I said.

"Me? No. I just make movies. That's my life. That's the only thing I love. But I've heard about her."

"Look, Adam, I really should be working today," I said. "It's not that I don't enjoy talking about sex and football, but that's not what Bruno promised when he asked me to leave my hotel in a rainstorm."

"All right," Adam said. "I'll get right down to it. My new film—it's called *Giants*—needs a rewrite. Your old friend X insists you do the fixing. I think X is right. You're the guy for the job."

"Thanks, but I don't even know what your movie is about."

"Does it matter?" he asked.

"Well, yeah, actually it does."

"Max Bloom will talk to you about the money, and then we will see if it still matters," he said.

"Max should talk to my agents, not to me."

"Max will act as your agent. He will represent both of us."

"No, thanks."

"X is going to ask you to do this as a personal favor to him," said Adam.

"X doesn't give a shit about Max."

"Doing the rewrite, I mean. *Giants* means the world to X. This one can put him up there with the big-money action stars."

I stood up.

"I wish X all the best," I said. "I will tell him so. I hope *Giants* is a blockbuster hit. But I don't want Max. I already have two agents in New York. I don't want to rewrite your movie. I have a job, and I must be getting back to it."

"You sit back down," Adam said.

"You sound like your mother."

"I heard you told my mother to go fuck herself last night," Adam said.

"You heard wrong."

"Sit back down," Adam said.

"What I didn't tell your mother to do, I am now about to tell you to do," I said.

"The picture you are writing now is quickly going to crash and burn," said Adam. "You don't even need to finish writing the script."

"What? Why?"

"Sit down and I will tell you."

I sat back down.

"Are you sure you don't want a joint?" Adam asked. "I've got some fresh Maui Wowie."

"Light it up," I said.

Eight

We passed the joint back and forth, and I found myself on my feet at a sideboard pouring two glasses of tomato juice over ice with a slice of lemon but no vodka. Bruno had left the room when Adam flashed the Ronson at the joint, which was the size of a number two pencil. It looked professionally rolled using oversized cigarette papers. I mentioned that to Adam and he began telling me about a Hawaiian healer in the mountains on Maui who rolled these joints for disciples of his healing circle.

"This shit will cure your head," Adam said.

I gave him a glass of tomato juice and sat back down. I heard a *whoosh* when I dropped into the chair. Adam's face grew larger. I could see the hairs on his chin. I gripped the arms of the chair to settle in more comfortably and felt myself becoming taller.

I took a gulp of cold tomato juice. I tasted every rich, red molecule of it sliding all the way down my throat. I almost shivered with delight.

"X and I did one of these joints last night after you left. We smoked the peace pipe. I am the Malibu Zulu, no question about it. X doesn't give a shit. We talked about *Giants*. What do you think of that kid, Sugar? Is she a Lolita, or what?"

"She looks like seven years in prison," I said.

"More like life without parole," Adam laughed.

I felt like tapping my foot and humming. What I really felt like was playing the piano. Bobby Short had a new album called *Moments Like This*. The way he sang the lyric in "Body and Soul" that goes "my life a *hell* you're making" gave me chills. Bobby Short comes into Elaine's after his late show at the Carlyle and sometimes sits with us at the novelist table. My mind was wandering. I looked around Adam's office, at the wall of bookshelves, at the photograph of Adam with The Juice, and back at Adam as he fiddled with the flipper on the Ronson.

I remembered Adam was going to tell me why my immediate future on the Jack Roach movie was headed for a wreck.

"Did you have thoughts of fucking that little blonde girl?" Adam asked.

"You keep changing the subject back to sex," I said.

"Sex is the subject of everything," said Adam. "Sex is the main thing everybody is interested in. Sex is all around you in a continual hum. The critics write that my films are violent, but what my films really are is sexy. I mean the kind of sexy that gets into a boy's shorts and wakes him up in the middle of the night with his fifth hard-on since he walked out of the theatre. You won't see any fucking or sucking in my films, but the, mysterious power of sex pervades them all and the draws people in."

Adam stared out the window, as if his imagination were trailing off into the gray sky.

"Good dope," he said.

"Weren't you going to tell me something important?" I said.

The joint had gone out, but neither of us cared. Adam sipped his tomato juice. He planted both elbows on the desk and shook his hippie hair out of his eyes and stared at me. He chewed his red lips, upper and then lower.

"Oh. Right," Adam said. "Well, the short of it is Jack Roach is dying of cancer. He has six months to live at the outside. The moment the news gets out, the money for the film you're working on will vanish."

I tapped each side of my head as if I had water in my ears.

"Excuse me?" I said.

"Jack is dying."

"I saw him last night," I said. "He looks fine."

Adam shook his head.

"Earlier last night Jack was at a very exclusive private clinic in Beverly Hills. He left the clinic to meet Claude Rimbaud and screw him out of a million bucks. Then he went back to the clinic and they gave him the fatal diagnosis."

"How would you know all of this?" I asked.

"I have a source at the clinic. Jack turned up with bad numbers on an insurance physical, but the exam report got changed somehow to give Jack a passing grade. Jack is going to somebody in Chinatown to treat the cancer in secret, stuffing himself with herbs and tea and getting his chi goosed. But last night they gave him the word that his number is up."

"I played golf with him yesterday," I said.

"He looks good, but inside he's not so pretty," Adam said.

"I have been with Jack day and night for three weeks," I said.

"You just think you have. Jack is slick."

I leaned back in the chair, making the leather groan, and shut my eyes. I called up an image of Jack striding up the eighteenth fairway yesterday, laughing, on his way to a par that would give him a seventy-nine. He had looked like the healthiest, happiest man this side of Shangri-la. I thought of Jack wearing that preposterous beard in the bar last night. I remembered laughing with him and toasting each other with shots of Stoli and swigs of ale.

"You know what, Adam?" I said. "With all due respect, I think I don't believe you."

"Why would I lie about this?"

"I don't know. But why would you tell me?"

"X and I want you to do the rewrite on *Giants* and we need to get to work on it. That's why. Max Bloom will step in and get you paid for this screenplay that you won't have to write for Jack. I understand you got a hundred and fifty thousand in front and are due another hundred thousand when you turn in the final draft of the screenplay. Is that right?"

I nodded.

"Max will get you the hundred thousand completion fee right now, ahead of the creditors who will come digging into Jack's remains. What kind of bonus do you get when principal photography starts?"

"Fifty thousand," I said.

"Piddly-ass money. You should have done better. I doubt Max can get you that fifty, since there won't be any principal photography. But he will get you a hell of a lot bigger bonus on *Giants*."

I fished a pack out of my jacket pockets and then lit a cigarette.

"Number one, forget Max," I said. "Number two is I am on information overload. I can't comprehend all this knowledge right now."

"Max will come to you with a deal for your three novels," Adam said.

"Max? You're kidding.'"

"What have you got against Max?"

"Why are you giving me this rush?" I asked.

"The Juice likes you, X likes you, and I like you," Adam said. "You should be working with X and me. I can make you into something out here. Of course you were something at *Sports Illustrated*, but I'm gonna make you into something more special—a million-dollar writer."

"What are you going to do with your so-called news about Jack?" I asked. "Am I how you're starting the rumor? You're using me to do it?"

"There won't be any rumor coming from my end. Nobody here knows except Bruno and me, and our lips are zipped. I'm not a cruel person. I don't get a kick out of watching a beautiful star die, not even when the star is an asshole like Jack Roach. His whole fucking world is going to fall on him while he is dying. But I am not going to start the feeding frenzy, not me. I can't vouch for the people at the clinic. You know the old saying—three people can keep a secret if two of them are dead. A tip that Jack Roach is dying is worth a lot of bucks to the *Enquirer*."

A buzz came from a small box on Adam's desk.

"No calls, Mrs. Buckham," Adam said.

"It's your mother," said Mrs. Buckham's voice.

"I'll take it on three," Adam said.

"No, your mother is here. She is outside your door, talking to Bruno," said Mrs. Buckham's voice.

"Oh, shit," Adam said. I saw a flash of what I would have to call fear in his eyes.

"She is coming in," said Mrs. Buckham's voice.

"Please, Richard, be nice to her," Adam said.

"This is my cue to be leaving," I said.

"Just don't be sharp with her. She gets migraines."

The big door opened. I figured Adam worked the door with a pedal under his desk, but it struck me that the Queen Bee might have her own means of opening Adam's door.

She walked a step ahead of Bruno. The Queen Bee was wearing a red-and-gold warmup tracksuit with the USC logo on it and white running shoes. Her hair hung down her back in a ponytail. Adam jumped up and came around the desk to hug her. Even with his long, dirty hair and his surfer bum outfit, Adam looked as old as his mother. He could have been her date at a pep rally. But you would have known on sight that she was the boss.

"Mom, do you remember Richard Swift, the great writer?" Adam said.

I stood still and smiled politely. The Queen Bee studied my face. I noticed fine lines around her eyes and a tiny scar beneath her nose. I wouldn't have seen them if she hadn't been staring at me so intently.

"You're the piano player," she said.

"Mrs. Wachinski, if in any way I insulted you last night, please accept my apology," I said.

"Accepted," she said.

I thought I heard a sigh go through the room as Adam's breath was released.

"You're a pretty good piano player. I might like for you to work a party for me next week."

"Mom, Richard is a writer," Adam said. "He's from *Sports Illustrated*. He knows The Juice. He's going to work for me."

"Poor boy," Queen Bee said, looking at me with a sadness in her large brown eyes, as if I were a cocker spaniel on my final trip to the vet.

"It's not exactly for sure," I said.

"Adam mistreats people," she said.

"I will keep that in mind. Thank you," I said.

I was edging toward the door and trying to signal Bruno with my eyebrows that I needed a ride.

"Now where do you think you are going?" the Queen Bee said.

"I need to go back to my hotel."

"Did you think I was through talking to you?" She arched an eyebrow.

"I didn't add it all up, no," I said.

"Mom, please. Richard needs to be going. He's got a lot to think about today," Adam said.

"Promise me, Richard, that the next time you come to my house, you will do 'My Way' for me at my piano," the Queen Bee said.

That was an easy promise to make. I didn't know "My Way," I felt sure I would never be at her house again.

"I promise," I said.

To my surprise, she kissed me. Her lips brushed my left cheek and then my right, a European sort of friendly kiss. She smelled like lemonade and perspiration. Her tracksuit felt damp, and I wondered if she had been running in the rain.

"You can be a sweet man," she whispered in my ear. "You must remember to behave." She pressed herself against me and gave me a quick, hard hug. I was surprised and just stood there like a piece of furniture.

The Queen Bee stepped away from me. I saw Adam scowling at us.

"Let me hear from you, Richard. Don't be stupid about this," Adam said.

I could tell that as far as the Queen Bee was concerned I had left the room the moment she turned her back, but Adam continued to stare at me. He was making little nervous, pursing motions with his red lips. He seemed to have gotten angry. I noticed the shaving mirror still lay on top of his desk. The Queen Bee went to the couch and flopped down and began taking off her wet shoes. I realized I was still standing there like a piece of furniture. Waves of Maui Wowie were washing through me.

"Come along, Richard. You were wanting to buy some typing paper, I believe?" Bruno said.

Nine

I paused at the front desk of the Westwood Marquis and rested my ream of high-quality-bond typing paper from the UCLA bookstore on the counter while I checked my box for messages. There was one message that had come in thirty minutes ago: "Call Bim Gump. Urgent."

I carried the typing paper onto the elevator and went up to my suite. I placed the paper carefully on the desk beside the Smith Corona typewriter, tidied up the other stack of paper, laid three ballpoint pens in a row, and then stepped back and observed my workspace. I needed more light. The housekeeper had closed the white wooden blinds. I opened them again and saw the rain was easing up. I switched on the desk lamp, adjusting it so the light shone just right.

I lit another cigarette—I had decided to quit counting them, just for today—and phoned the Beverly Wilshire and asked to speak to Bim Gump.

Jack Roach answered. He changed his name at the hotel desk every few days. During our trip to the bar last night he had told me his new phone name was Bim Gump. Jack had been pleased that I remembered the old comic strip. Bim Gump was Andy Gump's rich uncle.

"Oh Min!" I cried into the phone. The Maui Wowie put a little extra zing into my voice.

"What the fuck? Who is this?" Jack said.

"'Oh Min!' is what Andy used to yell when he got into trouble and needed his wife to rescue him," I said.

Jack laughed. "That's right. I forgot. Oh Min! And she'd come running and save his ass. How are you, Richard? Did you sleep well?"

"Yeah, I slept well. I've been out to buy some typing paper."

"Bingo, old buddy. We need to get words on paper pretty soon."

"What did you tell Claude Rimbaud last night?" I asked.

"I told him no. I said my whole mind and body are devoted to only one project, and it's my own. This man in our movie is the man I was born to be. Hey, I feel like talking. How about you?"

"We do need to talk," I said.

"I'll come by and pick you up. Let's run up to the Colony."

"In the rain?"

"Forecast is for the rain to stop this afternoon. I think we'll be playing golf tomorrow. But anyhow, so what? Fuck the rain. I need some kind of action. I'll pick you up in half an hour. Are we on?"

He sounded good and healthy to me.

Jack was driving a vintage yellow Thunderbird that sparkled in the rain. The doorman who had escorted me into Bruno's limo a couple of hours ago was bent down talking to Jack through the car window. The doorman jerked to attention and held his umbrella over my head as I went to the passenger door. I got the sense that the doorman was making a mental note to ask the concierge who the hell was I to be riding away with Jack Roach.

We flew down Wilshire in second gear spraying water. Jack drove racing cars when he was in the mood.

"Sorry I stood you up last night," Jack said. "Did you wait for long?"

"I left fairly early. I was tired."

"I'm sorry I jilted you. Something came up that I hadn't foreseen."

I glanced over at Jack's famous profile. His thick, closely cut wheat-blond hair was brushed forward in what I thought of as a "Roman senator" style. Drops of rainwater trickled out of his hairline.

"What was it?" I asked.

"Well, you know, I am basically off of women. I think I am gaining wisdom. Three ex-wives, six children, God knows how many in-laws and former in-laws that adds up to. You remember I broke up with my girlfriend Samantha during the three days you and I went up to Pebble Beach? Yeah, she was getting really heavy, and, man, I've got no time for heavy. I've gotta do my work. I've gotta do what I was put on this planet to do."

Jack braked for a red light. The car slid on the slick pavement but he handled it.

67

"You're running out of time?" I asked.

"Buddy, we're all running out of time."

The Thunderbird shot forward, and the passing scenery became a rain-streaked blur.

As we roared from behind a city bus into the oncoming traffic, I wondered which was more correct: we're running out of time, or our time is running out?

Jack cut back into the right lane at the last moment, barely avoiding a truck. He was laughing.

"My point wasn't about time, it was about women," Jack said. "You know I no longer have a steady girlfriend. I have practically sworn off women. I'm having nothing more to do with women until our movie is done. Do you know what I mean?"

"I guess."

"But every night about eleven thirty I've just got to fuck something," Jack said. "Last night it happened to be a woman I met in the coffee shop. We went to her house in Bel Air. I thought I'd be back at the hotel in an hour, but that didn't happen. Sorry."

"So you weren't at a medical clinic in Beverly Hills last night?" I asked.

"A clinic? What are you talking about?"

Jack was a great actor by my standards. Maybe he wasn't Olivier or Brando, but he could hold his own with Nicholson or McQueen. The look he gave me was pure puzzlement.

"Are you dying, Jack?" I blurted it out, Maui Wowie–style. "Wait, don't tell me we're all dying. I mean are you dying at a much faster rate than, let's hope, I am?"

"Are you drunk, man? What kind of a question is that?"

"That is not an answer."

"Am I dying faster than you are? Is that a real question?"

"I posed the question very poorly," I said.

"Did someone tell you that I'm dying?" Jack asked.

"Adam Wachinski told me this morning. Bruno came over to the hotel and picked me up and took me to see Adam. Adam told me you're dying of cancer. I'm asking if it's true."

"You're serious, aren't you?" Jack asked.

"I believe so."

Jack drove in silence for a few moments, staring straight ahead. I listened to the windshield wipers and pushed in the lighter to fire up another cigarette.

"We'll talk about this when we get to the Colony," Jack said. "I know just the place for this conversation. I'll take you into the Truth Room."

"The what?"

"You'll see."

He shoved a Grateful Dead tape into the dashboard and turned the music up loud to let me know we were through talking for a while.

Jack's house was behind the gates at the Malibu Colony, several miles north of where Adam and the Queen Bee lived. The house was nothing special for that neighborhood. It was just a brick ranch-style house that you might see in an upscale suburb anywhere in America, except for two things: the back porch of this house faced the Pacific Ocean across a few yards of beach, and parked along the street in front of Jack's house were fourteen vintage Thunderbirds like the one we arrived in.

As we cruised to a stop, the garage door raised, and I saw Jack's Filipino houseman, Roberto, standing in the garage, grinning, in front of a dozen motorcycles, most of them big Harley hogs.

"Boss man!" Roberto yelled.

Jack pulled the Thunderbird into the driveway and jumped out. The rain had become a windblown mist. I got out of the car and looked with awe at more Thunderbirds than I had ever seen at once.

"He do it again!" Roberto yelled. "By damn him, he do it again today!"

"Where did he do it this time?" asked Jack.

"On the front porch! I step in it when I go out to get the mail and the papers."

"I should go over there and whip his ass," Jack grumbled.

"What's the matter?" I asked.

"Rudy Zoo shit on my porch," Jack said.

Rudy Zoo was the drummer in a British heavy metal rock band that could sell out Dodger Stadium.

"The hairy little coward is renting the house next door. He's all bent out of shape because my cars are parked in the street. So he sneaks down here and shits in my driveway, in my yard, and now on my front porch," Jack said.

"Are you going to beat him up?" asked Roberto.

"Not right now. Richard and I have got to have a chat." Jack lovingly stroked the saddle of a silver-and-black Harley. "Make us a pot of green tea, hey, Roberto?"

"You should punch him," Roberto said.

"I think I'll call my youngest son, who is in junior high school in San Diego, and ask him to hitch a ride up here and kick Rudy's butt. That would be more of a fair fight."

"Your boy would take him easy," Roberto said.

"Yeah, I know," Jack said. "My boy is in the Golden Gloves. He's too young to drive, but he'd tear a hole in that tattooed rocker."

"Is Rudy Zoo the one who never wears a shirt onstage?" I asked.

"I think that describes all of them," Jack said.

Jack walked among his motorcycles, patting and rubbing them. He nodded and smiled. Then he entered a door at the back of the garage that led into the house. I followed him into a laundry room with a washer and a drier and a wicker basket full of dirty towels. We walked on into the kitchen, where Jack stopped at the tile counter and began poking through a stack of mail. Beyond the kitchen door I saw the living room with a floor-to-ceiling glass wall streaming with ocean spray and light rain.

Jack became absorbed by a handwritten letter that had the look of a family thing. I went into the living room. Three of the walls were covered with art. No old masters: it was modern stuff with a lot of color. There were a few photographs of mountains in silver frames.

I opened the door in the wall of glass and stepped onto the porch. I was still wearing my waterproof and my rain hat. Though the rain had almost stopped, the rising wind was blowing water into my face from the booming surf.

I saw a dim figure on the beach. He was standing at the edge of the water looking up at the house. He wore a yellow slicker and a rubber hat, like a fireman. As I watched he pulled something from under his slicker, and the first thing I thought of was a gun.

Then I saw two smaller figures in slickers emerge from the mist and join the man, who, I now realized, was holding a camera.

Jack strode onto the porch and waved his arms. He was bareheaded and was wearing a polo shirt and chinos.

"Hey, you out there, get the fuck away from my house!" Jack yelled.

The man on the beach began snapping photos.

Roberto handed Jack an electric megaphone that projected Jack's voice like the speakers at a football stadium.

"You think I'm just fucking with you?" Jack boomed. "You are violating my privacy! I have a God-given right to defend myself and my property. So get the fuck off my beach!"

The man paused from snapping pictures long enough to yell something. I couldn't exactly hear in the wind and surf from this distance, but it sounded like he said, "It ain't your beach, big shot!" "It ain't your beach, stupid!"

"Have you no sense of decency? This is a private home!" Jack announced.

The man stopped taking pictures. He pointed to the camera and conferred with the other two figures. I took them to be a tourist, his wife, and their child.

From the man's gesture of frustration, I guessed he was out of film. But he must have gotten some good shots of a bareheaded movie star blowing a gasket on a rainy afternoon. He could sell his photos of Jack to the tabloids if it occurred to him.

"They're leaving," said Roberto. "You scared them off."

All three figures in slickers waved at Jack and trudged away down the beach.

We went back into the house. Roberto poured cups of green tea for Jack and me. I didn't care for the taste of green tea, but my body could always use some antioxidants. Jack was walking around the room, growing more agitated and intense as he read page three of the letter written in ink on blue paper.

He stopped pacing, pulled out his silver Zippo, and lit a cigarette. While the Zippo was flaming an idea occurred to him. He set the blue paper on fire.

Jack disposed of the wrinkling black ashes in a red trash basket covered with an enamel dragon.

"Bad news?" I asked.

"What?"

"The letter you burned. I thought it might be a handy way to deal with bad news. Zippo it."

"That's what my boys did in Vietnam," Jack said, holding up the lighter so I could see the screaming eagle on it, and the engraving. "They Zippoed it. I never asked you, Richard. Were you in 'Nam?"

"I was in the 3rd Cav on border patrol in Germany," I said. "Vietnam was just getting started when I got out."

"But you kept the Russians from invading Paris," Jack said.

"So far I have reason to be optimistic."

Jack looked into the trash basket at the smoking remains of the letter.

"This babe says she is having my child. But I did the math. It can't be me. I'm in the clear by a good six months. The poor woman got sloppy with her calendar. She couldn't keep up with who she was sleeping with and when. I feel sorry for her, but she is asking for a hundred grand a year, and what I am wondering is how many other guys got this same letter? I bet I could get on the phone and find two out of my own Rolodex."

I felt the hot, sour taste of green tea on the back of my tongue.

"You're divorced, aren't you?" Jack asked.

"Yeah, about two months ago."

"Is this your only marriage so far?"

"Yeah."

"Being married is the best way to live," Jack said. "But it's impossible for some people. I mean, I admire people who can keep up a marriage in good humor and reap the blessings of shared experiences, like my mom and my old man. She taught the sixth grade for twenty-five years. My old man was career navy. He sailed a desk in San Diego. They were happy with each other when I was a little kid, and they're still happy with each other. They're retired in a neat little house with a beautiful view of the sunset over the ocean. They go to movies. They watch television. They go look at the seals. I think they're still making love. They're two happy people. For them marriage has been a lifetime thing. For me marriage is a tornado. Fucking devastation."

Roberto padded toward us down the hall, moving silently in his white sneakers.

"The room is ready, Boss Man," he said.

"You put sandwiches in there?" Jack asked.

"Sandwiches, green tea, coffee, cigarettes, vodka, Heinekens, and a bucket of ice."

"Did you check the system to make sure it's working?"

"I checked it, Boss Man. I'll be standing by."

"Don't interrupt us, not even if you see Rudy Zoo sneaking around."

"I'll be right here, Boss Man."

Jack turned to me and cocked his head to indicate I should follow him. I mashed out my cigarette, got up, and followed Jack down the hall into the Truth Room.

Ten

The Truth Room was about the size of the inside of a railroad box car. Its pine-paneled walls were inset with bookcases. Along one wall ran a polished wooden counter. A three-pound Bowie knife, a museum-quality piece, seemed to still be quivering where someone had stabbed it into the counter.

Jack slid the door shut behind us. I heard a click. He motioned me toward the black leather couch while he stood beside the coffee table upon which Roberto had laid out our lunch. Framed photographs of Jack's mother and father, of each of his three ex-wives, and of his six children decorated the wall at my back as I sat on the couch.

The opposite wall behind the Bowie knife was an arrangement of photographs of Katie Wynne. Two were studio glamour shots. The rest were candids blown up from an amateur's camera. I couldn't make out the backgrounds from the couch, but the pictures seemed to be studies of Katie in outdoor settings—the mountains, a beach, a boat.

At the far end of the room stood a gun cabinet with a glass door. I could see half a dozen rifles and shotguns inside on a bed of red velvet. On a counter beside the gun cabinet lay an old-fashioned western-style six-shooter and a handful of cartridges.

There were no windows in the Truth Room. I was starting to feel claustrophobic.

"You want some more tea? Help yourself," Jack said.

Instead of tea I poured a cup of coffee and a glass of water with ice cubes in it. Jack saw me looking at the photographs of Katie Wynne.

"Fascinating babe, isn't she?" he said.

"What is it about her that drives you guys nuts?"

"Us guys?"

"You and Adam. He gets a freaky look on his face when he mentions her name, which is fairly often."

"Oh yeah. Adam," Jack said. "We are going to talk about Adam. But first, let me explain the rules of the Truth Room to you."

Jack wrenched the Bowie knife out of the counter.

"Once we draw blood, truth is the only option. I mean there is no option but the truth. Once we draw blood in the Truth Room, if you tell a lie you pay with your life," Jack said.

"That's fairly drastic," I said.

Don't mock. "This is deadly serious. This room is consecrated to the truth. The kahunas have put a spell on it. Death soon strikes anyone who tells a lie in this room after blood is drawn."

Jack slid the point of the Bowie knife down his forearm, and left a ribbon of blood.

Then he handed the knife to me. I stared at the drops of blood on the blade.

"Now you do it," he said.

"I don't know, Jack," I said.

"You have to do it. We both have to be in the blood. It doesn't hurt much."

"I feel silly," I said.

"Go on, Richard."

I pinched a few inches of skin on my left forearm and lightly ran the knife blade across it. The blade was very sharp. I made an inch-long bloody trail on my arm.

Jack lifted his forearm toward me and I understood I was to press my bleeding arm against his bleeding arm to mingle our blood as the Truth Room ritual required.

"Does this mean I have to tell the truth, too?" I asked as our forearms mashed together.

"Absolutely," Jack said.

He stepped away from me and stood with his hands at his sides—at gunslinger level, slouching a bit: a familiar posture of his. Jack has just walked into a saloon or nightclub and is sizing up the place.

"Now ask me again why Katie drives me nuts," he said.

"All right. Why does Katie Wynne drive you nuts?"

"Hah! I've got you now, buddy boy." Jack clapped his hands. "The absolute truth is that I don't know why. Millions of guys are in love with Katie who will never know her as a person and have no idea why they love her beyond that Mona Lisa smile of hers. I've seen her in the bathroom, but I love her anyhow."

"That's not a Mona Lisa smile," I said. "She has an Ingrid Bergman smile."

"You see what you want to see, pal. Whatever you want to call it, it's the natural Katie Wynne smile. God gave her those teeth and those lips. No dentist had to build that mouth. It's a gift. Katie is an earthy girl. She can be very direct. If you disappoint her, she will turn on you and rip your ass. She can love you and shake you up, but with me she always held back. I could feel I wasn't getting all of her. She wasn't giving me everything she had. She never loved me enough. She never wanted me as much as I wanted her. I wanted her to love me more than I loved her, but the damned woman refused to do it."

"So you stayed in love with her because she wouldn't love you back?" I asked.

"I could give you a shorter, simpler answer. She puts a monkey in my pants. That's the truth, too."

Jack looked at his wristwatch.

"Did you notice a guy up working on the telephone pole when we drove in?" he asked.

"The truth is that since it was raining I didn't think to look," I said.

"They're tapping my phone," Jack said.

"Who is?"

"I don't know. Somebody's out to get me. I don't think it's the cops. I don't do blow any more. There's nothing here the cops would be interested in." He waved his bloody arm around the Truth Room at the gun cabinet and the Bowie knife and the pistol with its bullets spread out on the counter.

"You're sure your phone is tapped?" I asked.

"Not totally. It's a feeling I get that someone is listening on the line. I've never heard a tell-tale click or anything, nobody breathing heavy, but I feel like it's happening."

I thought of Katie Wynne's prowler.

"Did you get your phone checked?" I asked.

"I had the whole house swept for bugs. They didn't find anything but a big bag of Mexican weed that I'd hid in a closet and forgot about. Do you wanna smoke a joint?"

"Not just yet," I said.

My head was clear of the Maui Wowie by now. Pleasant though it had been to be lofted by the spirit of the islands, I thought it would be unwise to mix marijuana with the Truth Room.

Jack chewed a handful of cashews and poured two shots of vodka. He looked at me and raised his brows and I nodded. We toasted each other with vodka, clinked glasses, and drank.

"Are you enjoying this job, Richard? Are you going to like being a full-time screenwriter?" Jack asked.

"Truth Room speaking?" I asked.

"Hard-core Truth Room," he said.

"I'm having a terrific time on this job, but I am a little apprehensive."

"About what?"

"Well, there are two things that bother me at the moment," I said. "One is that I haven't written one single page of our script. The second thing is that I have been told you will be dead before I can reach the third act."

"What were you doing talking to Adam in the first place?"

"He offered me a job," I said.

"You've got a job. You're under contract to me for nine more weeks." There was a boss-man tone in Jack's voice that he had never used with me before.

"I never thought to ask about a death clause," I said.

"You're getting sort of uppity, aren't you, Richard? Listen, I don't give a damn if you know O. J. Simpson. I know O. J. Simpson myself. These days he's only another of us actors for hire."

"Sorry, Jack. I didn't mean to get cute about death. If the story is true, I am very sorry to hear it."

Jack went to the gun cabinet and looked at the weapons. He could also see his reflection in the glass. He turned his head and squinted at me. He seemed to be deciding something.

"I want you to swear an oath," Jack said.

"All right."

"Put your hand on your heart."

I did it.

"Everything I tell you in the Truth Room today will be kept secret for ten years," he said.

"Why ten years?"

"That's long enough. I don't ask the impossible. Do you swear?"

"Yes, I swear."

Jack sat down in a leather chair across the coffee table from where I sat on the couch. He rubbed his chin with his fingers, another familiar gesture that indicated he was thoughtful and very serious.

"I have a stomach virus," Jack said.

I waited. He twirled the Zippo in the fingers of his right hand. He opened his mouth and then closed it again.

"That's all," he said.

"Hey," I said. "This is the Truth Room. You can't get away with that."

Jack lit a cigarette and blew smoke toward the ceiling. "I want to impress on you that the insurance company must have no reason to doubt my health. I have already passed their physical. Our movie is bonded. We can't have two-bit rumors scaring the insurance people. That's why you have to keep quiet. I'm not sick. It's a low-grade virus that's been bothering me for a while. After we played golf yesterday I stopped by the clinic to see Dr. Feelgood and get a shot of antibiotics. While I was there I decided to do an IV drip of a vitamin cocktail, and I sort of took a nap while that was going on. When I woke up it was too late for me to go to the Queen Bee's party. So I went to the bar at the Beverly Wilshire and waited for you."

"Adam said you went to the clinic after you met with Claude Rimbaud."

"He knew I was with Claude?"

I nodded.

"Jesus," said Jack. "That son of a bitch has spies everywhere."

"But the spy in the clinic is wrong about your illness?" I said.

"Here's what happened. I wished Claude good luck. He left the coffee shop. There was a tall, dark, beautiful lady coming in as Claude went out. She and I locked eyes. I knew her from somewhere. She took me by the hand and led me to her Bentley and drove to her house in Beverly Hills. We were at her house for about an hour and a half. Then she drove me back to the hotel. On the way I stopped by Dr. Feelgood's office and got another B-12 shot for good measure. I returned to my hootch on the roof and found that my writer, Richard, had knocked off for the day."

"Your doctor's office is open in the middle of the night?"

"Dr. Feelgood is available whenever I want him. Do I detect that you are turning prosecutorial on me?"

"No, not at all. It's just that you surprise me sometimes."

"Anything Adam Wachinski says about me, especially if he acts like it's confidential, is a lie. You need to remember that he hates me and wants me to fail," Jack said.

"Why does he hate you?"

"He hates me because I'm Jack Roach and he's a two-bit asshole who got lucky."

Jack reached into the bucket and pulled out two frosty green bottles of Heineken.

"Adam was circling Katie when I first met her. He was just another young buttface in a USC sweatshirt and a baseball cap. He tried to break up Katie and me. He started rumors that she's a lesbian. Adam doesn't want anybody to fuck Katie except him, and he's scared to."

"But that was a long time ago," I said.

"Well, Adam doesn't forget. And also something more recent that deeply pissed him off."

Jack popped off the two bottle caps. He handed a beer to me.

"Adam walked in on me fucking his mother."

"The Queen Bee? *That* mother?" I laughed. I couldn't help it. Jack's upper lip quivered and then he grinned.

"It was about a month ago. We were in her bedroom in Malibu. It was the first time I'd nailed her in her own bed. She's a sex-hungry old doll. I've been fucking her occasionally for about ten years. But Adam never knew until last month when he walked in on us."

"What did Adam do?" I asked.

"Remember, you're sworn to secrecy for ten years."

"I swear."

"Adam started crying. He stood in the bedroom door and sobbed. It was enough to almost make me feel bad about what I was doing. The Queen Bee started yelling for him to get out. He was blubbering. I got up and put

79

my pants on and walked out. Man, the look in Adam's eyes as I passed him in the doorway—Well, if you could bottle that look you could sell it as eau de hatred."

I shook my head. "And yet you invited me to a party at Adam's house yesterday."

"No, I gave you the Queen Bee's address. She doesn't hate me. Far from it."

"Last night she cussed me out, and this morning she hugged me," I said.

"Hey, man, pharmaceuticals will do that. Don't take it personally either way."

Stunned by the thought of Jack and the Queen Bee getting caught in bed by Adam, I decided to make a sandwich. I smeared mustard on the whole-grain bread and piled on the cheese, ham, lettuce, and slices of pickle.

"What I'm telling you is Adam wants to hurt me. Adam is a liar," Jack said. He watched me fumbling at the food on the table. "What are you looking for?"

"I thought there was a tomato here," I said.

"I'll get you one."

"No, that's all right."

"Don't be silly. I've got tomatoes." Jack jumped up and went to the speaker box on the wall and pushed the buzzer. Nothing happened. Jack yelled, "Hey, Roberto! Bring me a tomato!"

He waited. It was eerily silent.

"Hey, Roberto!" he yelled again.

He walked to the door and pounded on it. The noise of his fists was muffled. I realized the Truth Room was soundproof.

"It's all right, Jack. I don't really need a tomato," I said.

"We're fucking locked in," Jack said. "The system has gone out. It's that guy on the pole. I knew it!"

I stood up and looked for the doorknob, but there wasn't one.

"The door opens only from the outside," Jack said.

The Truth Room seemed to get smaller when I heard that.

I sat back down to my sandwich. It seemed the Zen thing to do. I noticed the blood on my left forearm.

Jack began pacing in a tight circle. He was frowning.

"Don't worry," Jack said. "We have plenty of air."

I was about to light a cigarette, but I put it back.

"How did you get together with the Queen Bee?" I asked. "I mean the first time, years ago?"

"I met her at the Cannes Film Festival one of the years I won it. Adam had a movie there. She and Bruno were with him. I talked to her at a cocktail party. That night she knocked on my door."

"How about last month?"

"I ran into her at the bar at the Polo Lounge, and one thing led to another. I never should have followed her home. I feel kind of bad about that."

I finished eating the sandwich and stood and stretched. I wandered over to the wall and looked at the photographs of Katie Wynne.

"I took most of those pictures," Jack said. "The beach one is at Katie's house in Hawaii. She has a nifty hideout on Hanalei Bay on the north shore of Kauai. The photo on the boat is at Catalina. My favorite is the one in Aspen on the deck looking at the snow peaks."

I used to have a photograph of Paula on the wall of my office in New York in this same pose in front of a similar mountain. I had to wonder for a moment if Paula had ever met Jack Roach, even for an hour. But then I remembered the photograph of Paula was taken by Elrod when we were all in Vermont one Christmas.

"Is this your house in Aspen?" I asked.

"It used to be. Divorce claimed it."

Jack sat on the floor and took his shoes off. "I need to calm down," he said. "I'm going to meditate."

He settled into a cross-legged yoga pose with his arms folded in across his chest. A blissful smile appeared on his face. I looked at my watch. It was ten minutes until four. I looked at Jack. His blue eyes focused on a horizon only he could see. The Truth Room was growing smaller and smaller.

I returned to the couch and poured a shot of cold vodka and lit a cigarette. I could hear Jack breathing. He inhaled amazingly deeply and exhaled in long groans. I lay back on the couch and looked at the acoustic tiles on the ceiling. I thought about my dad. This afternoon he would be roaming his goat ranch in a valley in the hills or else be on the golf course at Kerrville Country Club. He'd retired from practicing law after a long career of winning big tort cases. Dad was a Jack Roach fan. In ten years I could tell him about today.

81

Eleven

Jack drove me back to the Westwood Marquis at five o'clock. We had been trapped in the Truth Room for forty minutes, but it had seemed much longer in the silence after Jack had stopped his deep breathing and settled into a sort of coma. His eyes fluttered open when we heard a humming sound from the door. The system was working again. The villain was not the guy on the pole, but a blown fuse.

Jack seriously frightened me at least three times on the ride home. The weather had cleared and the sun had come out, but the road was slick. He drove the yellow Thunderbird like we were at Le Mans and the Pacific Coast Highway was a road through French villages. I found myself hoping the cops would stop us.

But we arrived safely at the hotel.

"We're on the first tee at Bel Air at nine in the morning," Jack said as I was getting out.

"Do you want to work on the script tonight?"

"I've got a date," Jack said.

"Maybe I'll write a few pages . . ."

"Hey, Richard, we're doing the real writing now, talking the story, hanging out together, learning each other. Putting words on paper is just the typing part of it."

He reached into the breast pocket of his polo shirt and dug out a folded piece of paper. "Here," he said, sticking his hand out the window to give the paper to me.

It was a 213 phone number. I studied it, wondering what it meant.

"It's Katie's private number," Jack said. "I know you want it."

"Listen, Jack, if it makes you uncomfortable I won't try to see her."

"Oh, baby, it's a wild world," Jack said. "Do what makes you happy. I'll see you on the first tee at Bel Air at nine. We're playing with an Italian who is buying the European rights to our movie."

"I'm impressed. How could you get a nine a.m. tee time at Bel Air for a threesome on a Saturday morning?"

"It's the Italian's tee time, not mine. The Italian owns half of Chicago, so bring your best game. It's a foursome. Jim Murray is playing with us."

Jack watched for my reaction. He knew I was a fan of Jim Murray's sports column in the *Los Angeles Times*. Jack grinned and flipped me a wave, and the yellow Thunderbird shot away from the curb.

I watched the Thunderbird disappear down Hilgard Avenue into a strange early twilight of sun and smog and the remains of the rain. The air was damp and cool. I went up the steps into the hotel. I had three messages waiting at the desk. X had called, Max Bloom had called, and my mother had called. I went up to the suite, took off my shoes, got comfortable on the bed, and phoned Sag Harbor.

It would be nine o'clock at night in Sag Harbor. On a Friday night Mother and Herbie, her third husband but new at the marriage game, would have gone to Oscar's restaurant for a martini, a piece of fish, and a bottle of wine. I would leave a message on their answering machine, and I'd be in the clear with Mother when it came to returning her calls promptly.

"Hello," Mother said. There was a quality in her voice that made me think of sea spray, like hers was the only voice I could hear through the storm that was always crashing around us. She had loved sailing when she was a girl growing up on Long Island. She had done a little sailing on Lake Travis while she lived in Austin. Now with Herbie having moved in at her house in Sag Harbor, she was passionately into sailing again. Herbie was a very serious sailor. He wore his captain's cap nearly everywhere.

"What are you doing home? Is everything all right?" I said.

"Oh, Herbie's got a headache. He's lying on the couch."

"Tell him 'yar' for me," I said.

"We don't say 'yar' anymore," she said.

"That's too bad. It was a great word."

"Katharine Hepburn used it up. Have you ever heard anyone say 'yar' except her in *The Philadelphia Story*? I think not. People were afraid to say 'yar' after they heard her say it."

"So Friday night at Oscar's was shot?"

"I called Oscar and he sent dinner over here, including the wine and the martinis. Poor Herbie could hardly drink a drop. I think he got too much wind blowing into his eyes out on the sound. That starts his sinuses acting up. Look at him over there. He is in such misery, but he is smiling bravely."

I think Mother feels toward Herbie the way she would toward a favorite Labrador retriever.

"How is your new job working out?" Mother asked.

"So far, so bueno."

"Is Mr. Roach a nice man?"

"He's an interesting man. He's nice enough."

"I feel he is not a nice man," Mother said. "His vibe is not nice." She had seen most of Jack Roach's movies, but she preferred Ingmar Bergman, François Truffaut, Federico Fellini, and sometimes Woody Allen. "However, I suppose you know what you are doing. You've been doing it for a long time now. If you were going to learn anything about making a living by writing, I suppose you would have learned it by now."

"As a matter of fact, Mother, I have learned a lot of new stuff already today."

I heard the clink of ice cubes in a drink over the phone.

"I saw Paula at the Russian Tea Room," Mother said. "She was having lunch with two other women. She looked very unhappy. She cried into her napkin once."

"I hope Elrod hasn't been hit by a taxi."

Mother laughed.

"Is that why you called?" I said. "To tell me Paula is unhappy?"

"I thought you'd like to know."

"Did you say hello to her?"

"I waved to her on my way out. She was having a very serious, tearful conversation. But she did manage to smile at me. I always liked Paula. I feel sorry for her never having had the experience of giving birth to a child, of learning what it is like to be a mother. And now it's too late for her."

"She's only thirty-eight," I said.

"Well, one must move on. But she'll never have a family with that tall, poncy-looking photographer. Wait, Herbie is saying something. Herbie wants to know if you have met any movie stars."

"I met Katie Wynne last night."

"Oh, I love Katie Wynne. She has a good soul. It shines through. Herbie is nodding. He likes her, too. He says he likes her legs."

We talked for half an hour. Mother has always been open with me. When I was twelve years old she calmly explained to me that it made no sense for her to live with my father any longer. She took me out of school in Austin and I was suddenly living on the Upper East Side of Manhattan in the duplex penthouse apartment of her boyfriend, who was soon to become her second husband. He was a stockbroker named Robert. Mother had known him as a schoolgirl in Glen Cove and had run into him again the previous summer while we were visiting her family in Sag Harbor. It was love at second sight. They married at the Creek Club. Mother and Robert had been a great couple. They played tennis and bridge, went to lectures at the 92nd Street YMCA, shopped in local bookstores, and saw all the new shows on Broadway. Three years ago, seated at dinner on a charter yacht with two other couples in a bay on the north shore of Jamaica, Robert had been telling the others that the fishing that day with wonderful companions had made him the happiest man in the world, and then he had sighed and closed his eyes and died of an aneurysm. Bless his heart, Robert had left me a paid lifetime membership at the Creek Club in his will. I'd won him some large bets on the golf course at the Creek Club over the years.

After Robert died—those at the table said his passing during the course of a single breath at the end of a sentence was so natural that they couldn't believe he had died—Mother sold their Park Avenue duplex and returned to live full-time at her old family home in Sag Harbor, which she had inherited. She met Herbie at a boat show.

"Listen, Richard, you be wary of that Jack Roach person," Mother said. "Remember the film in which he played the detective with a terribly dark side who shot to death seven people including his own girlfriend? I feel that person is the real Jack Roach."

"Mother, you don't know him. He's an actor. He's a star. Nobody knows him."

"Well, you remember what I am telling you. Anyhow, I am glad you quit

85

your job at that magazine. At your age it's time for you to join the adult world and become a serious person. You've written quite enough about sports. What is your new movie script about?"

"Cattle rustlers."

"Oh my God," she said.

After she hung up, I went into the living room, where my typewriter was set up. I straightened the stacks of paper on the desk. I sat down and looked at the keys for a while. There was a lot of truth in what Jack had said—we were writing the story by being together and talking through it; the typing would be the easy part. Once I had the whole thing in my mind, it would write itself.

I lay on the bed and watched television until the seven o'clock news came on. Then I lifted the phone and called Katie Wynne.

Twelve

I picked up Katie at eight thirty and we went to Roy's All-American Bean-ery, a vegetarian restaurant that rambled down a hillside in Santa Monica.

A valet took my red Mercedes away at the street-level entrance and we were greeted by Roy himself, wearing a chef's hat and farmer's overalls. He led us down two flights of wooden steps into one of the several candle-lit dining rooms, all of which appeared to be full of customers. Roy took us to a table in the front of the room by a window, where we had a view of the boardwalk but also we could be seen from the sidewalk. It was not what I would have expected, but Katie seemed happy with the seating. We had, after all, been a last-minute call, and Roy's was a very popular place.

"Katie, darling, you look fabulous," Roy said. He wagged a finger at a waiter, who brought us a bottle in a bucket of ice. "This is the finest Chablis my vineyards have ever produced. With my compliments, may I pour for you?"

After we had sipped wine and ordered from the menu, Katie leaned forward with the candlelight flickering on her face and stroked the back of my hand with her fingers and said, "I'm so glad you called, Richard. I was afraid we might have chased you off with our craziness around the house."

Feeling the touch of her fingers, I had an electrical rush and a warm, sudden sense of well-being. I was conscious of being happy. Nobody knows what romantic love is, or what causes it, but when it hits you there can be no doubt that this is what you want.

"I like a little craziness," I said.

"Dolly said you wouldn't call, even after she gave you my number. She thought our prowler made you uncomfortable."

"I didn't get your number from Dolly. Jack Roach gave it to me."

The waitress was a hippie with a flower in her long hair. She wore a peasant blouse, a full skirt, and sandals. She set out baskets of chips, bread, radishes, and black olives. I poured two more glasses of wine.

"How is Jack?" Katie said.

"He's born to run," I said.

"What do you mean?"

The waitress lingered a moment to hear my answer, but I out-waited her.

"I mean he's in perpetual motion. He was born revved up to a much higher pitch than the ordinary human. A lot of big-league athletes are that way," I said.

"Haven't you found that people who are among the best in the world at what they do are born revved up to a higher pitch than the ordinary human?" Katie asked.

"Yeah, but I'm talking about Jack is in physical motion, not that his brain is revved up to superhuman pitch so he can sit in the library and dream up a new theory of the origin of the universe."

"Don't sell Jack short on dreaming. You should see him meditate. It's a technique he learned in the '60s when he went to Nepal with the Beatles. He goes deep."

"I saw him meditate this afternoon," I said. "It bordered on being spooky."

"Let's don't talk about Jack tonight," Katie said. "He has a way of filling up a room without even being there. Let's say goodnight to Jack."

She lifted her wine glass in a toast.

"Goodnight, Jack," she said.

"Goodnight, Jack," I said.

I wanted to ask Katie about Jack and herself, but I pushed the questions to the back of my mind as I looked into her eyes in the candlelight.

The waitress brought a plate of brown rice, squash, and black beans with salsa for Katie. For me it was a bowl of fettuccini Alfredo. I tore off a piece of brown bread and dipped it in the sauce. I watched Katie stirring rice and beans together and pouring salsa over them.

"I wish they had green chili here," Katie said. "Roy keeps telling me he'll get me some green chilies, but he hasn't done it yet."

"Green chili to me means New Mexico. You sound like a Santa Fe girl."

"I went to St. John's College in Santa Fe for two years. My dad said they taught me everything important in the history of civilization except how to write a check, ride a bus, buy an airplane ticket, or talk about sports. So he pulled me out of St. John's and transferred me to TCU, where I learned all of those things except how to ride a bus."

Roy stopped at our table, wiping his hands on his apron, and asked how we were doing. He indicated my bowl of Alfredo and said, "This one flirts with having too much dairy in the sauce to be vegetarian, but I feel it is worth the risk."

"It's a success," I said.

Roy beamed. He spoke softly to Katie. "As always, the staff knows to not let anyone approach your table."

I noticed that out on the sidewalk someone had spotted Katie and was pointing her out to companions. Roy was managing to exploit Katie and protect her at the same time. It was a true show-business relationship.

Roy hurried away to handle the crowd at the front door upstairs.

"How do you happen to speak Spanish so well?" Katie asked.

"I had a Mexican nanny who spoke Spanish to me from birth. Then I went to a private school in Austin where we took Spanish classes through the sixth grade. A young mind soaks it up."

"It's not the same for me," she said. "Foreign languages don't stick with me. Math is my thing. I had a devil of a time learning to conjugate in Latin at St. John's, but show me an algebra equation and I could knock it out of the park."

"Did you learn to read a financial statement?"

She laughed.

"No. I only read the bottom line. My lawyer, my agent, my manager, my accountant, and Dolly read the rest of it."

"Dolly can read a financial statement?"

"Her name is Dolly Rubenstein. She has a law degree. But she has never practiced. I'm not sure she ever passed the bar exam . . . She came to work for me as a temporary thing the summer after she finished law school, and she's still with me eleven years later. Dolly has read everything that has anything to do with me when it comes to financial matters. She sits with my accountant and looks at every check."

"Eleven years? So she has been with you through all of your serious romances?" I asked.

"Dolly is my rock," Katie said.

We ordered raspberry sorbet for dessert.

"Writing for *Sports Illustrated* must be an interesting thing to do," Katie said. "How do you get a job like that?"

"I was an English major at Columbia. I got lucky and sold a short story to the *New Yorker*. Well, I had been playing golf at Winged Foot, and I got to know the assistant managing editor of *Sports Illustrated*, a guy named Roy Barker, who was a member. Roy loves golf. I took him to the Creek Club at Locust Valley in Long Island for golf a few times. My *New Yorker* story appeared. There was about ten minutes of real excitement about it. About then, Roy was promoted to managing editor and offered me a full-time job writing feature pieces for *SI*."

"It sounds like you've been at that magazine your whole adult life," she said.

"What I haven't mentioned is there were several years between the time I received my diploma at Columbia and the week my short story made it into print in the *New Yorker*. I served in the army in Germany, and after I was discharged I leased a flat in Chelsea in London and set out to become an important novelist. I spent a year writing a novel that eventually got published, but it took a while, and few people noticed anyway. Eventually I fell in love with an American reporter from *Time* who was working in the London bureau. She left London to move back to New York to be an editor at *People* magazine, and I followed her to New York and married her."

I heard myself talking. It occurred to me that I might be telling her much more than she wanted to know. I paused to light a cigarette and checked to see if she was listening. Her eyes were on me. She seemed to be interested in my autobiography, so far at least.

"That's all the exposition I allow myself to use this early in the story," I said.

"But you are no longer married?"

"I am totally unmarried."

"Are you miserable and on the rebound?"

"I have never been happier in my life than I am at this moment."

"Let's drink up and go somewhere else," Katie said.

While I paid the check and put a tip on it that befit me being with a movie star, Katie made a call from Roy's phone, twisting its long spiraling cord around her finger as she talked.

"There's a place I'd like to take you," Katie said. She grabbed my hand as we climbed the stairs. "I phoned ahead. They're making room."

A cool breeze blew in from the ocean. The sky was clear and the air smelled clean after the rain. Katie wrapped a sweater around her shoulders. She took a beaded case out of her purse, removed a pair of horn-rimmed glasses, and put them on. She put on a blue cap with a small bill, like a Mao cap from Saks. She took her glasses off again, removed her contact lenses while leaning against the front fender of the red Mercedes, and put the glasses back on. She was wearing jeans and a blouse and white sneakers. But she was still obviously Katie Wynne. There are movie stars who when you see them in person on the street are shorter or fatter or older than you had thought, and have bad complexions. But Katie Wynne looked good anywhere.

I followed her directions and in a few minutes we were pulling into a parking lot outside an apartment complex in Marina Del Rey. I caught a strong whiff of Santa Monica Bay. Katie took my hand and led me along a sidewalk and through a bower into a courtyard that had a bubbling fountain. We came to a two-story white stucco building with bougainvillea growing on the wall. A discreet blue neon sign above one of the doors said Dunes. Katie pushed open the door and pulled me inside.

The room we entered was dimly but artfully lit with recessed lighting above the mirror that ran the length of the bar. Tiny spotlights shone down onto the middle of the tables and left the faces around them in flattering shade.

As we walked in I heard the great Rodgers and Hart song "My Romance" being played on a piano. I saw at the back of the room a black woman in a white dress seated at a white piano. She was singing in a rich, mellow voice: "Doesn't need a castle rising in Spain..." She looked up and smiled at Katie as a hostess in a long gown led us to a booth near the piano. Most booths appeared to be occupied, but it was hard to tell by how many customers because of the darkness.

"This is Minnie. She's fabulous," Katie whispered as she slid into the booth.

Katie was facing the piano player. I sat opposite Katie but turned sideways to the left with my back against the wall so I could see Minnie. I hooked my elbow over the back of the booth. Katie told the waitress that she wanted a ginger ale in a tall glass with ice.

"I have a photo shoot in the morning," Katie whispered to me.

I ordered a Black Label and water and settled back to listen to Minnie.

But at the end of "My Romance," Minnie nodded to acknowledge the scattered applause coming from the dark booths, then played a short signature riff and announced she was going on break.

Minnie stopped at our booth and kissed Katie's hand. Then she looked at me. "Is this the guy?"

"Minnie, this is Richard Swift. Richard, meet Minnie."

"Have a ball, Richard," Minnie said.

I wasn't sure I'd heard her correctly. "Pardon?"

"But please be gentle with her," Minnie said. "She's my best friend."

Minnie gave Katie another smile and made an exit, trailing cigarette smoke. The waitress brought our drinks.

"Sorry I can't keep drinking with you tonight, but I have to get up at six and look all cheerful and young and alluring, which is tough to do with a hangover and bad breath. It's for a magazine. I'm not sure which one. Which magazine does your wife work for?"

"Ex-wife, and it's *People*."

"No, this is artier. It might be *Vanity Fair*. I don't know. But I'm booked for five hours, starting at nine. So listen, Richard, we don't have all night. I'll just come right out with it instead of plying you with booze."

I had no idea where this was leading, but I did hope it might be her hot tub.

"Okay," I said.

"Play for me."

"What?"

"Play the piano for me. I heard that you played at the Queen Bee's party before I met you. Please, play for me now."

"I can't."

"Why not?"

"I'm not a professional," I said. "But I'm on a professional's turf. It would be rude to Minnie."

"It's all right with Minnie. I phoned her. That's what she was talking about, asking you to take care of her piano."

"I'm not really all that good," I said.

"Oh, please, Richard."

I figured she would make a crucial judgment of me not only for how well I performed, but of what I chose to play for her. I made another gesture of reluctance, and then smiled in surrender. I could hear the heels of my Guccis clicking on the wooden floor as I walked to the piano. I hadn't yet come up with the right idea as I settled down on Minnie's well-padded bench. I heard voices and rustling from the dark booths, and I noticed the bartender turn to look at me. The two waitresses paused and watched me. I kept my eyes on Katie. I doodled a few opening chords, and then it hit me. I started playing and talk-singing a Lane and Loesser song off the new Bobby Short album.

> "Sweet moments like this with the soft lights aglow
> make me long for your kiss though I know
> I'd be just one of all your affairs.
> But in moments like this, who cares?"

Katie's eyes told me I had made a good choice of tunes. I sang it through and put in a nice piano riff in the middle. I was hoping Minnie would reappear, because I was doing so well with "Moments like This" that I didn't want to have to choose an encore.

When I saw Minnie standing in the doorway to the parking lot, checking me out, I wrapped it up. Katie smiled and applauded, and there was clapping from the dark booths. I stood up. Katie shouted for me to play another. Some guy yelled from a booth, "How about 'Bewitched, Bothered and Bewildered?' Greatest lyric ever written!"

From another booth a woman called out, "Play 'April in Paris.'"

"How about a big hand for Minnie?" I said. I led the applause. I waited near the piano while Minnie walked slowly from the front door. I shook her hand and said, "Thanks." She gave me a peculiar look. She didn't like whatever I was up to with Katie Wynne.

As I shook Minnie's hand I slipped a hundred dollar bill into her palm.

"Won't you play some more?" Katie asked.

"I'm embarrassed," I lied. "I'll play for you later if you want."

Katie reached across the table and touched both my hands and looked at my fingers. "And these must be the same hands you use to type with," she said.

Actually I keep my typing hands in a jar of formaldehyde when they're not busy."

"That's an awful, ugly image," she said.

I should have said 'jar of cold cream,' shouldn't I?"

"How did you start writing movie scripts?" she asked.

"Paula and I went to see *Butch Cassidy and the Sundance Kid*. Afterward in the bar I said I thought I could write a script as good as that one. Paula said bullshit, I couldn't. It turned out she was right. But the script that I wrote while I was failing sold immediately to Fox and went straight into production and filming. I thought that was how things worked out here. Later I learned I had jumped over a huge pil of shit and didn't even know it."

"It must be strange to be a writer. I mean, to make your way in the world mainly with your imagination?"

"It's best not to think about it," I said. "If you start to question your right to be a writer, you're finished. To me it seems very strange to be an actor, to make your way in the world by pretending to be other people," I said.

"So we're both strange," she said. "Do we agree on that?"

She lifted her glass of ginger ale and clinked it against my Black Label.

"Agreed," I said.

Katie finished her drink and said, "Sorry, Richard, but I do have to go home now. It's been a long day."

"It has been a very full day, indeed," I said.

I paid the check. We got up and waved at Minnie. Katie took my arm. Minnie was playing "April in Paris" as we walked to the door. I felt lucky with Katie at my elbow. There was applause from the dark booths.

"That's for you," Katie said.

"Hardly likely," I said.

She was quiet in the car. She closed her eyes. She looked tired, but thoughtful, and it made her all the more appealing. I turned on the FM radio and found some soothing jazz. I lit a cigarette. Once again I was conscious of being happy in her presence, of feeling absurdly fortunate.

I was turning onto Benedict Canyon Drive when Katie opened her eyes and said, "Richard, what are you doing Saturday and Sunday?"

"No plans," I said.

I didn't mention the golf tomorrow morning at Bel Air because I wasn't mentioning Jack Roach tonight.

"I have an idea," she said. "I don't work Sunday or Monday and my call on Tuesday is late afternoon. Why don't you and I go up the coast to a place I know about two hours away? We could leave by four o'clock tomorrow afternoon and be at the inn in time for the sunset. I don't have to be back until Monday night. All day Sunday we could dig clams, or whatever people do at the beach. What do you say?"

"I would like that very much," I said.

"Me, too, Richard."

I stopped the Mercedes at her gate. She told me the code numbers to punch in. I remembered most of the numbers from the night before. It was a simple code probably based on her birth date. We entered the driveway. The blue pickup sat in a pool of floodlight. The garage doors were closed. I walked Katie to the front door.

On the porch she turned and kissed me. I put my arms around her and tasted her lips and her tongue. I felt myself go out of focus with delight and desire, and then come back together again and devote my whole self to kissing her and feeling her body.

"Oh, Richard," she said.

After a minute or so she removed her arms from my neck and placed her palms against my chest and gently pushed me back.

"Save some for tomorrow," she said.

"I am, believe me."

Her eyes widened and she sharply sucked in a breath.

"Someone's here!" she whispered.

I heard crashing in the hedges at the edge of the house. The noise didn't register on me for a second because I was dizzy with desire for Katie. Then I realized her wide-eyed look wasn't entirely inspired by me, and that I had heard something thrashing and moving.

Inside the house, Bananas, the poodle, began yapping. I ran toward the corner near the pool house then turned and ran along the strip of lawn between the two buildings. The floodlights popped on and lit up the back yard. I saw a movement at the rear gate. I ran toward the alley.

BALOOM! The garbage can bounced and rattled with pellets from Mrs. Garcia's shotgun. I sprawled on the grass and rolled over, my two years in the armored infantry suddenly taking over.

"Hey, it's me, it's Richard, don't shoot!" I yelled in Spanish.

I stayed in the shadows of the hedges until I was sure Mrs. Garcia was finished shooting. I saw Dolly come onto the back porch. The poodle rushed out of the house and ran straight to me, yapping all the way.

When I did jump up and go to the gate I saw it was open—it had a code box as well—and had swung into the alley. I stepped into the alley. Nobody was there.

This time there was no debate about calling the police. The neighbors had already done so. A private security cop in a white shirt and blue pants with a badge and a gun showed up within two minutes, followed by two Beverly Hills cops in a patrol car. We all gathered in the kitchen. I gave a statement.

I heard Dolly telling the cops this was the first time a prowler had ever bothered them.

Katie followed me out to my car when the police sergeant told me I could go.

We kissed and pressed our bodies together. I heard Dolly and the cops coming through the house toward the front porch, and Katie pulled away from me again.

"Four o'clock tomorrow, Richard," she said.

Thirteen

I ducked into the hotel bar to have a nightcap and listen to Gertrude play the harp. I wanted to sink into the overstuffed couch in the corner behind a fern where I could quietly smoke, drink, and observe the action on a Friday night while I smiled, stupidly lovestruck, and tingled as I remembered the sweetness of Katie's Wynne's lips against mine.

"Richard! Fickya in the butthole!" cried a familiar voice.

I stared at Gonzalo, the bartender, a boxer, who squared his shoulders and tugged at his red vest and straightened his bow tie and rolled his eyes toward the ceiling. His mustache crinkled as his lips turned down. Gonzalo was almost at the limit of his professional tolerance for the man doing the shouting.

Adam Wachinski sat at a table against the wall, waving his glass. With him were Bruno, Max Bloom, and the impressive figure of X wearing a white jumpsuit with sequins.

Gertrude was a veteran of entertaining in bar rooms. She kept a smile on her face and sat elegantly erect at her instrument, her graceful fingers caressing the strings of the harp as she played "Hey There" from *The Pajama Game*.

I turned and started out, but X slid out of his chair and in two strides was between the door and me. I looked up into his dark, shining face with three tribal marks on each cheek. His eyes were large and brown and streaked with red. His teeth were brilliantly white. His deep voice carried authority.

"Richard," he said. "This movie is my chance to live above the smog line. Come to the table. Let's talk. Please."

"I'm sorry, X," I said.

"Did you notice I said please? Don't make me go Erazmo Jones on your ass."

"Punching me out in this bar would be a terrible career move," I said.

"Hey, what are you buttholes talking about?" Adam yelled.

"Richard, please. Just talk to the man," said X.

I smiled at Gertrude as X steered me to the table. Adam had cleaned up. His hair was washed and brushed neatly and his face was shaved and pink. He wore one of the handmade suits I had seen in his closet. It was midnight blue silk. His shirt collar was glowing white. His pale blue silk necktie set off his aggressive chin and his red lips.

"Richard. Fickin with ya . . . fickin with ya!" he said.

He seemed to be sober. His eyes took me in, then left me and shifted to a couch on the other side of Gertrude. I followed his gaze and saw Claude Rimbaud sunk into the upholstery with a drink in his hand and a cigarette in the corner of his mouth.

"Sit down, man," said X, who pulled out a chair for me.

Max was rolling his silver bullet between his palms. He grinned as if he were glad to see me. Bruno wore a white suit with a blue open-collar shirt. He barely looked at me.

I ordered a drink from Trudy, the waitress. She was working her way through graduate school at UCLA.

"You see Claude Rimbaud over there?" Adam asked.

"Yeah," I said.

"He's one of the great men in the business," Adam said. "I worked for him on *The Blue Baboons* fresh out of film school. I was a production assistant. I didn't sleep for eight months, keeping up with everything that was going on around me. Claude taught me how to produce a movie."

Trudy brought my scotch in a tall glass with ice. As she bent over to put the drink on the table, Adam placed a hand on the hip of her wine-colored velvet dress.

"I'd like to fick ya right up the butthole, darlin'," he said.

Trudy straightened up and stared at him. Adam looked back calmly. Trudy was working on her master's in psychology. She raised an eyebrow at me, a good tipper, and walked away.

"Remember the *Baboons* movie, Richard?" Adam said.

"Sort of," I said.

"I'll bet you didn't see it, but you remember the promotion of it," Adam said. "You know there was a tribe of blue baboons that had one big king baboon that fell in love with a missionary's wife on the jungle island. You remember the publicity that the movie cost twenty-five million bucks in the days when twenty-five million was huge. Without having seen the movie, do you remember anything else?"

"They had to build a hotel on the island to house the actors and the crew," I said.

"The hotel was in the budget for five million. The way the deal worked, Claude would own the hotel. He charged the production rent for a property the production had already paid for. He shot the movie for four million. He put another six million in his pocket. Then he spent five million selling the story of blue baboons fucking white women to the press to spread it to the world audience. And that adds up to the twenty million."

"You said it was twenty-five," I said.

"It was never more than twenty. Claude told the *Mirror* in London that it was thirty. *Variety* settled on twenty-five. But it was never more than twenty, including the hotel. Claude sold parts of the distribution for seventeen million upfront and got another three from a German syndicate. And it did two-hundred-eighty million worldwide. Everybody made money. Claude has a yacht in St. Barts with a blue baboon painted on the stern."

"You admire him for stealing half the budget?" I said.

"I didn't say I admire him. I said he's one of the great men in our business. In my movies, the money is all on the screen. The similarity is that Claude has made a lot of money for his investors as well as for himself, and so have I."

"I was tempted to feel sorry for him for the million Jack Roach lifted from him last night, but I guess I won't," I said.

"How is Jack?" asked Adam.

"He's fine."

"No cough or anything?" Adam asked.

I shook my head.

"Why? Has Jack been sick?" asked Max.

"No. He's fine," I said.

"You didn't fuck Katie Wynn tonight, though," Adam said.

"How do you know?"

I thought of Katie's prowler but dismissed the idea that it could have been Adam.

"Did you nail her in her hot tub?" asked Max.

"It's too soon for Katie to be giving it to you," Adam said. "Next date you'll fuck her."

I glanced at X. He kept his eyes on Gertrude at the harp.

"Why don't you ask Katie out yourself?" I said to Adam.

"She hates me."

Bruno looked at his watch. So I looked at mine. It was nearly midnight.

"Listen, you guys," X said. "Let's talk about something Richard wants besides pussy, and that would be money. I want to see the big Malibu Zulu making a deal right now with Richard."

"Hey, you're acting a little above your pay grade, aren't you, chief stud?" Max retorted.

"Mandingo! Revolt of the slaves! Fickem in their buttholes!" Adam yelled.

"What did you call me?" X said.

Adam smiled.

"Just fickin with ya, X," Adam said smoothly. "Don't take offense, big man. I'm on your side. Max, toss me that bullet."

Max rolled the silver bullet across the table. Adam did a snort in each nostril and then passed the bullet to X, who did two delicate sniffs and then offered it to me. I shook my head. X gave the bullet back to Max. Bruno was sipping a green stinger and observing.

"What do you say, Richard?" asked Max. "Just nod your head and go to bed. I'll make the deal for you. You'll wake up rich."

I had to laugh.

"If I were writing this story I would never make the protagonist face the obstacle of being too desirable," I said. "Let's change it all around. You don't want me, Adam I don't like you, and besides, I'm an asshole. Max, I don't want to play golf with you, ever. Bruno, you're creepy. X you are a good guy and I hope you get your house above the smog line—which, by the way, is the same thing O. J. told me he wanted—but you don't need me."

Adam's red lips smacked twice as he chewed on a straw.

"Your trouble, Richard, is you think you're the protagonist, but you're only a second lead," Adam said. "You're not the star, Richard. You work for the star. And the star you are working for is falling fast. Take a moment for common sense to speak to you. Max put it well. Nod your head, go to bed, and wake up rich. Well, not rich like I'm rich, but rich like you have never been, that's fer fickin sure."

"Jack told me you're a liar," I said.

"Look, boys, he's a star ficker," Adam said. "See his eyes light up when he says 'Jack'?"

I stood up.

"Good luck, X," I said.

As I walked out, Gertrude was playing "Isn't It Romantic?"

Trudy was serving a table near the door. I slipped her a twenty to help with her education. I could still hear Adam's loud and arrogant voice behind me.

Fourteen

When you catch the ball in exactly the right spot on the club face, a 260-yard drive feels like a whiff.

Bel Air is a short course designed for rich people to have fun on. I swung my beautifully polished persimmon-headed Tommy Armour driver on the first tee and felt nothing but air and knew my Titleist had been creamed. My partner, Jim Murray, cackled with joy. I was thirty yards in front of Jack Roach.

The first hole is a par five, only 485. I pulled out my 1-iron and laid the ball ten feet from the flag. I felt this was going to be one of those great days. I was hitting the ball like a natural, and Katie Wynne would be waiting for me at the end of the game.

"The blade on this club looks like a butter knife," Jim Murray said, inspecting my 1-iron. I play with a twenty-year-old set of MacGregor Tourney muscle back irons. "You could open your mail with this."

Jim and Jack and the Italian investor, whose name was Carlo, had switched to the new metal-headed Taylor Made drivers and the Ping cavity back irons that Murray called pipe wrenches. Golfers rush to any new thing that promises to make the game less difficult. But I learned to play with blades and persimmon when I was a kid, and I was too proud to change.

"He's showing off with that 1-iron," Jack said.

Carlo said, "Lee Trevino told me he uses his 1-iron as a lightning rod. He says even God can't hit a 1-iron."

Jim and I glanced at each other. Both of us had heard that same Trevino story from so many different people that it had become a folktale.

I was playing Jack a $500 Nassau with automatic two-down presses. I intended to clip him for a couple thousand dollars and collect the $1,100 he already owed me from earlier games. This would be my tip money and spare change for the weekend with Katie.

Jim and I were matched against Jack and Carlo for a $10 Nassau. Carlo was also playing against Jack for a thousand dollars in a straight-up match. Carlo suggested he play me for a thousand dollars in medal play and I should give him six strokes, the same as I gave Jack. As gracefully as possible, I negotiated that bet down to a hundred dollars. But Jack made a thousand dollar bet with Carlo that I would beat Carlo, giving six, so I was playing both against Jack and for him.

Crossing the footbridge over the canyon to the tenth green, I had Jack out, out and out, two down, and even. I was three under par. Jack hadn't broken forty; I was eight shots up on Carlo. Jim Murray was winning all his bets. He was laughing and telling baseball stories. Life was sweet.

I was listening to the pleasing sound of our spikes clicking on the bridge when I heard Jim say, "What the hell is this?"

Sean Connery stood on the back edge of the tenth green, glowering, brandishing a putter in his hand like a sword. "Hey, you arseholes, I'm damned sick of you dogging our heels. Keep the hell back from my four-some. You bloody well nearly hit me two holes ago!" Connery yelled.

"Get away from the green, you sheep-shagging Scottish shit-ass," Jack retorted.

The two stars glared angrily at each other, each of them armed with a putter.

For a second I thought of how Paula would love a photo of this for *People* magazine.

"Clash of the titans," Jim Murray said.

"Hey, Jack, calm down," said Carlo.

The caddies stood beside their golf bags, watching.

I marked my ball with a dime and tossed the ball to Huey, my caddie. He was looking at the two movie stars, but he saw the ball coming out of the corner of his eye and caught it. Caddies observe extreme behavior on the golf course—grown men weeping, cursing, hurling their clubs into the woods or into a pond, but just as often there are grown men howling with joy that can be heard three fairways over as a putt rattles into the cup.

"Look at me funny and I'll beat your arse," Connery shouted.

"That'll be the day, fatso!" yelled Jack.

"Fatso!" Connery turned to his caddie. "Toss me my driver. A putter isn't enough for this cocksucker."

Jack stepped forward with a swagger, chest out, chin tucked in, boxer-style. He dropped his putter on the green and raised his hands with his fists half-clenched into claws, as in martial arts. I noticed the little fingers on each hand stuck out crookedly, showing they had been broken.

"I've been wanting to deck your fat ass," Jack said.

One man from Connery's foursome trotted over to be a peacemaker. The other two kept their distance. I lit my first cigarette of the day.

Carlo walked across the green. He was not a tall man, but he was solidly built, dark and hairy. He moved in between the two stars and stuck out both arms with his palms up in a universal "stop" gesture.

"Stop it, Jack," Carlo said.

"Step aside, Carlo," Jack said.

Connery let his driver fall to the ground and raised his fists in a classic boxing stance.

"Leave it be, Sean. Somebody will get hurt," said the man from Connery's group.

"That's the bloody idea," Connery growled.

Carlo placed a palm against each star's chest. Jack had told me Carlo owned half of Chicago. I could see how he might.

"Back up, Jack," Carlo said.

"Who the hell are you?" asked Connery.

"I'm his money," Carlo said.

"Oh." Connery backed up a few inches.

"Come on, Carlo, I can take him out fast," Jack said.

"Your tongue is wagging out of your arse is what is happening," Connery said. "You're talking shit."

Jack moved sideways to step around Carlo. But Carlo swiftly blocked him.

"If you break your hand again, Jack, I'm taking a walk on this film," Carlo said.

"Sean, please. Think of the lawsuits this could cause," the peacemaker said.

"You have to catch a plane to Hong Kong tonight, Sean," called a man from his foursome.

Connery turned to Jim Murray.

"Jimbo! You saw him hit into me two holes ago," Connery said.

"I guess I wasn't looking," said Jim, glancing at me. I shook my head. We had been pressing Connery's foursome pretty closely. Jack liked to play fast—he'd walk to his ball and hit it without much apparent thought or indecision, so we'd had to wait for Connery's group on every hole. I had learned to be Zen about delays on a golf course. The waiting didn't upset me. Today I had been talking to Jim Murray and enjoying our game.

But Jack had begun cursing loudly two holes back. By the time we reached the tenth green and found Connery waiting, Jack was boiling.

"I respect the etiquette of golf!" Jack said. "I wouldn't hit into your fat, lazy ass, but for God's sake, man, speed it up."

"Hey, Jack, one of our guys just had a hip replacement. He can't move so swiftly," said the peacemaker.

"Do I know you?" Jack asked. "Do you think I care?"

"I'm just trying to smooth things over," the peacemaker said.

I leaned close to Jim and muttered, "I wonder what Steve McQueen would do?"

"McQueen is dead. He didn't play golfanyhow," Murray said.

"Clint Eastwood then. What would he do?"

"I don't know what Clint would do, but Dirty Harry would clock 007's ass," Murray said.

"Come on, guys," said Carlo. "This is ridiculous. I'm asking you again, Jack. Calm down."

Jack lowered his claws and stepped back.

"You're right, Carlo. Why should I break a knuckle over something like this?" Jack said.

Connery dropped his hands and picked up his driver. He brushed grass off the persimmon head. The peacemaker touched the star's elbow and gestured toward the next tee, where the other two guys were smoking and waiting beside the caddies.

"I accept your apology," Connery said to Jack.

"Same here," Jack said.

Connery squinted at Jack.

"You're apologizing to me, is that what you're saying?" Connery asked.

"Not fucking likely," said Jack.

Carlo stepped in front of Jack. "You guys have too much class for this," he said. "I'm apologizing to both of you for both of you. This is my final word on the matter."

Jack studied Carlo and then turned to me. "You hear the way he said that? 'This is my final word on the matter.' That's the line our guy will say at the cattle auction at the end of act two. It's the perfect line. I've caught the tone!"

Jack repeated, "This is my final word on the matter."

"Jesus, but you're a lunatic. Just give us some room, will you?" Connery said.

He and the peacemaker walked away.

For the rest of the back nine, "This is my final word on the matter" was Jack's mantra. He repeated it a dozen times. I noticed Carlo listening closely to be sure it wasn't mockery, but he seemed satisfied that it was truly Jack rehearsing a line for the movie Carlo was buying a piece of.

The mantra didn't help Jack any play any better. As we had drinks at the men's grill afterward, we counted the numbers on the scorecard. Jack brought in a suede pouch that he dug out of his golf bag. He unzipped the pouch and licked his thumb and dealt me thirty-three one-hundred-dollar bills. I was one under par for the day and took three hundred, with presses, from Carlo. Jim Murray and I as partners clipped them for another hundred and sixty each. I was stuffing cash in every pocket of my blue cashmere jacket. In an hour I would be picking up Katie Wynne. I began humming the "Rose's Song" tune from *Gypsy*.

Carlo was a Cubs fan. He had a box at Wrigley Field and also a box at Dodger Stadium. Carlo and Jim talked baseball over drinks. I sat back and tasted my beer and loved my life, waiting for enough time to pass that I could excuse myself and speed out of the Bel Air gates and turn onto Sunset and hit the road to Katie's house.

I lit a cigarette and caught Jack staring at me.

"You got the place for it, don't you? He's on his horse with his rifle in his hand and he's facing the mob."

"Yeah." I could see the scene in my head. "He's slowly backing up on his horse, keeping the crowd at bay. 'This is my final word on the matter.'"

"Not backing up. I don't back up. They see my eyes. My eyes say I could kill them in an instant and enjoy it. I've got the big .40–.60 Winchester rifle on them. The bad guys back up. I freak them out with my eyes. They back up some more. Then I make a classic turn and gallop away on a beautiful horse and leave them in my dust."

"I like it," Carlo said.

"Who's directing this epic?" asked Jim.

"We don't have one yet," Jack said.

"Jack has fired two directors already." Carlo smiled at his star. "He's very picky about finding the right man, I am happy to say."

That two directors had been fired was news to me. I looked at Jack.

"I may direct it myself," Jack said.

"I don't think that is wise," said Carlo. "It's too much stress. You've got enough to do with writing it and starring in it."

I studied my glass.

"Richard is writing it. I'm just supplying encouragement and a few ideas, and of course I furnish the dope," Jack said. "The Writers Guild insists on that."

Everybody laughed. I looked at my watch and stood up.

"I enjoyed it, guys," I said.

"Where are you off to?" asked Jack.

"Got a date," I said.

I shook hands with Carlo and with Jim Murray. Jack caught me outside as I was waiting for my car.

"The two directors were way before you came into the picture," he said. "Neither of them was actually hired. It was just talk for Carlo. He loves show business gossip. I like to make him feel he's part of things."

"You're going to direct it yourself?" I asked.

"Cocktail bullshit. Don't worry. Oliver is finding us a top director. What would you think of Peckinpah?"

"I met him in London when he was making *Straw Dogs*. He showed me a script he had just finished writing. It was sixty pages long. He said a script longer than that is a waste of pages."

I saw my red Mercedes turning toward the clubhouse.

"Hell, sixty pages is sixty pages more than you've got now," Jack said. "Look on the sunny side."

A skinny white kid wearing a white shirt and white pants and white sneakers got out of my car and gave me a stoned smile. I reached into a coat pocket and pulled out a bill. It was a hundred. I gave it to the kid anyway. He blinked. Money was being thrown at me today and I was throwing it back.

"I'll see you Tuesday morning," I said. "You want to meet for breakfast?"

"What's wrong with Sunday and Monday?" asked Jack.

"I'm taking those days off," I said. "I'm tired. Running with you is tough. I'll meet you Tuesday morning and we'll start putting words on paper."

"You've got a shifty glint in your eye," Jack said. "Could it be that you're going up the coast with Katie?"

"Why would you think such a thing?" I asked, looking at him across the car roof.

"Buddy boy, I talked to Katie on the phone this morning. She told me." Jack caught my eye and held me with his famous squint. "You don't know shit. Faking it and think you're making it. Enjoy yourself, but watch out. She'll eat you alive, starting today."

Jack lit a cigarette with his silver Zippo, exhaled a stream of smoke, clicked the lighter shut, and an icy look froze his blue-gray eyes. "This is my final word on the matter," he said.

Jack backed into the clubhouse, sitting on an imaginary horse with an imaginary rifle in his right hand, keeping me at bay with his eyes.

"Is that Jack Roach?" asked the stoner parking attendant with the hundred dollar bill in his hand as he held the Mercedes door open for me.

"You mean you're not sure if that's Jack Roach?" I asked.

"I didn't know he was so old," the kid said.

Fifteen

Dolly buzzed me through the gate and met me at the door with an expression that she might be wearing if Katie had died in her sleep.

"You're late," she said.

"I'm early," I said.

"Park your car over there under the basketball goal and get your suitcase out. You did bring a change of clothes, I hope?"

"But I'm driving," I said.

"Wrong. Katie is driving," said Dolly.

I glanced at the blue pickup truck.

"She'll be out in a minute," Dolly said, and shut the door in my face.

I parked my red Mercedes under the goal and took my small black Italian leather suitcase out of the trunk. I put the suitcase in the bed of the pickup and leaned against the fender and lit a cigarette. I would rather go riding up the coast in my red Mercedes, but with Katie at the wheel a pickup truck would be the vehicle of the gods, or so I reasoned as I blew smoke and studied the mockingbird that landed on the hoop above my car and cut loose a stream of curses at me.

When I finished the cigarette I field-stripped it and crumbled the paper into a tiny ball and flipped it in the direction of the mockingbird, which flitted down and deliberately left a blob on the windshield of the Mercedes.

I shifted from foot to foot, looked at my watch, shook another cigarette out of the pack and then stuffed it back in. I opened the passenger door of the blue pickup and got in. I sniffed the familiar new-car scent. I looked at the odometer. The faithful old family pickup had 787 miles on it.

Katie came out carrying a hanger bag and with a duffle slung over her shoulder. She was wearing jeans, a white shirt, and a gray cashmere sweater.

"Have you formed a romantic attachment to Ava already?" she asked.

"I will learn to love her," I said.

I opened the door to get out and help with Katie's bags.

"But Ava is not going with us today," Katie said. "We're going with Lamby."

The third garage door rattled as it slid upward.

Dolly was standing inside the garage. I wondered if she was Lamby. Then she stepped aside and popped the trunk on a yellow two-seater hardtop sports car that even standing still looked like it was going two hundred miles an hour.

Lamborghini.

"I'm driving," Katie said as I fetched my suitcase out of the truck. "It's a big treat for me. I don't get to take Lamby out for a run anywhere near as much as I like."

I had never been inside a Lamborghini. From where we sat low to the ground, I looked up at Dolly's scowling face as the car backed out of the garage with a muffled growl. Katie twisted the wheel and spun the car in the turnaround and the gate swung open as we hit the drive going twenty already.

It is about one hundred miles from Beverly Hills to Santa Barbara. On a Saturday afternoon, with the weekend traffic, it takes two and a half hours unless you run into a rockslide or a bad auto accident. We encountered both. A delivery van and Cadillac had collided and created a twisting, smoking metal sculpture on the coast highway. The detour sent us up a canyon road, where we met the rockslide.

But I never looked at my watch even once.

I looked at Katie almost constantly. My heart swelled and I felt happy.

Katie whipped the Lamborghini onto the shoulder to get around the rockslide. A state highway patrolman stepped away from his parked cruiser and flagged Katie back into line, but when he recognized her he grinned and waved us forward.

I told her about the scene Adam had put on in the hotel bar the night before.

She smiled. "He's courting you, Malibu Zulu–style."

"I don't think so. I think he was doing it to keep X happy."

"He has X under his thumb already. No, Adam has drawn a bead on you. He wants you on his team."

"Why on earth would he want me? He could open the Writers Guild directory and hire any Academy Award winner in it."

She steered the Lamborghini around a Volkswagen bus and mashed her white sneaker against the pedal. My head rocked backward from the thrust.

"Adam may be a billionaire with a string of hit pictures but he's also a scared, formerly fat kid whose daddy ran off with a couple of hookers and never came back. Remember the Bill Goldman axiom that in the movie business nobody knows anything? Adam has made up his mind that you might know something. You have published three novels. That impresses him deeply. Adam can't write a novel. He can change your story later, but he can't assemble the words from scratch that make a book into something he can hold in his hands. He loves it that you're a writer for *Sports Illustrated*. That means much more to him than the two movies you wrote. He probably phoned O. J. Simpson yesterday and checked you out. O. J. must have approved. So Adam now has it in his head that he needs you. He's got to have you. He'll get you. And listen, Richard, write a big juicy action part for me, will you?"

"I'll never work for Adam," I said. "But I'll write a big juicy part for you in everything I ever do."

"Adam wants you. He needs you. He'll get you," she repeated.

"It's very far-fetched to think Adam might need me," I said.

"About the movie business you don't," she said with a grin. She sounded like Jack Roach, and it reminded me that Jack told me he had spoken to her on the phone this morning. But I didn't bring it up now.

Katie shook a cigarette out of a pack on the seat. I punched in the lighter on the dashboard.

"Really, Richard, never underestimate the massive inferiority complexes you run into in this business. All artists are hiding something, which is why they become artists, and we know for sure all the bosses are hiding something."

I looked out the window at the hills flying past. They were green from the rains.

She said, "I think to Adam you represent a possible safe haven in a world of enemies. X trusts you. The Juice trusts you. Adam wants to trust you. You're good as gold. Don't sell yourself short when you sign with Adam."

"You seem to know Adam a lot better than I realized," I said.

"I'm an amateur shrink, that's all. But I did know him a little before he became a big shot."

"What did you mean about Adam's father running off with hookers?"

"That's the untold story," she said. "The fishing trip that he never came back from involved Adam's daddy and two hookers. They took the boat to Central America and stripped it and sold it. Daddy gave the metaphorical finger to his wife and son and disappeared into a new life. What does that do for Adam's self-esteem?"

"Daddy bailed out on fifty-seven Dairy Queens?"

"The Dairy Queens are hers. The Queen Bee? The rumor is a few million dollars disappeared along with Daddy. So Daddy chose a villa on a beach in Costa Rica or someplace with a lapful of ladies over the love of his son and whatever it was he was getting from the Queen Bee."

"I must admit I sort of admire Daddy's outlook," I said. "I'll bet Daddy plays golf."

"Daddy did one great thing for Adam before he left. He hired Bruno."

"How authentic is this rumor?" I asked.

"It must not be very authentic. The *Enquirer* ran a blind item a few years ago, but nobody followed up on it. I think Daddy is legally dead."

We curved up around a crest and saw the ocean shining below.

"We're nearly there," Katie said. She grabbed my hand and squeezed it. "You're going to love this place, Richard."

She turned the Lamborghini through an open redwood gate between tall pines. We followed a twisting road to a redwood lodge that sat among trees on a lawn of rich, wet, green grass that sloped down to a view of the ocean rolling in the sun. A small sign on a pine board said Brother Jonathan's Inn.

It occurred to me that Katie might have booked us into one of those hideaways for upscale hippies where we would sit naked around a campfire with our comrades and smoke weed and confess our spirituality, or lack of it, to each other, and then all plunge into the hot tub. I took Paula to Esalen a few years ago. Truth-telling sessions made things worse between us.

Brother Jonathan came out the front entrance with two bellhops dressed in white turbans, long white blouses, and white trousers. While the bellhops took our luggage away, Brother Jonathan gently gripped each of us by an elbow and guided us into the lodge. A contented look on his face made him almost glow. Brother Jonathan was six feet tall, thin, maybe sixty years old. He had a black mustache and curly gray hair.

"You honor us with your friendship," Brother Jonathan said to Katie.

He showed us to a suite that had a terrace facing the ocean. This wasn't *Mother Jones*; it was a picture out of *Town & Country*. Our luggage was being laid out in the large bedroom. A man in a turban was building a perfect fire in the fireplace using piñon logs.

After Brother Jonathan and the others cleared out, I caught Katie as she was walking past. I drew her close and kissed her.

"Not yet, Richard," she said. "Let's have a drink on the terrace and a nice dinner in the dining room and then another drink or two in the bar and talk about lovely things. Let's have a real romance."

The suite had two bathrooms, which is a good way to keep the romance going. We showered and dressed. Katie put on a blue shirt, cream-colored slacks, and a dark jacket. I wore my usual khakis and Navy cashmere sport coat. Paula called that outfit my uniform. Why was I thinking of Paula?

It was too cold for drinks on the terrace.

We took a booth in a corner of the bar with a view of the cove below the inn. There was a little slice of beach. Surf pounded and the sunset turned a glorious red. I saw Brother Jonathan padding silently through the bar, smiling serenely at the customers and the staff.

"He used to produce movies," Katie said. "Sandy Ginsburg was his name. He had a nasty divorce and a total disaster at the box office and he fled the country a step ahead of an army of lawyers. He went to Kathmandu and disappeared for a few years. One day he turned up in Santa Barbara with that damned beatific smile on his face and enough money to open this inn."

"How do you know him?" I asked.

"I used to date him when he was Sandy Ginsburg."

"But you don't date Brother Jonathan?"

"Brother Jonathan doesn't date anybody. He goes around bestowing his blessings."

The dining room was darkly elegant with candles on the tables and walls of glass facing the night and the wind and the water. We both ordered fish. Brother Jonathan sent over the first bottle of wine with his compliments.

The second bottle went on our bill, along with the coffee and the cognac.

Katie told me about being a child in Weatherford, Texas, where her daddy was an oil wildcatter who went where the action was. Her mother had been a teenage rodeo queen. When Daddy Wynne got flush with a major strike in East Texas, Mother began shopping in New York and spending summers in Santa Fe, where she took up painting in oil and got good at it.

"I took drama classes at TCU and came to LA thinking that with my math ability and knowing who Ionesco was, I could get a job in an office in some area of show business. I had loved show business since I used to see Broadway shows in New York with Mom. I thought it would be thrilling. I became a receptionist at Fox. Max Bloom was constantly in and out of the building. He always flirted with me. Max put it in my head to go to an audition one morning."

"And you came back a star?" I said.

"It took me two years to get a speaking part and another year to get a part that had some soul. It was in a western with Jack Roach. After that I kept getting lucky with my choices.

I used the candle to light Katie's cigarette.

"Let's have one more cognac," she said.

I motioned to the waiter.

"I want to drink it in the bar while you play the piano for me," she said.

"But there's no piano in the bar," I said.

"Brother Jonathan has arranged it. Come on, Richard."

My pockets were bulging with hundred-dollar bills from the golf game. I dropped a couple on the table and followed Katie into the bar.

She took a seat on a bar stool, crossed her legs, smoked her cigarette, tasted her cognac, and looked at me expectantly. I noticed Brother Jonathan in the back of the room, smiling.

I thought I knew what she would like. I sat down at the piano and talk-sang "At Long Last Love," the Bobby Short arrangement without the benefit of his stylish voice but with some nifty work on the keyboard. I was just exactly the right amount of drunk to be very entertaining. Katie smiled and applauded. Brother Jonathan smiled and gave a few dainty little claps. Everybody in the bar was staring at Katie and wondering who the lucky piano player was.

I showed off. I played "Lullaby of Birdland," the old jazz tune, and gave it a sort of Bach style with some fancy finger action. This was a little beyond my ability, but I'd had just exactly enough to drink and I had practiced that tune for years in private. I played it well. The jazz seemed to surprise Katie, but it pleased her. Her lips parted and glistened in the dim light.

She snubbed out her cigarette and stood up.

"That was lovely, Richard," she said.

Brother Jonathan smiled and nodded good evening as Katie and I left the bar.

Sixteen

She asked me to undress her.

In my novels I approached descriptions of sex and everything around it very carefully. Adam said it was one big reason my novels didn't sell very well.

I could reveal to you that the moment we got inside the suite Katie turned and kissed me and wrapped herself around me for a long, hot, delicious spell. Then she stepped back and her eyes smoldered as she looked me in the eyes and said, "Undress me, Richard. I am taking you to bed."

That is how it started happening, but since this is a memoir and not fiction it would be ungentlemanly to describe how it was with Katie and me that night.

I wouldn't have said this much except it pisses off Paula.

From the moment she asked me to undress her until room service arrived with eggs Benedict and brandy Alexanders for breakfast at about dawn—I leave this part to your imagination. According to Adam your imagination is already pumping out such juicy images that my words would pale beside it anyhow.

After breakfast we made love again and then slept in each other's arms until noon.

In the afternoon we put on sweaters and pants and went down to the beach. Brother Jonathan sent two fellows with red turbans who laid out a picnic lunch and built a fire. The men were Sikhs. Brother Jonathan was keen on Sikhs, Katie told me, because their religion held hospitality to be a high virtue.

"Were you in love with him?" I asked.

"Was I in love with whom?"

"I mean before he became Brother Jonathan."

"No." She smiled. "You have such a pained expression on your face all of a sudden. Aren't you enjoying yourself? Shall I fetch you a chili dog?"

"I hate to think about you with other men."

"Oh, Richard, please. Don't behave like a schoolboy."

"I can't help it. I'm falling in love with you."

Katie got up and went to the fire, where she skewered a wiener on a stick and held it over the flames. She glanced back with a wickedly knowing smile.

"You had better not do that, Richard."

"I know."

She laid the wiener inside a bun, smeared it with spicy mustard and relish, ladled on a scoop of chili, and brought it to me. She knelt in front of me and offered me the hot dog wrapped in a napkin.

"I could fall head over heels for you, Richard," she said.

I leaned forward to kiss her, but she stuck the tip of the hot dog in my mouth.

"But I'm trying not to," she said.

"Why?"

"You're on the rebound. You're in an emotional state. You don't know how you really feel."

"I'm not on the rebound. I'm a new man. I know exactly what I want."

"What is it you want?" she asked.

"I want you."

"You want the woman you see in the movies. But the woman you'll wake up with is me. We are not the same person. You will be disappointed in the real me."

"I've never seen you in the movies," I said.

"What?"

"You right here in person is the only Katie Wynne I ever knew."

"You haven't seen even one of my films?"

"I promise."

"You don't need to be proud of it," she said.

She got up and returned to the fire. She opened the picnic basket and

117

dug around inside until she found a carrot. Katie took a bite of the carrot and chomped on it like Bugs Bunny.

"Do-do-do you recognize me now, doc?" she said between chews.

I followed her, dropped my chili dog in the basket, and reached for her to kiss her. She smiled and wriggled away. I lost my footing in the sand and fell onto all fours. Katie danced in front of me.

I looked up and saw a tall figure shambling toward us from the hotel. I recognized him and had a premonition that something had gone wrong.

"Uh-oh," I said.

"Is that Oliver Weintraub?" Katie asked.

"Yeah, that's him."

"Did you tell Jack we were coming to this place?" she asked.

"I didn't know where we were going."

Oliver waved as he trudged through the sand toward us. He had powerful shoulders and arms and a comfortable belly. He wore a Dodgers baseball cap on his bald head. His graying beard matched his bushy eyebrows, and his suede boots trudged through the sand in long strides.

"Kiddos! Hallo, kiddos!" Oliver's voice boomed over the sound of the waves and the cries of the gulls.

"Have you met Oliver?" I asked.

She nodded and waved back at him. I should have realized she would know him.

As he grew closer, Oliver stopped for a moment to gaze out to sea, taking a deep breath. He struck a pose as if he were the captain of a pirate ship, which in a way he was. The breeze ruffled his beard, and there was a glint in his eyes.

"Katie, my dear girl." He kissed her on the cheek.

"Richard, my expensive writer. How are you feeling this fine day?"

"I feel great, Oliver."

"Katie, do you think there is a Coca-Cola in that little fridge? Not a diet drink, dear. I need the full experience with the delightful sugar rush."

Katie bent to the box and opened the door.

Oliver unfolded one of the aluminum chairs that had been stacked near the fire. I wondered if the green plastic mesh seat would hold his heft. His bottom hung over the sides and the material sagged deeply, but Oliver sat confidently and reached for the bottle of Coca-Cola that Katie had opened for him.

"Want a glass, Oliver? Ice?" she offered.

"I like it out of the bottle," Oliver said. "It makes me think of my youth in the Bronx. Drinking Cokes in Uncle Abe's newsstand and grocery store and listening to my elders debating the human situation, I learned something important. I learned I had to get out of the Bronx as soon as any opportunity presented itself."

"How did you do it?" I asked.

"I got a job running numbers in Harlem. It is not a career path I would recommend, but it worked for me."

Oliver produced an alligator cigar case from one of the many pockets of his safari jacket. He offered a Cuban to me. When I declined, he stuck a long brown panatela in his mouth, but he didn't try to light it in the breeze. He rolled the cigar around in his lips, tasting the tobacco, and smiled with satisfaction.

"It is fortunate I caught the two of you together," Oliver said, as if he had wandered across us by accident. "I have something to tell the both of you that I will not tell to anyone else in this world. I must ask you to swear on whatever you hold sacred that you will not repeat what I am about to say."

He looked at us.

"All right, I swear," I said.

I felt a shudder go through me. I knew what he was going to say.

"I promise," said Katie.

"Jack Roach has a large mass in his right lung and small tumors scattered here and there in both lungs. He has nine months to a year to live by the most optimistic prognosis. The probability is four to six months."

Oliver paused to let us digest the news. Neither of us appeared to be surprised.

"My God, so it's true," Katie said.

"Jack told you?" asked Oliver.

"He told me if I heard the rumor"—she glanced at me—"that it's a lie."

"Jack is completely in denial," Oliver said. "He thinks he will beat it. But he has run into something that he can't beat."

"So you're saying the movie is over with?" I asked.

Oliver smiled. "Ah, my expensive writer thinks first of the movie. You are learning our ways rather quickly, Richard."

"Cut it out, Oliver. You know what I meant," I said.

"I know exactly what you meant. This is Show Business. But some of us are all heart. We are going to make Jack's movie. It will be the last thing he ever does, and it will be the best thing he has ever done."

"But you don't have time," Katie said.

"Dear, I have been actively prepping this film for Jack for a year. I have put all the parts in place. We will shoot it in the desert starting next week. You know, Katie, how Jack has wanted for years to make this movie. We are going to make his desire come true. I believe we can get the film into theaters just about the time Jack dies. You talk about critic-proof? What kind of asshole would put the rap on Jack at his funeral?"

"Oliver," I said.

"Yes, Richard?"

"I haven't written one page of the script."

"I didn't hire you strictly for your literary abilities," Oliver said. "I hired you because you are fast and reliable. You turn out those long features in *Sports Illustrated* at a high rate of speed. I checked with Jim Murray about it. He says you can do six thousand words in two or three days. Isn't that true?"

"I can do it faster than that," I said.

"You are the sixth writer we have had on this project," Oliver said.

He saw the surprise on my face. I didn't know there had been other writers. I had seen no scripts or heard other writers mentioned.

"But you are the first writer Jack has liked," Oliver continued. "I had to fire all the others. You don't want to read their scripts, believe me. They're all pieces of shit. Every unmade script is a piece of shit. Tell me, Richard, how long did it take you to write your first script, the one you did on spec?"

"About two weeks."

"That was your best work, I believe. But this script for Jack will be even better. You have one week to write it."

"One week? Listen, Oliver—"

"I have taken the liberty of checking you out of the Westwood Marquis. We have moved all your stuff—including that ream of blank white paper that you bought two days ago after leaving Adams's office—into a suite at the Universal Hilton."

"I don't like it in Burbank," I said.

"I am sure you would prefer I moved you into a suite at the Beverly Hills Hotel, but we can't afford it. I have three million dollars to spend on this movie and not a penny more. You are at the Universal Hilton under the name Gerard Manley Hopkins. Nobody can find you. Not even Adam. You have one week. Seven days. Give me fifteen pages a day. I will come rip them out of your typewriter if I have to."

"That's only a hundred pages," I said.

"It is one hundred and five pages. That is plenty of script," Oliver said. He looked at Katie. "Why are you smiling?"

"Gerard Manley Hopkins," she said. "The British poet. Sprung rhythm. See, Richard? I wrote a paper on him at St. John's."

"Is that right? A poet? My assistant is playing a trick on me. Well, no matter. Sorry that I had to interrupt your idyll on the beach, but it's up and at 'em now, Richard. You and I are riding back to town in my limo. We will talk story on the way."

I saw the two Sikhs walking toward us from the hotel, coming to pack up our picnic.

"I'm sorry, Katie. I do need to take Richard from you."

"Who's directing the picture?" Katie asked.

"Lonnie Holmes is coming back from London tonight. I will have him in for a chat," said Oliver.

"Lonnie Holmes doesn't do action very well," she said.

"Jack says it is a character piece," said Oliver.

"And what do I think it is?" I asked.

"Let's not take an attitude here, Richard," said Oliver.

The aluminum chair stuck to him as he stood up. He shook it off.

Katie hugged me and kissed me on the lips.

"I'll come see you tonight," she whispered.

"I love Gerard Manly Hopkins."

Seventeen

The offices of Jack Roach's independent film company were in a bunga-low on the lot at Twentieth Century Fox. That was the only place I had encountered Oliver Weintraub. I'd had lunch with him a couple of times in the commissary at Fox and sat in his office later and listened to him talk about his hobby of raising quarter horses on his ranch in Thousand Oaks. A hundred acres wouldn't qualify as a ranch in Texas, but in the rolling hills of Thousand Oaks, a hundred-acre horse ranch within view of the ocean was quite a prize.

Now I learned that Oliver's own production company, where the kung fu movies came from, had offices in the Black Tower at Universal, next door to the Hilton where Oliver had stashed me.

"Anything you need, any little problem you have, pick up the phone," Oliver said, delivering me to the suite on the twenty-first floor. "I will be here within ten minutes if you need me."

I walked around the parlor room, where my Smith Corona typewriter was set up on a table in front of a large window with a view of traffic moving on the 101 Freeway far below.

"You and I have never spoken about this subject, but I have taken the precaution of placing an ounce of cocaine in the drawer of your desk," Oliver said. "Please try to make it last for the whole week."

Oliver took off his Dodgers cap and wiped his forehead with a napkin from the room service table, where a club sandwich sat bristling with toothpicks. On the wet bar stood a bottle of Black Label, a bottle of vodka, a bottle of vermouth, a bowl of olives, a bucket of ice, and six glasses.

I looked inside the large bathroom that opened off the bedroom. My shaving kit was on the counter above the sink. I unzipped it and saw my bottle of orange Dexedrine pills.

"I wish you'd take the coke away," I said. "I won't need it."

"I was hoping you would say that," Oliver said. "I have noticed that cocaine produces some brilliant work from writers early on, but the work diminishes rapidly and the writer gets delusional and starts raving at me about winning the Oscar."

"But for a seven-day sprint, you're willing to stuff me with coke?"

"I am willing to do whatever it takes, Richard. This movie has come to mean a lot to me because of Jack. I admire the man. I did a stretch in reform school, too, just like he did. I served in the Navy like he did. I made my own way in the world like he did. I'm a fan of his movies. When he came to me personally and begged me to take over this production and save him, I was deeply moved. I felt tears on my cheeks. I have devoted myself to this project since the day I said yes and shook Jack's hand."

"There were really five writers before me? Why did nobody tell me?"

"Listen, there were two producers before me. There were two directors. This picture has been in development for eight years. They have wasted millions of dollars and what now turns out to be years of very precious time for Jack Roach."

I said, "I heard an improv actor say we all have exactly as much time as what we use up."

"Save your good lines for the script," Oliver said.

He opened the bottom drawer of the desk, removed a small brown paper bag and stuffed it in a pocket of his safari jacket.

"We talked this through in the limo, but I would like you to run through the basic structure for me one more time so I am totally sure you and I are working on the same movie," Oliver said.

"All right," I said. I poured a glass of ice water. "The setup is Jack is Dirty Harry of the Old West. He is noble and sexy, but he is getting old. Prudish assholes fire him as a marshal in Denver. He is alone. Maybe he has a dog. Jack takes to booze. One day a stranger shows up. The stranger is president of a cattlemen's association in Wyoming or Idaho—"

"California," said Oliver.

"Or maybe California. Anyhow, the stranger hires Jack to deal with gangs of cattle rustlers who are stealing big numbers of cattle from the association and terrifying and killing the cowboys. The stranger appoints Jack as a range detective, whatever that means. Jack goes to Wyoming or Idaho—"

"California," Oliver said. "We have the locations already."

"And that is the end of act one," I said.

"What happens in act two?"

"Jack meets his love interest: the school marm. She is way too young for him, but she falls in love with him. She can't help herself. Her love cracks open Jack's old heart. He is starting to love her, too. The rest of what happens in act two is Jack kills all the rustlers, but he gets betrayed by some politician in the cattlemen's association and is arrested and charged with murder."

"Good, good," Oliver said.

"Act three is Jack's trial. He is found guilty. He is sentenced to hang."

"And then?"

"I don't know," I said.

"Yes, you do. Jack makes a rousing speech at the gallows saying he is an honest man of the Old West who believes in a code of honor, but the cattlemen's association is a bunch of fucking sleazy hypocrites. So they spring the trap door. Jack falls through. But wait! Down below, out of sight from the crowd, Jack isn't dead! Maybe his deputy friend sawed the rope, I don't know. But Jack slips out and escapes to the mountains, where you can see his face in the clouds even still today."

"That is very neat," I said.

"What is our movie about?" asked Oliver.

"It's about changing times."

"Very good," Oliver said. "Now I will let you go to work."

"Jack hates that ending," I said. "He wants to hang."

"You don't need to tell him," Oliver said. "Seven days from now, when you give me the final page, I will tell him."

Oliver patted his pockets to be sure he had the bag of cocaine.

"By the way, Gerard Manley Hopkins is not accepting phone calls," Oliver said. "You may call out, but no incoming calls will get through."

"Who would be calling Gerard Manley Hopkins at this hotel anyway?" I asked.

"Katie Wynne, for one."

"I'm not allowed to see Katie?"

"Watch out for her, Richard. That is my friendly advice."

"What do you mean?"

"You don't have time to get involved with Katie Wynne, believe me. There is another advantage to your phone being blocked—Jack cannot call you. If he is going to bother you, he has to come all the way to Burbank to do it. Otherwise he might have you on the phone all night."

"Let me ask you something, Oliver."

"Please. Fire away."

"Is this story exactly the same story those other five writers were working on?"

"Not exactly, but pretty much."

"Then why has it taken so long?"

"There are various reasons why the other writers failed. But one main reason is in each case Jack decided he didn't like the writer personally or respect his work and suspected the writer was here to steal his money."

"What did you think?" I asked.

"Well, one of the writers had won an Academy Award, but that doesn't mean he wasn't here to rob Jack. I don't know. They were all fired by the two earlier producers before I came onto the project. You are my first writer on this movie, and you will be the only writer with his name on the screen. I'll see to it."

Oliver opened the door to the hall. He looked at the latch. "Lock this," he said. He went out.

I stared at the Smith Corona. The moment always came when you had to sit down and type the first word.

Eighteen

As a hazy red sun set beyond the 101 Freeway on Sunday evening, I rolled a piece of paper into the Smith Corona.

On Tuesday evening, I lay on the couch in my underwear while the messenger from Oliver's office picked up the last twelve pages of act one.

I had showered once since Sunday, but I hadn't shaved. I had been dead drunk twice. The suite smelled pungently of Winston cigarettes. I had begun wishing I hadn't been so hasty in asking Oliver to take away the bag of cocaine.

I also hadn't heard from Katie Wynne.

I could have phoned her, but I didn't. I had expected her to show up at the suite Sunday night as she said she would. The desk told me there were no messages for Gerard Manley Hopkins.

I was thinking that it was just as well Katie hadn't come. As I go into a long piece of writing I become psychotic. I hear voices that I can't control. Being an editor and a writer herself, Paula had understood what was going on with me even if she didn't want to be around it. Paula gave me a lot of room when I was writing a novel or a screenplay.

After the messenger left I lay on the couch smoking a cigarette and drinking Black Label and water. I was trying to think of a title for the movie. Right now it was called the Jack Roach Project. The title of the movie was to be the name of Jack's character. I was sure the previous five writers had faced this same problem. They must have thought of some crappy names if none had survived eight years of study.

So far in the script I was calling the character Jack.

I was running through names in my mind. All I could think of were names like Flint Ridge, Rock Studly, Prey Hunter—I mashed out the cigarette and sat up. I was losing my mind and it was only Tuesday.

The doorbell rang. I figured it was room service to pick up the food debris I had scattered around the parlor and bedroom and both bathrooms: tin dish covers, plates, catsup bottles, coffee cups.

I opened the door. A tidy-looking man in a white linen suit with a dark blue necktie stood in the hall. I caught him spitting on his comb, but he went ahead and ran it through his thin blonde hair before he spoke with a slight English accent.

"I assume from your attire that you are my writer, Richard Swift?" he said.

"Who would you be?" I asked.

"I am your director, Lonnie Holmes. May I come in?"

"Yeah. Sure. Make yourself comfortable."

Lonnie Holmes had directed a western that won the Oscar for its lead actor four or five years ago. That was all I knew about him.

I slipped on a pair of khaki slacks and clawed at my hair. Barefoot, I returned to the parlor and saw Lonnie Holmes examining my typewriter and the top of my desk and reading my notes.

"I haven't read the latest pages, but I did glance through the earlier stuff," Lonnie said. "It is nice, very nice. I will have my chap tweak it a bit, of course."

"My chap? Who the fuck is my chap?"

Lonnie's eyes widened. "Don't take offense, old boy. I run through all the material myself with a pen in my hand making notes, and then I have my chap vet it. This is what you call standard operating procedure on a Lonnie Holmes film."

"This is a Jack Roach film," I said.

"We shall see. We shall see."

Lonnie tossed a stack of newspapers out of a chair and started to sit, but instead he straightened up and gave me a big grin. "On the airplane I had an inspiration for a great scene. Are you willing to listen? Are you ready for this?"

"Go ahead."

Lonnie walked to the plate glass window and posed against the red sunset. "Imagine those clouds behind me are the Rocky Mountains out there," he said.

I nodded.

"Jack is sitting by the campfire just where you are now. He looks up at me. I am Geronimo."

"What?"

"I am Geronimo."

"How did Geronimo get in this movie?"

"Jack was his friend. Just hear me out."

I put my head in my hands and closed my eyes.

"No, really. This is quite good," Lonnie said.

"All right. I'm listening."

Lonnie handed me two folded pieces of typing paper and a ballpoint pen. "You will want to make notes," he said.

He returned to his pose by the window and folded his arms like you see in old sepia photos of Indian chiefs. He showed his profile against the sunset. He slowly turned his gaze to me.

"Geronimo looks at Jack and says, 'Dah a dah a dah dah deed ah.'"

Lonnie proudly reared his head. "And Jack looks back and slowly says, 'Dah dah de dah.'"

"Yeah?" I said.

"So Geronimo looks back at him and with great profound sadness says, 'Dah dah dah deed ah dah dah.'"

"What does Jack say to that?" I asked.

"Jack leaps to his feet and cries, 'DEE DEE DEE!'"

"Then what?"

"You're not writing this down," Lonnie said.

"What am I supposed to write down?"

"I am giving you the rhythm of the scene, all the beats, how it will play. I see it vividly in my head. I imagined the scene on the plane. It photographs beautifully. You put in the words. You are being paid to write the words."

It was nearly seven o'clock but I picked up the phone and called Oliver Weintraub on his private line. I caught him as he was about to leave his office.

"Would you please stop by and see me on your way home?" I asked.

"Are you in trouble? It's not the police, is it?"

"I want you to hear this new scene."

"Richard, please. I told you to call if you have a serious problem. By serious I mean if you get busted or you decide to jump off the roof. I don't want you to call to read me your brilliant writing. I have a family, you know. I need to go home."

"Lonnie Holmes is here," I said.

"I'll be there in ten minutes," said Oliver.

At Lonnie's request I fixed him a martini with three olives. He lit a cigarette that smelled like an electrical fire. He said it was Turkish. Lonnie was thrilled with his scene. He rehearsed Geronimo's moves. I turned on the television to catch the end of the news and poured another Black Label.

It entered my mind that my next phone call might be to Roy Barker in New York to ask for my job back at *Sports Illustrated*.

Or there was Adam Wachinski to think about. *Giants* with Erazmo Jones, now known as X, and little blonde Sugar, and Bruno and Max. How desperate would I be?

Oliver arrived in less than ten minutes.

"Have a seat and watch this," Lonnie said. "Richard, make him a drink."

"I don't want a drink," said Oliver. He sat on the arm of the couch. "Let's hear it, Lonnie."

Lonnie went through the same act he had performed for me. I am not sure the dees and dahs were all the same, but the action was a little more robust than before.

"Geronimo? Where did he come from?" asked Oliver.

"Richard can work that out and put in the words. I see the scene vividly in my head, Oliver. I see the mountains, the sunset. The noble red man and the noble white man sharing a bond that is heartbreaking. Civilization is coming to fuck both of them."

Oliver said, "Lonnie, I want you to do something for me."

"Of course, I will do anything within reason."

"Your idea is not good. I want you to get out of here and leave Richard alone."

"Oliver, you cannot sit there ex cathedra and criticize me and order me around."

"Ex cathedra? Is that what you say in the Ivy League?"

"You know perfectly well what it means."

"Lonnie, you are jet lagged. Go to Newport and get aboard your yacht and take a long nap. Let us work here," Oliver said.

"I warn you, if I walk out this door right now I am not ever coming back to this project," said Lonnie.

"That is fine with me," Oliver said. "Give my best wishes to your wife and kiddos."

Lonnie slammed the door. I started to say something, but Oliver held up a hand for silence. "Lonnie walks out and then comes back. It is his tactic," Oliver said.

In a moment the doorbell rang. Oliver opened the door. Lonnie was standing there.

"Perhaps I was hasty," said Lonnie.

"Go to Newport, Lonnie. We will talk tomorrow."

Oliver shut the door in Lonnie's face. After waiting a moment to see if the doorbell would ring again, Oliver picked up his briefcase, adjusted his Dodgers cap, and made ready to leave.

"Is there anything else?" he asked.

"Is that the end of Lonnie?"

"You did Lonnie a favor. I haven't made a deal with him. I had him in for a chat, as I said I would, and Lonnie took it from there. You saved him from a major embarrassment. Jack would have fired Lonnie within two or three days of meeting him."

"I thought you said Jack wanted him."

"Lonnie was a three a.m. idea."

"Do you have anybody in mind?"

"Next week I am bringing in George Sigal. George is a big, tough guy. He can whip Jack's ass. Jack will respect him. George will shoot the script you write, and do it beautifully and fast."

"Where is Jack?"

"Jack is at a clinic in Mexico. They are pumping him full of vitamins and herbs and stardust. He took his Chinese healer from Chinatown with him."

Oliver paused at the door.

"Jack might have taken Katie Wynne to Mexico with him, too, but I don't know for sure," Oliver said. "Well, good night, Richard. I have to go feed my horses. I will leave you here to throw peanuts to the gorilla."

Nineteen

Thursday evening at sunset I was lying on the rug in the middle of the parlor floor, reading *Variety* and studying the light fixture in the ceiling.

There was a note in Army Archerd's *Variety* column that Lonnie Holmes had quit Jack Roach's troubled, untitled western because of creative differences.

I had taken several Dexedrine tablets, smoked two packs of Winstons, and was fairly drunk. The script was well into act two. Jack was killing rustlers left and right with his Winchester rifle. His tough old heart was opening to romantic love for the beautiful school marm. It turned out the school marm was born on Long Island and went to college in New York City before she chose to go out west to teach children and have an adventure.

Meeting Jack the range detective was a hell of an adventure.

I realized I might be writing a part for Katie Wynne, so I gave the school marm a background that was more like Paula's. I was pissed off at Katie. Sunday she was in love with me, maybe. Now it was Thursday, and not another word nothing. She knew where Gerard Manley Hopkins was hiding. If she had gone to Mexico with Jack, that was all the worse.

But that wasn't why I was having an existential meltdown.

The doorbell rang, and it was Oliver coming in response to my phone call. He tossed his briefcase on the counter, poured a Coca-Cola over ice, lit a panatela, sat down, and crossed his legs.

"I can barely see you for the fucking smoke," he said.

"I have a creative problem that involves the production department or whatever you call it."

"Are you feeling all right? Have you been eating regularly? Why don't you shave and shower and change clothes? You will feel much better."

"I feel fine. Maybe just a little bilious, a touch of diarrhea, but you don't want to hear about that."

"Please, Richard. You know I have horses to feed." He looked at his watch. "I have ten minutes for this. What is your problem?"

I lit another cigarette and chewed on a peanut butter cracker.

"Well, you understand that I need to visualize all this stuff as I'm writing it?" I said. "The actors in my head act out the story and the dialogue against a backdrop of scenery?"

"Yes, of course," said Oliver.

"I can't visualize cattle rustlers rustling cattle in the desert. I can't see hundreds of cattle being herded through the sand to an oasis of palm trees. What are cattle going to graze on in the desert? I can't see Jack chasing rustlers through the dunes. I don't see the school marm with sand in her teeth. My imagination fails me."

Oliver laughed. "Forgive me," he said. "I had not anticipated this. I should have told you. We are not shooting in the desert. We are shooting at Ted Berne's movie ranch near Santa Barbara. Our sets are being built already. There is a good western town there with a wonderful court house for the trial."

"But Jack told me—"

"Let's not mention this to Jack. I will tell him when the time comes. Imagine any action you want in this town—hotel, barroom, pharmacy, this place has it all. What are you calling the town in your script?"

"Jackville."

"How about calling it Black Rock?"

"Could I?"

"You're the writer. Just don't tell Jack."

"I am hearing that sentence quite a bit—don't tell Jack."

"You know Jack pretty well by now. Do you really want to pick a fight with him?"

"No."

Oliver dug into his safari jacket and pulled out a hand-rolled cigarette the size of my middle finger.

"This is fresh off the plane from Jamaica," he said. "Smoke it and dream a while. Relax."

Oliver laid the joint on the counter and left. I went back and sat down at the typewriter. I typed "EXT. JACKVILLE—DAY."

I tore out that piece of paper, wadded it, and threw it at the trash basket. I rolled in another piece of paper and typed "EXT. BLACK ROCK—DAY." I knew that somewhere down the line someone would decide we couldn't use that name because it was already the title of a famous movie. But the image of a town called Black Rock excited me and started me typing madly.

I phoned room service. I ordered a New York strip steak, a baked potato, a bowl of creamed spinach, a bottle of red wine, and an ice cream sundae. Yet when the waiter wheeled in the table with my dinner on it, I hardly noticed. I was typing. The waiter uncorked the wine and brought me a glass for my approval. I tasted it, signed the check with an enormous tip, and returned to typing.

At midnight I heard the doorbell. I hadn't touched the food on the room service table, but I had drunk the bottle of wine. The waiter was here to clear the dishes and take the table away.

"Come in," I yelled.

I expected the waiter to use his house key. The doorbell rang again.

"Come in, damn it!" I yelled.

The doorbell rang three times.

I jumped up and hustled to the door and yanked it open.

Katie Wynne stood there. She warmed me with her gorgeous smile. Jack was right: this was a unique smile, a gift from God. She was wearing jeans and a cashmere jacket over a white blouse.

"I can't talk to you right now," I said.

"What?"

I did feel I was losing my mind. As recently as Tuesday, I had thought about Katie night and day, as Cole Porter would have put it. Staring at her now I could hardly remember what she had looked like.

"Richard, it's me, your lover," she said. "My God, how stoned are you?"

"Katie, I'm working."

She brushed me aside and entered the suite. Then she made a face and pinched her nose. "This place smells like a toilet," she said. "No, not just a toilet, like a bus station toilet. I am calling housekeeping to come up here at once and scrub and fumigate."

"No, not now. That would ruin everything," I said.

She opened the refrigerator in the wall behind the counter and found an unopened bottle of chardonnay.

"I got that for Sunday night. I mean last Sunday night," I said.

"Is that what this attitude is about?"

She popped the cork on the wine.

"I've got everything just the way I want it right now. You are interfering," I said.

"You're angry because I didn't show up on Sunday night?"

She walked over and looked at the page in the typewriter. She sipped the chardonnay and thumbed through the stack of pages on the floor beside my chair.

"Page seventy," she said. "You're getting there."

Katie noticed the bomber joint Oliver had left on the counter. "Let's fire this up," she said.

"Are you drunk?"

"Me? I am not the drunk person in this room."

"Can't you hear me? I'm working tonight. Go away."

She sat down on the couch and patted the cushion beside her. "Come sit by me," she said.

"Have you been in Mexico with Jack for the last few days?"

"I have been at home every night and working every day. Why haven't you called?"

"I was waiting for you on Sunday night."

"Oliver asked me to stay away and let you work on the script."

"He did?"

"But I can't stay away any longer. Come sit by me," she said again.

I am not going to write in this memoir what happened next on the couch, but it was something Paula gave up doing with me several years ago..

When Katie came out of the bathroom I was sprawled on the couch with a cigarette and a drink, looking beyond my bare feet to the desk where my Smith Corona stood above a pile of pages I was happy with.

A writer's life is a peculiar life. Most writers understand that it is a roller coaster ride. If the idea is to capture that enormous, gut-wrenching rush as your hair flies in the air and you zoom to the top, I had it in that moment.

Twenty

On Sunday night not fifteen minutes after Oliver Weintraub's messenger took away the final pages of the script, Jack Roach showed up at my suite and wanted to read the whole thing. Rather, he wanted me to read it to him. And if I were too tired to perform, then Jack would have his Chinese friend read it aloud.

Jack said he was completely cured of his stomach virus. The clinic in Mexico had jacked him up. I must say that Jack did look very healthy. He was glowing with sun. His eyes were sparkling blue.

"The script is gone," I said. "Oliver has it."

"Didn't you keep a carbon?"

"No."

"Didn't you keep a photocopy?"

"No."

"You hear that, Mr. Li? No copies," Jack said.

His Chinese friend smiled inscrutably.

Jack glanced in the bedroom and saw my suitcase open on the bed. "What's this?"

"I'm moving back to the Westwood Marquis tonight."

"You're not leaving town, are you? You work for me for eight more weeks, you know," Jack said. He was smiling but his tone was edgy.

"I want to see this picture all the way through," I said.

"You'll have to clear that with George Sigal. I don't know how he feels about having the writer on his set."

"What's the matter with you?" I said. "What have I done wrong?"

"You should've saved me a copy of the script."

"I'm sorry. I didn't know."

"Is it the same story you and I have been working out between the two of us?"

"Yeah."

"What about the ending? How does it end?"

"With a rope around your neck," I said.

Jack's Chinese friend placed a large brown envelope on the coffee table and sat down in front of the television . He poured himself a glass of ice water and turned on the eleven o'clock news.

"Listen, Jack," I said, "Katie will be here in a few minutes. She'll drive me back to the Westwood Marquis."

Jack paused in fixing a drink and slowly turned to search my face with his eyes.

"Really?" he said.

"Yeah. Really."

"Nice work, buddy boy. Having Katie Wynne drive you around makes you hot stuff, doesn't it? Where's your Mercedes that I'm paying for?"

"Oliver Weintraub took my car away for this week. Why have you got a bug up your ass? You knew I was seeing Katie."

"I'm sorry, Richard. I have a lot on my mind. It's not personal."

"It sounded personal."

"I'll tell you what. When Katie gets here we'll go celebrate your finishing the script. We'll go to Chinatown and have a banquet, just the four of us. Right, Mr. Li?"

Mr. Li was watching the news about a car chase on the San Diego Freeway. "I know a fine place," said Mr. Li, never shifting his gaze from the television screen. He lit what smelled like an herbal cigarette.

"Jesus, it stinks in here," Jack said.

"I don't smell anything anymore," I said.

"How long is it since you've been in the fresh air?" asked Jack.

"Seven days."

"Has Katie been spending time over here? How could she stand the smell?"

"If we're gonna fight about Katie, let's do it now and get it over with," I said.

"Do you mean fisticuffs? You want to duke it out with me?" Jack clawed

137

his hands into the martial arts look he had shown to Sean Connery. Then he grinned. "Hey, buddy, you're my writer and my golf partner and my drinking pal. You've been in the Truth Room. That gives you privileges."

"What you told me in the Truth Room is the truth, isn't it?" I asked.

"In the Truth Room nothing is spoken but the truth, Richard. It's sworn in blood."

"Your blood and my blood," I said.

"We're going to make a great film, you and me," Jack said.

"I have high hopes."

"Am I on every page of the script?"

"Just about."

"What happens on the pages I'm not on?"

"Plot points."

"How can our movie not be great?" Jack said. "Man, I'm excited and ready to go."

I said I had to finish packing. I went into the bedroom. Katie had left a blouse draped across the back of a chair. I folded it and put it under my shirts in the suitcase.

I didn't hear the doorbell ring, but I heard Katie's whoop of delight, and I heard Jack cry out her name. When I turned and looked, they were embracing. They kissed on the lips. It was a long kiss.

Katie stepped back holding both of Jack's hands and smiled gloriously. "Look at him, will you, Richard? Doesn't he look great?"

"He looks very life-like," I said.

"I am well, Katie. I'm cured!" Jack said. "My stomach virus is done. It's over and gone."

"I pray for you every night," she said.

"At this clinic on the Pacific Coast they have brujos who come down from the mountains and jungles with healing remedies that our tight-ass medical establishment has never heard of and wouldn't allow anyhow."

"Hey, Mr. Li, show them the X-rays," Jack said.

Mr. Li opened the brown envelope. He removed two X-ray photos of a human torso.

"Take a look," Jack said.

We examined the X-rays against the light of the desk lamp.

"This is my stomach. Clean as a baby. This second one is my lungs. See? No infection. Not a cloud in the sky."

Jack took out his Zippo and patted his shirt pocket. Mr. Li glanced at him, wagged a forefinger, then returned to the car chase on TV.

"Mr. Li won't allow me to smoke." Jack said. "Smoke gets in my chi and fucks me up."

Mr. Li let out a squeal. "Breaking news! Breaking news!" he cried, jabbing a finger at the television screen. With the remote he turned up the volume on a gabble of loud voices. The television screen showed an excited scrambling of people on a corner of Sunset Boulevard near the Hyatt Hotel, which was a favorite of rock bands and other touring musicians and performers.

A tall woman with bright red circles of rouge on her powdery pale cheeks was being shoved by a uniformed police officer toward a squad car. Her wig was knocked askew and her off-the-shoulder gown was ripped, revealing a fleshy white arm.

Her crooked red-lipped grin was aimed directly at the television camera. Flashguns lit up her face as more paparazzi came running from the hotel. The crowd was growing rapidly. The woman stumbled but caught herself and thrust her shoulders upright with dignity.

Her arms were behind her back, her hands in cuffs. But she favored the cameras with a broad wink as she was shoved into the back seat of the police car.

"My God, do you realize who that is?" Katie gasped.

"I don't believe it," Jack said.

I recognized the woman just as the TV reporter spoke her name.

She was Adam Wachinski.

Twenty-one

We stood stunned as the announcer told the story on the TV news.

A tall, awkward-looking woman who called herself Brenda had apparently offered to perform oral sex on a longhaired rock fan for twenty dollars, but the fan turned out to be an undercover vice squad officer. The officer recognized that Brenda was not a woman. Had Brenda been a woman, the officer would have ignored her or dismissed her with a warning.

Three hot rock bands and one major country group were staying at the Hyatt, the sidewalks and the lobby were crowded with fans, and the officer was scouting the crowd for much bigger game than a twenty-dollar blow job.

"I heard the cop tell this creep he ought to go home and sober up, 'cause he looked disgusting and was making a fool out of himself. You could tell the cop felt sorry for this person," a skinny young man in tight leather pants told the TV news reporter.

But Brenda then pushed the officer in the chest with both hands.

"The man in the red wig said very loudly, 'I want to [BLEEP] your [BLEEP] big boy,'" the witness said.

When the officer tried to subdue her, Brenda took a swing at him, hitting him on the shoulder. Brenda's wig fell off. As Brenda bent over to pick up the wig, the officer was able to subdue the wigged assailant and call for backup.

Photographs of Adam Wachinski and news clips of him at the Academy Awards, the B'nai B'rith banquet, and other elite occasions, began appearing on the screen while the reporter in the studio narrated Adam's history as a fantastically successful show business figure.

"Did you know he was a cross-dresser?" cackled Mr. Li.

"That's not drag behavior," Jack said. "That is pure sick."

"I wonder where Bruno is," I said. "How could he let this happen?"

"Poor Adam," said Katie. "This is so humiliating."

I glanced at Jack. He was squinting at the screen with the small ironic smile he was known for. I thought of Adam sobbing in the bedroom doorway with Jack putting his pants on and the Queen Bee screaming at her son to shut up and go away.

"Adam is not gay. He doesn't know what sex is," Jack said. "He's afraid of it. He doesn't feel what other people feel in sex. He's looking for the thrill, but he can't find it. That's how I see it."

"What do you think, Richard?" asked Katie.

"Adam is not a sex man, he's a filmmaker," I said.

"What does that mean?" Jack asked.

"I don't know. It's what he told me."

"I don't think Adam even has any sex," said Jack.

"He has no dick?" Mr. Li asked.

"I didn't say he has no dick. I said he doesn't understand sex."

I picked up the phone and asked the bell captain to send up a bellhop to carry my suitcase downstairs. It was the same small black leather suitcase I had packed for the weekend with Katie a week ago.

"What the hell am I doing?" I said. "I've been in this hotel too long. I have to get out of here," I said.

"Good idea, Richard. Let's go to Chinatown and celebrate your script," Katie said.

She took me by the hand and squeezed my fingers.

· · ·

I could imagine Paula rushing into the art department at *People* magazine in New York and digging through stacks of file photographs of Adam as himself to print next to fresh, new paparazzi and wire service photographs of Adam as Brenda. I remembered Adam in his office showing me stacks of photographs of naked women and saying, "Look at the titties on this pig!" I remembered Adam poking a finger at the vagina of one woman in the photos and comparing it to the face of Adolph Hitler, and another to Groucho Marx. Recalling the look of disgust on Adams face, I smiled and shook my head.

"What's funny?" Katie asked. Her blue pickup shot through a yellow light that was turning red.

"Just about everything," I said.

"I don't see Adam as funny," she said. "I think this is very sad."

Katie steered the pickup around a van full of hippies. They gave us the finger.

The television above the bar in the Chinese restaurant was tuned to a local station that was turning Adam's bust into a never-ending circus featuring frequent updates and reactions from around the US.

"I ordered for everybody," Jack announced when Katie and I arrived at the booth. "I told Mr. Chow to bring us everything on the menu."

Jack held up his empty glass and pointed to it, and the waiter hurried to get him another. Katie and I slid into one side of the booth. Mr. Li nervously spun a cup of tea in its saucer. He was trying to see past Jack into the bar, where the television flickered with Adam's public disgrace.

"Getting here you must have set a land speed record for cities of over five million," Katie said.

"I have the black T-bird tonight. It rides six inches above the pavement."

My thigh pressed against Katie's thigh. I looked across the table at Jack. I noticed a small frown as he watched Katie and me so close together.

Jack poured each of us a cup of rice wine. He lifted his cup in a toast. "This is history in the making," he said.

The four of us touched china cups above the center of the table.

"This is the night Richard finishes our script and Adam Wachinski goes down in disgrace," Jack said. "We're on our way to many Academy Awards and Adam is on his way to the jail house. This is sweet."

"I want to make it clear that I feel sorry for Adam," Katie said.

"I do, too," I said.

"Forget him," said Jack.

We drank to our success and Adam's personal disaster.

"Is he ruined now?" Mr. Li was happy at the thought.

"That gurgle you hear is Adam drowning in the toilet," Jack said.

I glanced at Katie. She was studying Jack's face as he relished Adam's disgrace.

"The tabloids will murder him," Jack said. "Every mother in the world who shops at a supermarket will see Adam in his off-the-shoulder gown and his red wig scuffling with a vice squad cop. Every time there is reason to mention Adam in the future, the tabs will drag out that same photo. When they get a juicy item like this, they use it forever to define a person."

Jack wore the smile that he flashed whenever he wiped out the bad-ass villain in the movies. "That sick bastard has had it," Jack said. "Let's eat."

• • •

I woke up in my bed at the Westwood Marquis with the throbbing skull of an early hangover. The clock on the nightstand said it was 3:56. I rolled over and touched the place in the bed where I expected to find Katie.

I found her standing in the dark in the living room. She was looking at the big hospital across the street. Red and yellow lights were flashing on the roof as another helicopter delivered a sad bundle onto a gurney. Somehow the lights flashed on Katie's face. She was wearing my blue Brooks Brothers shirt.

"Do you believe Jack is cured?" she asked.

"I wish I did."

"Why would he show us X-rays of a virus? Can you even take an X-ray of a virus?"

"You can take an X-ray of viral pneumonia. My grandmother had it."

She hugged her elbows and took a deep breath. She watched the helicopter soar up from the hospital landing deck, its lights vanishing into the night.

"We have to stick with him, Richard," she said.

"He can count on me," I said.

"Promise me you won't leave him until this is finished."

"I promise."

• • •

Adam was the star of the morning newscasts and his photo appeared on the front page of the *Los Angeles Times* in its full glory—a proudly defiant Brenda in a red wig and a torn gown.

His attorney, Bert Fields, announced that Adam was suffering from overwork and exhaustion and had checked into an establishment in the Malibu vicinity that specialized in rest and rehabilitation. The charges against him were being negotiated.

143

Katie and I ate a room service breakfast and watched *Good Morning America* personalities speculate if this scandal would destroy Adam's career. How dare he, this maker of films that scored so heavily with the teenagers, put on a dress and solicit a policeman on Sunset Boulevard?

We flipped through the channels. Every station was talking about Adam and sex, sex, sex, sex. I smiled. Adam might have performed this spectacular act to prove his point that sex was all everyone thought of, except for Adam, who only thought of making films.

The phone rang. A teamster in a Ford van was waiting for me at the curb.

Katie walked me to the door with her arm around my waist. She was wearing a white terrycloth robe.

"As soon as we wrap this show I'm in now, I'll be up there to stay with you and Jack," she said.

She kissed me. A long, slow kiss.

"I love you," she said.

Her words thrilled me. I felt amazingly happy and optimistic on the strength of those three words.

"I love you," I said.

The phone began ringing again. Katie smiled and turned me around and pushed me out the door. I was on my way to Black Rock.

Twenty-two

Oliver Weintraub presided at our first general meeting in the production offices of the Jack Roach Project at the Wizard Motor Inn on Highway 101 north of Santa Barbara.

The heads of each department sat around a long table with their scripts, papers, and notepads in front of them. Wearing his Dodgers cap and a striped rugby shirt, Oliver sat at the head of the table. To Oliver's right was a large, hairy man wearing shades. I had not been introduced to him yet, but I knew he was George Sigal, our director.

Oliver discussed a few items like housing, parking spaces, makeup and wardrobe trailers, and the need for being frugal but wise with our money.

"As all of you know, we planned on a forty-five day shoot, which is not a lot of time to put this work of art together," Oliver said. "I continue to stress that we are working on a very tight budget. Last night George Sigal and I and our brilliant production manager, Cyrus Brooks," he nodded toward a chubby bald man in a blue denim shirt, "sat up until dawn putting a pencil to every aspect of this production."

Oliver looked to his director and his production manager, and they nodded. "We have decided to shoot this show in thirty-seven days," said Oliver.

The department heads glanced at each other and then looked back at Oliver.

"George has generously agreed that we will use the second unit extensively to shoot our cattle roundups, ranch life, postcard shots, chases, ride-ups, and ride-aways. We have brought in Trent Roberts to direct second unit. Say hello, Trent."

A lanky man I had never seen before lifted a hand and said, "Hello."

"Everyone will begin at once to make adjustments in your plans," Oliver said. "But first, pick up your scripts."

There was the sound of scripts being shuffled on the table.

Then Oliver said, "Everyone open your scripts to page one."

We did as instructed.

"Now turn to page twenty. Remove pages one through twenty from your scripts. Toss these pages in the wastebasket. We are losing Denver."

"What?" I said.

"Write us a new opening this morning, Richard. Jack rides into town. That is how our story starts."

The Denver pages were my jewels. In Denver Jack was drunk, violent but with humanity and wit, and he loved his cat. His speeches to his cat were my best writing. His puritan enemies were sharply drawn. You felt Jack's hurt pride when he got fired as the marshal. He was talking to his cat when the cattleman showed up to hire him to kill rustlers in California.

"But Denver—"

"Denver is subtext," George Sigal spoke up. He had a surprisingly soft voice. "Jack rides into town. He's a tough, mean, horny, mysterious stranger, and we're into the meat of our story right away."

"But we need to know—"

Sigal interrupted me again. "Jack's past life in Denver we can see in his face. Jack can do that whole back-story with a look," Sigal said. "We pick him up riding into town. It's a long, slow ride. The townspeople gape at him. Who the hell is this? He rides to the bank. The cattlemen's association is meeting in the back room."

I felt my face and neck turning red.

After the meeting was done and the department heads scattered to their domains to tell their troops the new plans, I caught up with Sigal as he was getting into a van in the parking lot.

"George, I'm Richard Swift," I said, and stuck out my right hand.

"I'm pleased to meet you, Richard. Your script is a nice piece of work."

We shook hands.

"A stranger rides into town? How many times have we seen that opening?" I asked.

"This is no ordinary human being riding into town. This is Jack Roach. Here comes trouble."

"But the setup in Denver—"

"We see what happened in Denver in his eyes and his walk," said Sigal. "Hemingway said eighty percent of a great story is under the surface. What you can't see is what gives it power. Now, please excuse me, Richard, but I have work to do. I'd like to see those new pages after lunch."

The van drove off, heading down the road to the nearby movie ranch.

I had used that same Hemingway line on Paula more than once. I went to my motel room and rolled a sheet of paper into my Smith Corona.

• • •

Four hours later I was eating a club sandwich in my room with a view of a truck stop. I was chewing and watching the truckers. The sheet of paper in my typewriter was blank. Half a dozen sheets of paper lay crumpled in the vicinity of the wastebasket.

I was expecting a messenger from Sigal to pick up the new pages.

I remembered something Sam Peckinpah told me in London years ago. He showed me the new script he had written that was only sixty pages long. In several places the script read, "Director stages chase through mountains here," or "Here Director stages fistfight."

I wondered if I could get away with writing "Director stages Jack riding into town."

That was exactly what was going to happen anyhow, so why should I describe it? Sigal already knew what it was going to be. He and the director of photography and the art director were probably working it out right now.

I typed, "Jack rides into Black Rock—mid-morning, the main street is busy. People notice Jack and dare to stare at his back after he passes."

Nobody had changed the name of the town yet.

I heard a knock at my door. I rolled the sheet of paper on out of the typewriter and took it to the door to give to Sigal's messenger.

"Hi, pal." Jack Roach was wearing a yellow golf shirt and his white linen Ben Hogan cap pulled down low on his forehead above a pair of aviator sunglasses. "You have time to play nine holes at the muny down the road?"

"I left my clubs back at the Westwood Marquis," I said.

147

Jack entered my room. He walked to the window and looked at the truckers. "I'm at the other end of the building and around the corner on the second floor. Number 2606. I look down at the pool," he said.

"It must be awfully noisy over there with all the poolside beauty contests," I said.

Jack grinned.

"Anyhow, your clubs should be here any minute," he said.

"What do you mean?"

"Oliver checked you out of the hotel in Westwood. It costs too much to have our writer living two places at once. Your stuff is on its way here. I think he turned your Mercedes back in at Hertz this morning, too."

Oliver had forgotten to mention any of that to me.

Jack lit a cigarette with his silver Zippo.

"Smoking fucks up your chi," I said.

"My chi has never been stronger, buddy. We are starting our movie. I'm excited, aren't you?"

"We lost Denver," I said.

"I heard."

"Sigal says you can do Denver with a look."

"He's right. I can."

"What do you need me for?" I said. "Maybe you can do the whole rest of this thing with a look."

"Hey, Richard, don't go all temperamental on me. I loved the Denver section, believe me. But this is show business. Sometimes you have to kill your darlings."

"Yeah. I've heard that advice before. I never believed it." I sat on the bed and looked at the piece of paper in my hand.

"Killing your darlings just means that above all you must keep the story moving," Jack said.

"Denver was all about character."

"Action is character," Jack said. He took the two-sentence opening out of my hand and read it. "This is good."

I nodded.

"I would like to add one sentence," Jack said, rolling the paper back into my typewriter. "Type it for me, will you?"

I moved to the chair, sat down, and looked up at him.

"Type 'Peeping out of Jack's saddlebag is his pet tabby kitty cat.'"

"Are you kidding?"

"I love that cat. It's a character thing."

"People will laugh."

"They won't laugh at me. I promise."

"Sigal won't like the cat."

"He damn sure will."

"Sigal doesn't like me. He doesn't want me here," I said.

"Did he say that to you?"

"No. But I could feel it."

Jack mimed playing a sad violin.

I typed the sentence about the tabby kitty cat. I started smiling.

"We're in this together, pal. It is you and me, making our movie," Jack said. "This is our vision. We're doin' it."

"All right. I'll stop sobbing."

"There's one more thing while we're thinking of the script," Jack said. He pulled the paper out of the typewriter and read it with approval showing on his face. "This is very good. Now let's look at page thirty-seven. I have a long speech telling the schoolteacher about the miserable condition of the Chinese laborers in the west, how exploited they are."

"Right."

"Cut that speech. She and I are walking past a Chinese laundry. Instead of all those words, I can do it with a look."

The messenger knocked. Jack opened the door and gave him the new page.

· · ·

I clipped Jack for three hundred dollars at the nine-hole muny course down the road that afternoon. I watched him closely. I was looking for any sign of illness, a cough or a wheeze or a stagger, but Jack didn't even sniffle. He hit the ball strongly, too. He lost because he pressed the bets on both the eighth and ninth. He showed the confidence and self-assurance and physicality that Jack Roach was noted for.

We were about to go for another nine holes when a production assistant showed up in a van to fetch me for a meeting with Sigal. Jack jumped into the back seat.

We arrived in Black Rock in a cloud of dust.

It was my first look at the town on the movie ranch. I noticed with surprise that the sign painted on the window of the building we entered said Black Rock Savings & Loan. George Sigal was bent over a table littered with papers. Oliver Weintraub was in the back of the room talking to the director of photography. Lights were being moved.

Sigal clawed his beard with three fingers and looked up at me. "Where the hell are we going with this cat?" he asked.

Jack stepped up beside me. "I love this cat," he said.

"Why?"

"It's a character thing."

"You're a cold-blooded killer," said Sigal.

"I am not cold-blooded. I love my cat."

Sigal frowned at me. "Did you talk him into this?"

"The cat is my idea," Jack said. "This is my fucking movie, too. Keep that in mind if we continue this conversation."

Oliver hurried over to join us.

"What does the cat do in the story?" asked Sigal. "Do you know?"

"Sure," I said.

"Does the cat die?" Sigal asked.

"Ummm . . . Yes," I said.

"Oh, Christ. Hello, animal lovers," said Sigal.

Oliver clipped the end off a Havana cigar so that the brown tip fell on the table. "Sorry," Oliver said. He brushed the tobacco away. He gave me a patient, understanding look. "Richard, we are going to have to hire a cat wrangler with four or five backup cats. Cyrus will have to know at once how many days you need the cat for."

"Ten days," I said.

"Twenty days," said Jack.

"How about five days?" Sigal said.

"How about you don't act like an asshole?" said Jack.

"Oliver, let's take a walk," Sigal said.

The producer and the director, both of them large men with beards, stepped out onto the street. Jack and I could see them through the window. Sigal waved his arms while he talked.

"I should fire the bastard," Jack said. "I'll call Carlo in Chicago and get Sigal's fucking legs broken."

"We don't have time for that, do we?" I said.

"No, not really. But I'll call Carlo and get him to come keep an eye on this prick."

"I thought you liked Sigal," I said.

"Nobody is always right all the time. Remember that," said Jack.

Oliver and Sigal came back into the bank and returned to the table. "You guys haven't seen the new shooting schedule," Oliver said. "Why don't you go back to the hotel, Richard, and write us the new pages that the cat is in. Then we can adjust the schedule and count up how many days we will need the cat wrangler. Agreed, Richard?"

"Okay," I said.

Oliver turned to the production assistant who had stood quietly listening and watching. Oliver made a hitchhiking gesture with his thumb and said, "Please take Richard wherever he needs to go."

Oliver smiled at me.

"Jack, you stick here for a while, will you?" Oliver said. "Anabel has a lot of wardrobe choices for you to make. It's important for you to see these clothes."

"See you later, buddy," Jack said over his shoulder as I followed the PA to the van and Jack walked with Oliver and Sigal toward the wardrobe trailer.

• • •

That night I talked to Katie on the phone for two hours.

I had a rush of feeling good from hearing her voice, and a feeling of being exceptionally lucky that it was me she was sharing herself with. I told her that I loved her. She said she loved me. We kissed over the phone.

Then I watched the action at the truck stop and drank scotch and water from a bottle of Black Label that Oliver had sent me.

Late that night I wrote the cat back into the story with a ballpoint pen on my copy of the script.

Twenty-three

I was roaming the back streets of Black Rock at eight o'clock in the evening. The first shot of the movie was underway in the bank building. It was a night for day setup with the building tightly wrapped and sealed and so hot and crowded inside with actors, lights, scenery, crew, and equipment that I didn't hang around to watch.

Two streets ran parallel to the main street where the bank was. There were fake houses on one street that looked like a neighborhood where families might live with kids. The other street had warehouses disguised as barns and period feed storehouses, and a row of cabins that were dressed to look like offices and shops next to a livery stable.

Here and there in the night stood young production assistants with walky-talky radios. They would shout, "Quiet! Rolling!" when the camera began running inside the bank to capture the meeting of the cattlemen's association as the actors awaited the arrival of their newly hired private range detective, the righteously deadly killer known as Jack. I had never thought of a better name for the character in the script. I understood why the other five or six writers had failed. Jack was Jack, after all.

In the dark I nearly collided with a tall young woman wearing a headset and a small microphone. I had become friendly with her. She was a graduate student in the USC film school. She wanted to be a screenwriter.

"Hi, Gwen," I said.

"Hey, Richard. He's over there in that room with the light in the windows but the curtains drawn."

"What?"

"You're looking for Jack, aren't you? He's in that room at the corner of the livery stable."

"Who is with him?"

"Nobody."

"Are you sure? I would hate to walk in on him—"

"I opened the door for him. I found the light switch for him. Actually, between you and me, he's pretty drunk."

My first thought was that Jack really was sick with the cancer.

"Quiet. We're rolling," Gwen said.

I walked across the dusty street to the plank sidewalk beside the livery stable. I stepped quietly on the boards. Not making a sound, I stood outside the door to the room Jack was in. I noticed a crack of light. The door wasn't shut all the way. I stood silently, listening for an okay from Gwen before I made any noise by knocking.

I heard a moan.

The boards creaked beneath my feet as I shifted my weight to lean closer to Jack's door.

Again I heard a moan, a low keening sound that trailed into a soft "Nononononononono . . ."

I pushed the door open. Jack didn't see me. He sat in a wooden chair at a dressing table and stared at himself in a big mirror framed by light bulbs. He was bareheaded, and his cheeks were swollen and red. He was staring deeply into his own eyes. His mouth turned down with disapproval. A half bottle of vodka sat on the dresser within reach. Jack wore a denim shirt, jeans, and boots, his wardrobe for tonight.

I stepped inside and eased the door shut behind me. My heart froze with foreboding at the thought that Jack was dying.

He hunched forward and stared at himself, probing with his eyes the face that looked back at him from the mirror. He began to cry. He wasn't weeping, but he was crying, tears running down his cheeks.

Jack picked up the vodka bottle and swigged from it. As he drank he noticed me in the mirror where I stood behind him, also framed by the light bulbs.

"Buddy boy," he said.

"Can I have a drink?"

He passed me the vodka bottle. I took a swallow and handed the bottle back. Jack drank again. He set the bottle down in front of the mirror.

"Is there anything I can do?" I asked.

"For me?"

"You look like you might not be feeling so well," I said.

"Like I'm dying faster than you are?"

"That was a stupid thing for me to say."

"Not really stupid, just honest."

Jack lit a cigarette with his silver Zippo. He turned back and studied himself in the mirror. "You're a smart guy, Richard, but you don't understand what's going on here."

His eyes never left his own face in the mirror.

"It's always the same the first day," he said. "Before the first shot, it is always the same. I always have the same fear. I always turn cold with fear and I wonder—Is this the day they find out I'm a fake? Is this the shot that shows the whole world that I don't know what I'm doing? Are they going to catch on that I'm faking the whole way? Tonight everyone will suddenly realize that I'm just pretending to be a movie star. I will be exposed. I will be done. I will become a laughingstock."

We heard a loud hum as generators began running again. Jack continued staring at his face in the mirror. I could hardly believe what I was hearing. Jack doubted himself? I had the craziest thought, looking at Jack, that I was beginning to see in his face that tortured soul who had been fired in Denver.

"I must be Zen. It's the only way," Jack said. He drank heartily from the bottle.

I frequently have the thought—not to call it a revelation—that I am faking my way through life, that I don't know what I am doing. But Jack Roach? Jack Roach is having stage fright in a totally existential way?

Could this be an actor's trick? Like an athlete psyching himself up for a big game, was Jack prepping as an actor who could do Denver with a look?

But to me, Jack looked just plain scared. I didn't believe Jack could be this frightened of starting a new movie. I remembered him coolly taking a million dollars off the international film tycoon without showing a moment of self-doubt.

"Truth Room?" I said.

"This ain't the Truth Room." He looked up at me from his seat at the dressing table. "But I know what you're asking. So let me tell you that anything I said in the Truth Room is the truth."

"You're not sick?"

"Sit down, Richard. Have a drink. Smoke a cigarette. Act like you're my friend."

I sat on the army cot and poured vodka into a dusty glass.

"When I was fourteen years old, I was a wild kid," Jack said. "I got in fights. I shoplifted small stuff like record albums. I didn't do anything really bad, just sort of wild. Then one night my buddies and I boosted hubcaps in a parking lot and sold them for five bucks each to a greaser in Long Beach. I stole eight hubcaps myself. That was forty dollars I earned in cash."

Jack looked into the mirror again.

"We got caught. In the courtroom the judge looked down from his throne and frowned at me and sentenced me to three years in detention. Three years! For eight hubcaps, forty bucks total. I stared up at the judge. There was a big American flag on the wall behind him. I thought, what? This is reality? This is really happening? Well, if this is reality, I reject it. So long, reality. I will live in my own world from now on. And that is what I have done. I got out of detention by joining the Navy. But ever since that day in the courtroom I have lived in my own head."

He turned his icy blue eyes onto me. The dark spots beneath his eyes had deepened, giving his face a buggy effect that startled me.

"I don't know what the fuck I am doing," he said. "So what I do is do it. I just do it. I am Zen. I am Zen. I am Zen. But on the first day of every picture my Zen cracks under the pressure of my inner knowledge of myself and the way of the world, which is that everybody thinks I know what I'm doing and they love me for it but when they discover they are wrong and I'm a fake they'll come piss on my grave."

We heard knocking at the door. I opened it and saw Gwen standing on the planks with her headset and microphone and clipboard.

"I'm here to take Jack to makeup," she said.

Twenty-four

The next ten days were a blur. I was up at six in the morning and some nights I was still working at midnight. Jack wanted me to stick close to him. George Sigal stayed polite to me. I began to admire Sigal. He was polite to everyone. He made thoughtful decisions every few minutes. Scenes were altered and lines of dialogue were changed for reasons that the writer could not have anticipated, such as the head of the cattlemen's association breaking his leg while falling off his horse. I was consulted on each change. Jack always took my side.

I phoned Katie every night at nine. Usually she was home to answer. She was doing re-shoots and couldn't get free to come to Black Rock just yet. The first thing we always talked about was Jack's health. Jack was working long hours at a pace that would tire anyone, but he was still a vigorous Jack Roach. On Sunday I wanted to sleep late, but Jack ordered a van to drive us to the Montecito Country Club in Santa Barbara at eight a.m. There, in the dining room eating breakfast and drinking coffee, was Carlo from Chicago. The club pro joined us for what turned out to be the first eighteen. On our second round after lunch, a wealthy pal of Carlo's completed our foursome. I lost twelve hundred dollars. Jack won quite a bit. In the van on the way back to the Wizard Inn, he told me he had been extraordinarily happy of late. He told me he felt strong and full of energy. He said he was taking pills furnished by Mr. Li. Jack's low-grade virus was no match for traditional Chinese medicine.

Whenever I got a chance, I watched Oliver Weintraub watching Jack. Oliver would study Jack, the way Jack walked, and listened closely to Jack's voice. I asked Oliver if he had changed his mind about Jack's prognosis.

Oliver looked at me for a moment and then put a finger to his lips, signaling for silence.

"This is not a matter for discussion," he said.

I told Katie all these things on the phone. Most nights we talked about Jack more than anything else.

We always signed off with pledges of love for each other.

• • •

I had stepped out of the shower and was drying off with a towel when I heard a familiar voice on the television playing in my room at the Wizard Inn. It was a talk show. I realized the talk was about Adam Wachinski, and the speaker was O. J. Simpson.

"—a quiet guy, really, the kind of guy that just stands around looking and listening," O. J. was saying.

O. J. wore a white cashmere sweater, dark slacks, and loafers without socks. He is a dynamic man, handsome, with a confident gaze. I'd hung around with him for three weeks in the summer of his rookie NFL season, and then I saw him from time to time over the years. I was with him at his first Buffalo training camp when the coach told him he would never be strong and tough enough to play running back. I saw O. J. score his first exhibition season touchdown by catching a long pass. I went with him to a family reunion of the Simpson clan in a suburb of Detroit, where we ate barbecue. He and I never played golf together, but I lost money to him at gin.

"Surely you do not mean Adam Wachinski?" the host asked on television. "A quiet guy? A listener? Adam Wachinski? The Malibu Zulu?"

"This was when we were at USC. In college, I mean. Adam would come around. He was shy. He always had his man with him, Bruno. Maybe you didn't see Bruno but you knew he was there. We had a game called Where's Bruno?"

"I know Bruno. What a piece of work," the host said.

"Well, Adam certainly was not the quiet type when I worked for him."

The camera pulled back to show a blonde woman—a buxom person with plump cheeks and a rather cute face—sitting on the couch beside Simpson. She was leaning so that her knee scraped O. J. She touched his thigh with her fingers as she made her point.

"He used to come around the set and just verbally destroy people that didn't please him." I could imagine Adam taking her photograph and showing it around and calling her a pig. "I was terrified of him."

"Why do you think Adam would do such a sick, ridiculous thing? Why would he put on a dress and get into having sex in public with a vice squad cop?" asked the host.

"Sex makes a person do unusual things," said the blonde woman. "I mean, things that if you stopped to reflect for a moment, you probably wouldn't do them."

"What do you think, O. J.?" the host asked.

"I have never worked for Adam. I don't know why I haven't." He looked into the camera. "Hey Adam, baby, if you're watching this I'm on your side."

"But why would he put on a dress and proposition a cop? What satisfaction would a man get from that?" asked the host.

"Do I look like Sigmund Freud?" O. J. said. "Man, I majored in athletics. I'm no shrink. I don't understand why people do things like this. I try to keep my own life pretty much straight down the middle. But listen, Adam, be good in rehab. I'm rooting for you. Call me when you get out, pal."

I did hope Adam was watching. To be encouraged by The Juice was bound to make Adam smile.

• • •

Sigal shot the "this is my final word on the matter" scene at nine o'clock on a chilly morning. The wind was from the north. Gray clouds were blowing in. I heard Sigal and the director of photography discussing the clouds and wondering whether to tear up the schedule and go to a covered scene indoors. Everyone was assembled: a dozen cattle buyers attended an auction held by a crook who got his three hundred head of cattle from half a dozen rustlers, who lounged against the cattle pen rails and watched the crowd with sinister sneers—that is, until Jack arrives on his big, fine Kentucky horse with his .40–.60 Winchester held across his saddle horn.

Jack started coughing that morning.

He and I were having breakfast in a tent. Other actors and crew were standing in the food line or sitting at tables. Jack had taken a table for two in the rear of the tent and sat with his back to the room. I was across from him, holding a tin cup of hot coffee in both hands.

Jack's leather spurs creaked and his spurs jingled as he shifted in his seat and raised a hand to his mouth. He tried to hold it in, but the cough came out, then another and another. Jack smothered the sound of them with his hand.

"Damn dust," he said.

I noticed the actress who played the school marm. She was carrying her tray and chatting with a writer from a newspaper as they searched for seats at a table. Jack turned and glanced at her, then looked back at me.

"She's a spinner. I can tell," he said.

The coffee burned my lips. I blew on the cup.

"What do you hear from Katie?" Jack asked.

"Last night she said it'll be at least another week before she can get free to come up here. She's taking diction classes, they're rehearsing, the do-overs aren't finished yet, there's looping to do—"

"Do you believe her?" Jack said.

"What?"

"Is she running around on you, buddy boy?"

"Running around?"

"You've heard the term? Is she going out with other guys?"

"I don't think so. I talk to her every night."

"I warned you not to get hooked on her," Jack said.

"Why do you bring this up? What are you trying to tell me?"

Jack poked a fist against the middle of his chest and frowned. "Gas," he said.

"Do you know something about Katie you're not telling me?"

"I know miles and miles about Katie that I am not telling you."

Jack picked up his gray, wide-brimmed, well-battered hat off the table. He smoothed back his hair, which he was wearing longer for the character so that it stuck out in wisps around his ears. Looking at me, Jack put on his hat.

"That is my final word on the matter," he said. He stood up. "Let's go to work."

He walked out of the tent ahead of me. He had adopted a rather bow-legged gait and chaps flapped like wings.

· · ·

Most nights shortly after dinner they showed dailies on a big pull-down screen in the Black Rock Saloon.

I usually sat on a folding chair on the back row beside Jack. It was a magical thing to glance at this person slouched next to me with a toothpick in his mouth and a slight rasp in his breath—and then to regard this magnificently powerful and complex creature I was seeing on the movie screen. The transformation was fascinating.

I would watch Jack doing a scene on the set and I couldn't catch him doing any acting. I could barely hear his voice. I would wonder why Sigal didn't call "cut" and tell Jack to speak up, quit muttering.

Then I would see the same scene on a big screen in dailies and right before my eyes was the magic of a movie star in action. The camera picked up and illuminated qualities of Jack Roach that lifted him apart from ordinary people. The tiniest gesture Jack made on the set, the slightest lifting of an eyebrow or curl of a lip, when seen on the big screen carried a load of subtext.

Some nights I went with Jack to his suite that had a small balcony looking down on the pool. Usually we would be joined by a stunt man or two, and maybe two or three minor actors Jack had become momentarily attracted to. Jack's stunt double would set out the bottles and the bucket of ice on the counter, and the guys would start telling stories about other shows they had worked on, or talking about golf and baseball and women.

Then about eleven o'clock there would be a rap at the door.

Jack would open the door and a woman would be standing there. She was never anyone from the crew, though some of the actresses took turns. Tonight Jack was in the bathroom when the knock came, so I opened the door.

It was the school marm. She looked embarrassed to see me and then to see the stunt men and others rushing around finishing their drinks and stubbing out their cigarettes and getting ready to leave.

"I'm sorry," she said. "Is Jack here?"

"He'll be right with you," I said. "Can I make you a drink?"

"No, thanks. Well, maybe a glass of water, please."

The other guys cleared out as I poured her a glass of Pellegrino.

The school marm was a very pretty woman, about thirty, with long blonde hair.

"What do you think of the film so far?" she asked.

"It's going well," I said.

"Am I doing okay? Is this how you saw her when you wrote her?"

"You are much better than I imagined," I said.

She smiled gloriously.

"I'd better say good night," I said.

"Are you sure Jack is here? I need to run some lines with him."

"I'm sure."

"Would you tell him I am here, please? He might have gone to sleep or something."

I went into Jack's bedroom. The bathroom door was open. I saw Jack standing at the sink. Once again he was staring at himself in the mirror. His face looked haggard. He was leaning on the sink, and his hand slipped. He caught the mirror with his other hand to stop his face from hitting it. I thought he was going to fall. I rushed into the bathroom and grabbed him under the armpits.

Jack whirled on me. He glared and shoved my chest with both hands. He pushed me back three feet.

"What the fuck are you doing?" he yelled.

"Are you okay?" I asked.

"Are you okay?" is the line they say in every movie and television show. You can be in a car wreck, an explosion, laid out on a slab—and someone will ask, "Are you okay?"

"Hell, no, I am not okay!" Jack yelled.

"Are you sick?"

"You fucker, stop asking me if I'm sick! I am not sick! I am not okay, but I am not sick! I might be getting sick of you, Richard, but physically I've never felt better."

"Fuck you, then," I said. I started toward the door and felt him touch my back. I wondered if he was going to try to karate me. I turned. Jack hugged me.

"I'm sorry, buddy boy," he said. "I'm not happy with myself tonight."

"You have a visitor," I said.

"The spinner?"

"I guess. Goodnight, Jack."

"Goodnight, Richard."

When I got back to my room I phoned Katie. I told her the story of the whole day, including the scene in Jack's suite. I shouldn't have used the school marm's name, but I felt so comfortable with Katie that I felt I could tell her anything. If Katie had asked for the secret numbers on my Swiss bank account, I would have told her.

Being apart from Katie had become a physical strain, a tension. I could smell her hair and feel her body. The urge to join with her, to put my arms around her, was close to overpowering. Her voice on the phone was exciting and comforting.

That night she told me she was head over heels in love with me. I felt a rush of joy. I told her I missed her so terribly that I could hardly sleep. I said I was counting the seconds that I spent waiting for her to come see me.

Twenty-five

In our fourth week on location, Thursday morning, eleven o'clock, I hitched a ride in a van from Black Rock back to the Wizard Inn to fetch the script I had left in my room. The script on set had some newly revised blue pages in it that I wanted to read to see if Sigal and Oliver had changed my words during the night.

This was the scene in which Jack discovers someone has hanged his cat. It was pretty well established that Jack would do it with a look. But Sigal wanted to shoot it with a bit of dialogue also—a couple of lines with the school marm—on the chance that we might produce a memorable phrase.

"Hey, man, look at that snazzy car."

Hearing the driver's voice, I looked out the window and saw the yellow Lamborghini parked in front of the Wizard Inn.

My heart leaped. I folded the newspaper I was reading and tucked it between the windshield and the dashboard. I jumped out of the van the moment it stopped rolling and ran into the lobby of the Wizard Inn, where I saw Dolly at the check-in counter arguing with the clerk.

Then I saw Katie in the coffee shop that opened off the lobby. She was standing beside a booth by the window. She was wearing faded jeans tucked into stovepipe boots with walking heels. Her hair was tousled and she looked tired. My Gucci loafers, now quite battered after a month in Black Rock, made scuffing sounds against the tile floor as I hurried past the cashier and caught Katie at the booth.

She turned into me and I hugged her and kissed her. This would have been a terrific photo for *People* magazine, the writer passionately kissing a movie star in the middle of a coffee shop before noon.

"I've missed you so much," I whispered into her ear.

"I've missed you, Richard."

"I love you. Let's go to my room," I said.

"Oh, Richard."

"I've really missed you."

She kissed me and pressed herself against me. Then she stepped back and smiled her famous, heart-rending smile.

"I'm tired and hungry, Richard. I want a grilled cheese sandwich and a Coke. Sit down with me."

"We could call room service. No, we could do two grilled cheeses to go. I know the chef here."

"Please, Richard. Sit down with me."

We took a booth with a view of traffic speeding by on the highway.

"You look gorgeous," I said.

"You're sweet to say that. I know I'm a mess."

Katie ordered a grilled cheese on whole wheat toast, a Diet Coke, and a chocolate milkshake. The waitress was accustomed to customers from the movies, but her smile showed she was impressed to have Katie Wynne at her station. I ordered a BLT and a glass of iced tea.

"Oh, I have news," Katie said. "Last night the cops caught our prowler."

"So it wasn't Adam?"

"Adam?"

"I'm kidding. Who was it?"

"A twelve-year-old boy who lives in the neighborhood. The cops caught him in the yard at Pickfair trying to peek in a window."

"Are you sure it's the same prowler who was at your house?"

"He confessed that he got inside my house one afternoon and stole my panties from the laundry basket."

The waitress brought our food. Katie sucked the chocolate shake through a straw.

"They make a good tuna salad sandwich here," I said.

Katie bit into her grilled cheese. "I'm starving," she said.

I told her about the hanged cat scene while we ate. I said we had debated whether to hang the cat or cut its head off. She asked why the cat had to die. I said it was a plot point, and also the cat wrangler and his trained cats had been gone for three weeks. She smiled and licked melted cheese off her fingertips. I could tell she wasn't as interested in the cat's fate as I was. I said the cat was a dog in my first draft. Katie looked at me and drank her Diet Coke. That's the thing with telling about shooting your movie to people who were not involved with it—they're just never as interested in it as you are.

Dolly appeared at the booth. She gave me a look that was cordial but not warm.

"You're still here?" Dolly asked.

"I'm here for the duration," I said.

Dolly handed Katie a room key and returned through the glass door into the lobby. I saw her talking to the bellhop, who had their luggage stacked on a cart.

"Where did they put you?" I asked.

She looked at her key. "I'm in 2612."

"Look, Katie, I'm sorry if I'm coming on too strong. I know you've had a long drive and you need to go to your room and wash up or something. It's just that I've missed you so much and I've been so excited to have you join me up here and take part in what we're doing. It's a great adventure for me, and I want to share it with you."

She reached across the table and put her hand on mine. She gave my fingers a little squeeze.

"You know I love you, Richard," she said.

"I know."

"The last thing in the world I would want to do is anything that hurts you. You mean so much to me." She smiled rather sadly. A chill shot through my heart. "You're such a wonderful, talented man. In many ways you're the best thing that ever happened to me. I will love you forever. That will never change."

"What are you trying to say?" I said.

"Please don't be hurt. Please try to understand that I will always love you."

"All right. I'll try. What is it?"

"There is someone else, Richard."

"You drove up here to tell me that?"

"He phoned me last night. He needs me."

The door from the lobby swung open and Jack Roach came in.

Jack ambled over to our booth. He wore his wry little grin and had a toothpick in his mouth. He looked down at me.

"Katie is with me now, buddy boy," he said.

Jack slid into the booth beside Katie.

I felt I was slowly turning to ice.

"You traitor," I said.

"Please, Richard," Katie said. "Don't be that way."

"Jack, are you dying?" I said. "Is that what you did? Call up Katie and tell her you're dying and you must have her before it's too late? Level with me, you bastard."

Jack studied me with his unflinching electric blue eyes. He removed the toothpick from his mouth and tossed it into the ashtray.

"No way am I dying," he said. "I've never been healthier."

"You're a back-stabbing SOB."

"You might want to put a governor on that mouth of yours, old sport," Jack said.

"'Old sport?' Now you're Jay Gatsby?"

"You're getting very loud, Richard," Katie said.

I looked at her. "I talked to you last night for half an hour," I said. "You might have mentioned this."

"I just couldn't bring myself to tell you. I'm sorry."

Jack lit a cigarette with his silver Zippo. He coughed.

"The Truth Room?" I said.

"I keep telling you this ain't the Truth Room. This is the world," he said.

"Please don't be so upset, Richard. I've never seen this look on your face," Katie said.

"You know what? I am not upset. You're both phony assholes. You belong together. Fuck the both of you. Fuck this movie."

I grabbed the check. At the register I stopped and gave our waitress a hundred dollars. Without looking back, I entered the lobby. Dolly was waiting for the elevator. The bell rang but she let it go and turned to me instead.

"You know the best thing you could do for everyone concerned?" she asked.

I looked at her.

"You could just haul ass out of here and get lost," she said.

Twenty-six

There was an Avis rental counter at the Wizard Inn. With my typewriter, a suitcase, a hanger bag, and my golf clubs packed in the trunk of a new Buick, I drove off madly down the highway toward Los Angeles.

I didn't know where I was going, but I was getting out of Black Rock.

I'd had plenty of warning that Jack took what he wanted when he wanted it, but I had thought he wouldn't do it to me, his old buddy from the Truth Room. Several people, including Jack himself, had warned me not to fall for Katie Wynne. But I did it anyhow.

I drove for hours with the radio turned up loud. I would hit the scan button and move from station to station. I found a disc jockey playing ballads and sang along with them. Later he faded away and I got into the Mexican music. I sang corridas. I started wanting a shot of tequila. I wanted a quart of tequila in straight shots with salt and lime on the rim of the glass. I could taste the tequila burning my throat. About then I caught a look at a sign in my headlights. An exit for Toluca Lake was coming up.

A few nights ago a stunt man in Jack's suite had told me if I ever wanted to pick up some cocaine I should go to the China Trader in Toluca Lake and ask for Captain Fluff and say I am a screenwriter and a special friend of Clifton's.

Cocaine and tequila—that sounded just like what I needed.

I was familiar with the China Trader. I went there one night a couple of years ago to have dinner and listen to Bobby Troup and his jazz group. I turned the Buick off 101 and headed for Toluca Lake.

Toluca Lake is about fifteen miles north of Los Angeles between Burbank and Universal City with the Santa Monica Mountains all around. There are many mansions among the palms. I had played golf with Jack at the Lakeside Golf Club, which wraps around the lake. Warner Brothers and Universal are nearby. The China Trader is a dinner club with Chinese food and entertainment. I found the white stucco building under the neon sign.

The parking valet, a Latino boy, stuck his face in the window of the Buick. "Good evening, sir," he said.

"Take good care of my car," I said in Spanish as I got out. I gave him several twenty-dollar bills. "And listen, friend, if I come out of here way too drunk to drive, you call me a taxi and then follow me and bring my car to wherever I go, and I'll give you another handful of twenties."

"Hey, man," he answered in Spanish, "you have made a brother out of me."

I found a seat at the bar. The bandstand up behind the bar was empty, but the bass fiddle and the drums were set up, and I noticed a big brass ashtray on the piano. I ordered three egg rolls and a bowl of wonton soup to lay a base for a night of heavy drinking. Chinese food and tequila might not seem like a proper mix, but that's the mood I was in.

I asked the bartender if Captain Fluff was in the house. The bartender studied me for a moment and then asked if I was a special friend of Clifton's. I said I was a screenwriter and was working on a picture with Clifton.

I had finished eating and was rubbing a lime on the rim of my third shot of tequila when the musicians took the stage. I recognized the trumpet player, Kenny Willis, from New York. The piano player wore a hat, needed a shave, and smoked. They played my kind of music—cabaret stuff, Johnny Mercer, Harold Arlen, Cole Porter, George Gershwin, Sammy Cahn. I nipped more shots of tequila, licked the salt off my lips, and became aware someone had deftly slid in beside me at the bar.

"What picture is it that Gilbert is working in?"

Captain Fluff had long red hair parted in the middle and a red beard and a gold earring and yellow teeth. Yet he looked stylish in a tan linen suit, white buck shoes, and a navy blue open collar shirt.

"It's the new Jack Roach picture."

"What do you have to do with it?"

"I wrote it. Well, I wrote some of it, anyway."

"Listen, man, I respect your craft," said Captain Fluff.

"Thanks."

"What you do, it's a hard world to make a living in. People aren't honest, and it's not a steady business. It comes and goes. You can't count on it."

I nodded.

"I have several appointments this evening or I'd like to have a drink and swap stories with you," Captain Fluff said. "But as it is, I've got to rush away. So here's the deal, man. I have a quarter in my pocket in an envelope. A quarter it is, nothing smaller."

"I'll take it."

"Rock and roll discount for a writer, man. Eight hundred dollars."

"Okay."

"I don't have time for you to test it."

"Clifton said you're a solid citizen."

"I don't take checks."

I had a roll of golf money in my coat pocket. I took the cash out, peeled the rubber band off it, and started counting out eight hundred dollars. Captain Fluff raised a hand.

"Are you sure you're a writer?" he said.

"I'm in the guild. I have two feature credits."

"Not so obvious with the cash, man. We don't know who might be taking our picture."

Captain Fluff departed as magically as he had arrived. I went into a stall in the men's room and opened the envelope. The coke was indeed fluffy. I rolled a twenty dollar bill into a straw and stuck it into the envelope. I made two enormous huffs. Pain shot through my sinuses. The back of my throat burned, then froze, and a sour drip began going down my pipes. Not great coke, I thought.

I stuck the straw into the envelope again and did two more snorts. I got a pain above my eyes. Pretty good coke after all, I decided. My stomach heaved, but I held it down. The green door of the stall leaped into my vision. My shoulders began to twitch. I felt terrific.

I licked my right forefinger and dipped it into the coke. I rubbed coke onto my gums to get a freeze. I looked all around when I left the stall. No one had been listening. I looked in the mirror at my face. I looked sort of demented, but it had been a long day. I combed my hair and returned to the bar.

The bartender leaned across the bar and said, "Wipe your nose, pal."

On the theory that tequila would make me way too drunk, I switched to vodka and began drinking it like water.

When the jazz group took their next break, the trumpet player came around and shook my hand. He asked if I would like to sit in on the next set. The piano player had a sick kid at home and needed to be gone for a while.

"You're not too drunk, are you, Richard?"

"I am just exactly perfect."

Sitting on the piano bench on the bandstand up behind the bar, I could see the big, crowded dining room. A lot of show business people live in Toluca Lake. Every seat at the bar was filled, and people were standing behind them. I was drinking vodka and orange juice. I would now and then stick a wet finger into the envelope in my pocket and then either lick my finger or stick it in my nose. I missed a few chords that way. It seemed to me that nobody noticed.

The set went well. We got applause at the break. I went backstage with the players into their dressing room. I took out my envelope and laid out lines on the Formica counter. We each did two snorts. Then the drummer produced a glass vial with a tiny spoon on a chain attached to the lid. He passed the vial around for another hit.

The piano player phoned and said he had to take his kid to the hospital. The bass player lit a joint and we passed it around. I sat in a leather easy chair that had an arm broken off. I was feeling pretty great. I had kept up with the guys better than any of us expected. That was a satisfaction I was treasuring. Someone knocked on the door. We went back out for another set.

The next set was even hotter—or perhaps cooler—than the previous one. We returned to the dressing room. The piano player phoned again and said he wouldn't be coming. Out came the envelope, the glass vial, and another joint. I drank more vodka with orange juice. I was having moments of wooziness, but I was very happy.

We went out for the final set. It was midnight by now. The crowd had thinned out. Show business people have to get up early. I placed two vodka drinks on the floor where I could reach them. I dipped a finger into the envelope in my pocket and sucked the finger. We led off with "Here's That

Rainy Day." It's a difficult tune for a singer to sing, but for my style of talk-singing, more or less reciting it like a poem, the lyric was a big hit with the late, drunk audience still left at the China Trader. It could have been that I performed it with emotion.

A voice from the bar cried out, "I love that piano, man!"

I looked down and saw the Queen Bee smiling up at me. Her blonde hair was free now and curled down onto her shoulders. The neckline of her dress was cut exceedingly low across her breasts.

I asked the guys if they would back me on "I Get a Kick out of You." I realized about then that I was really drunk and very much loaded, but I couldn't make myself stop. Instead I dipped into the envelope and then performed the tune. At the line "I get no kick from cocaine," I looked down at the Queen Bee. She laughed and pulled an envelope out of her purse and waved it at me. It looked the same as the envelope in my pocket.

We made it through the final set somehow. We went back to the dressing room and did another round of envelope, vial, reefer. I drank another vodka and orange juice. I shook hands with the guys and thanked them for letting me sit in. I knocked over a stool on my way to the door. "Be careful, man," the trumpet player said.

"You better call a cab," said the bass player.

I pulled myself together and left the dressing room and walked down the hall in the direction of the front door and the parking valet.

"Piano man! I love you!" The Queen Bee clutched my right bicep in a strong grip. She kept me from staggering. "My baby," she said. "Don't worry. I'm taking care of you."

I was going in and out of focus. I remembered Jack Roach rejecting reality and I laughed. I leaned on the Queen Bee. She put a strong arm around my waist.

"He's riding with me," the Queen Bee told the parking valet.

"Follow us and bring my car," I said in Spanish.

I gave the attendant a handful of bills. I don't know how much, but he was pleased.

The Queen Bee was driving a BMW. The ride was so smooth it was like flying inside a plush leather cockpit with all the instrument lights glowing.

"How is Adam?" I asked.

"Let's don't talk about Adam. He's doing fine. That's all you need to know."

I took out my envelope and a rolled up bill.

"Put it away," she said. "A cop might see you. They know to look for heads bobbing at this hour. When we get to my house, we have to use up all of this . . ."

She pointed to her purse where her own envelope was waiting.

Twenty-seven

Wearing only my boxer shorts in the moonlight I sat at the Queen Bee's piano and played "My Way" while the Queen Bee, who had changed into a silk robe, stood beside me and sang it.

We had both dumped the contents of our envelopes onto the top of the piano in a fluffy white pyramid. It was growing rapidly smaller. The Queen Bee had opened a bottle of champagne, but I stayed with the vodka mixed with juice.

She sang pretty well. I wondered if she might have been an entertainer in her youth. I applauded her at the end of "My Way." She smiled and bowed.

Her robe fell open. I reached over and took her hand. We walked into her bedroom. The bed was enormous and the sheets were very white. I kissed her. She grabbed my face in both hands and devoured my mouth. Her robe slipped off. I turned her around and we fell onto the bed. She fell on top. I could hear the surf outside her window.

• • •

I opened my eyes and looked at my watch. It was 5: 20 a.m. I must have slept an hour or two. The Queen Bee sprawled naked on the huge white bed. She was sleeping deeply. I saw two pill bottles on the night stand. I found my boxer shorts on the floor and put them on and crept out of the bedroom. The rest of my clothes were scattered around the living room.

The two envelopes from Captain Fluff were ripped apart on top of the piano. There was a dusty-looking layer of fluff left. I started to scrape together a couple of lines with the edge of a matchbook, but my stomach did a flip-flop at the thought.

My khaki slacks were crumpled on the floor. My Guccis were under the piano. I couldn't locate my socks. My shirt was draped over a chair. I put on the shirt and was struggling with the buttons when I heard a rough, hoarse voice.

"Good morning, Richard." Bruno was sitting in a dark corner of the room, wearing a white suit, his legs crossed at the knee.

"I am rather glad I stopped by to check the videos before returning to see Adam at the rehab resort. This one might have slipped by me otherwise, and made it into a delivery to Adam. My God, I hate to think of his hurt and crushing disappointment if he saw this."

Bruno held up a VHS tape.

"Adam has thought so highly of you," Bruno said. He tapped a forefinger on the tape carton. "I also am very disappointed in you, Richard. But I would guess you don't need to hear that. At this moment, you are highly disappointed in yourself, I would imagine."

I carefully buttoned my shirt and tucked it in.

"Does the Queen Bee know you have a camera in her bedroom?" I asked.

"No. Adele has her bedroom swept for cameras and bugs quite often. But I hire the firm that does the sweeping, you see. She trusts me."

"Adele?"

"The Queen Bee. She was Adele Shropshire, a minor actress but very beautiful. She married the Dairy Queen king when she was eighteen. He was an elderly gentleman. He died of a heart attack within a year. Then she met Mike Wachinski."

Bruno stood up. He slipped the videotape into a coat pocket.

"You need a cup of coffee," Bruno said. "Follow me."

In the kitchen Bruno stirred two cups of instant coffee and stuck a plate of Danish pastries into the microwave. In my mind I was sorting through events of the previous night. I remembered "My Way." I felt foolish. I felt guilty. I felt ashamed of myself and sick at my stomach. I glanced at Bruno's pocket that held the videotape.

"Have you heard of Mike Wachinski?" Bruno asked.

"No."

"I thought with you being a writer of sports, you might remember him." Bruno brought the two coffees to the breakfast alcove. I sat down. He went back to get the pastries when the microwave dinged.

"Mike Wachinski was a professional light heavyweight who fought mostly in California," Bruno said. "If a Mike Wachinski fight was on the card, every seat at the Olympic Auditorium was full because everyone knew there would be blood."

Bruno sat across from me at the table. I chose a pastry off the platter and chewed into the sweetness. I noticed a tiny scar in Bruno's eyebrow, and then another tiny scar near it.

"I was Mike's trainer. I worked in his corner as his cut man. Mike was a bleeder. He was a handsome man, black-haired, mean, and with a great smile. Women were mad for him. He married Adele and quit the ring. He kept me on as his personal trainer and handyman—driver, masseur, valet. I began training Adele, too. We would go on long runs on the beach. When she became pregnant with Adam, Mike threw a fit. He slapped her around. I stopped him from giving her a real beating. Mike knew the baby wasn't his. He had girlfriends all over California, but he hadn't slept with Adele in a year. Adele is a devout Catholic, so she wouldn't give Mike a divorce. They made a financial deal. He stuck around and acted like her husband, and she paid his bills and shut her eyes to his women and his gambler friends. Mike never liked Adam. So he assigned me to take over the little boy and watch him."

There was something in Bruno's expression, a twisting of the lip, an eyebrow lifting, that gave me the sudden realization.

"You're Adam's real father," I said.

Bruno didn't answer. He sipped his coffee.

"This arrangement lasted nearly ten years," Bruno continued. "Then Adele fell in love with some actor and wanted to marry him, but Mike was in the way. They devised a plan for Mike to get lost at sea and declared legally dead. Adele paid him quite handsomely to get lost."

"Does Adam know you are his real father?"

"Adam believes his father is Mike Wachinski."

"What's to stop Mike from turning up unexpectedly and claiming his share of the Dairy Queen and Adam's empire?" I asked.

"Mike will not be turning up. I understand he was shot to death in an alley in Mexico and his body was thrown into a jungle ravine."

Bruno took the videotape out of his pocket and laid it on the table.

"Adam watches these tapes. However, the fairly recent tape starring Adele

175

and Jack Roach he happened to be watching in live action in his office next door. That performance seemed to hurt Adam worse than any others. He watched the tape of Jack Roach again the evening he got away from me and pulled his distressing stunt with the vice squad cop."

Bruno pushed the tape across the table.

"There is no other copy of this," he said. "I trust you will destroy it."

"Thank you," I said.

"What are you doing here anyway? I thought you were on location," Bruno asked.

"I was. I left yesterday."

"Did they fire you?"

"No."

"Did they ask you to leave?"

I shook my head and finished the peach pastry. I selected another that had a dusting of sugar on it. "No. I quit."

"You should go back. You must not get the reputation out here as a writer who walks away, who doesn't show up when needed. Adam and I heard you were being very helpful to Jack and the production. Somehow Adam doesn't mind so much that you are having an affair with Katie Wynne. He's usually very jealous."

"Why doesn't Adam hire her? Why doesn't he date her? She actually seems to like him."

"Adam was born with an unusually small penis. He is terrified of sex with a woman he truly desires, like Katie. But it seems to be okay with him that she is with you." Bruno smiled. "He doesn't consider you a threat."

"The reason I quit the movie is that Katie showed up at Black Rock yesterday, but she came to be with Jack, not with me," I said.

Bruno watched me finish the sugary pastry. "Would you like another cup of coffee?" he asked.

"Yeah. Please."

Bruno poured the hot water, scooped the Hawaiian coffee, slowly stirred the cups, and then returned to the table.

"Katie Wynne is a sweet girl," he said. "She is not mean or underhanded or selfish. But face it, Richard—is there a woman in the world who would choose you over Jack Roach?"

"My mother doesn't like him," I said.

"Your mother must have never met him," said Bruno.

"Anyhow, I can't go back to Black Rock."

"For your own good, you should go back," Bruno said. "There's only another week or so of shooting left, isn't there? How is Jack holding up?"

"He seems very fit."

"Jack has cancer in his blood. There's no way around it." Bruno looked at his watch. "I must get back to Adam," he said. "Some young man left your car in front of the house. You should get in it and return to the movie. If for no other reason, Richard, go back and watch the son of a bitch die."

Twenty-eight

I had left the Do Not Disturb sign on my doorknob and hadn't bothered to check out, so it was easy to sneak back into the Wizard Inn. I caught a ride in a van from the motor pool and returned to Black Rock, where they were shooting in the courtroom

The set was closed, but Gwen let me in. I stood in the rear of the room beside Oliver Weintraub. Sigal was shooting close-ups of Jack reacting to lies that were being told about him on the witness stand. Oliver glanced at me between takes.

"You look like hell," he said.

"I've got the flu."

"Then maybe you haven't heard that Katie Wynne is visiting."

"Really? Where is she?"

Oliver looked me over. His rugby shirt had dark sweat stains at the armpits. "Are you all right, Richard?" he asked.

"I might still be a little feverish."

"I mean are you all right with Katie being here with Jack?"

"Sure. I just want to say hello. Where would she be, do you think?"

"You're not going to do something stupid, are you?" asked Oliver.

"Of course not. Katie and I have been over for a while."

"George and I will want a meeting with you tonight. We need to noodle with the speech Jack makes on the gallows," Oliver said.

The hanging sequence was saved for last because it was still uncertain whether Jack would do it as Oliver and Sigal wanted. In this instance, I was on the side of management.

"Fine," I said. "Where did you say Katie is?"

"I don't know. She might be in Jack's trailer."

I watched another take of Jack doing it with a look. Sigal called a halt and asked that a light be moved. I left the courtroom during the pause before Jack could see me.

The star's motor home was parked on the back street near the livery. A young man wearing a black security T-shirt was stationed outside the door of the vehicle. He recognized me.

"Jack's not in there," he said.

"I know. Katie Wynne is in there. Jack is going to meet us here in a few minutes."

"She is some doll. I could fall in love with her myself," said the guard. "With all due respect, of course."

I knocked. I heard Katie's voice saying come in. I opened the door. She was standing at the counter, stuffing bananas, strawberries, blueberries, and vanilla ice cream into the blender.

"I said I would stick this out to the end, didn't I?" I asked.

"Richard! I'm so glad you came back!" Katie hugged me and kissed me. "I felt like a dog when you stormed out of the coffee shop," she said. She stepped back and made a face. "You sort of stink. You smell like booze and smoke and drugs and sex."

"I could use a glass of whatever that is in the blender," I said.

She pushed a button and the blender began to whirr.

"I want you to understand," she said. "I've been in love with Jack since the first day I met him. That has never changed. It has nothing to do with you."

"Jack told me you dumped him and broke his heart."

"He called what I did dumping?" She smiled. "He practically chased me out of his life. Jack was impossible to live with in those days. But I have always been in love with him, and now that he finally needs me—"

"Why does he finally need you?"

"I am not going to say any more. Jack will be here in a few minutes. We have some news for you."

"Actually I don't need any more news," I said.

The blender turned itself off. Katie poured me a glass of creamy pink fluid. I took a long, cool drink and felt the smoothie coat my throat. I was a bit hoarse from performing last night at the China Trader and from cigarettes. My vow to restrict myself to ten cigarettes a day had long ago been forgotten.

"Did you know Jack has a wall of photos of you in his Truth Room?" I asked.

"Truth Room?"

"That's what he calls it."

"A whole wall of me? Really?"

The thought pleased her.

"Why did you never tell me this before?" she asked.

"I must have been jealous."

"I'm not asking you to forgive me, Richard. But it is important to me that you believe I do love you."

I nodded. "Okay." I lit a cigarette. "Okay, I believe it."

"Do you love me?" she asked.

"Yes."

"Then don't go away again."

"This movie will be over in another week. What then?" I asked.

The plastic door of the trailer rattled. It was stuck for a few seconds. Then it was yanked open, and Jack appeared, dressed in his courtroom wardrobe—brown wool suit, boots, white shirt with the collar buttoned at the neck. His hair was brushed forward onto his forehead and curled out from behind his ears. He looked at me. His icy blue eyes widened, his forehead wrinkled, and he favored me with a lopsided, friendly smile. "Buddy boy. Welcome home."

Jack stepped up into the motor home. Behind him I saw the security guard. Jack shut the door and loudly turned the latch to lock it.

Jack looked back and forth from Katie to me.

"You must not have told him yet," Jack said.

"You know I wouldn't tell," she said.

Katie poured a glass of smoothie from the blender and handed it to him. Jack drank half of the smoothie in one long swallow and then kissed Katie on the cheek and flopped onto the couch. He peeled off his boots and wiggled his feet in white socks. He leaned over and massaged his toes. "Sigal had me standing for hours. I don't see why I couldn't do this sitting in a special criminal's box or something."

He lit a cigarette with his silver Zippo.

"They want to look at your gallows speech again tonight," I said. "Is there anything you want to change?"

"Be sure I call them pasty-faced."

I nodded. I finished my smoothie and started to get up to go back to the Wizard Inn and catch a nap.

"Wait a minute," Jack said. "I have to tell you this. I promised Katie that I would. You've got to keep it quiet. Nobody in the world knows but just us."

He took Katie by the hand.

"Buddy boy, it's true. I have cancer. It's pretty bad, but it's not the end. They give me a year, maybe eighteen months. Maybe by then there will be a cure. I've hired the best doctor in the world. He's the top specialist in my particular illness. The kahunas are working for me, too, and the healers in the jungle in Mexico, and my friend Mr. Li with his herbs. Everybody wants to help me. So I'm going to start chemo and radiation as soon as we finish this picture."

He paused. He studied my face. I was having a rush of complicated, conflicting thoughts.

"But there is a very good chance that I'm dying faster than you are, Richard," he said. "Therefore, I have claimed the right to be happy even at your expense. I have asked Katie to marry me."

He turned her hand over and kissed her palm.

Katie smiled down at him. Then she looked at me.

"We're driving to Vegas on Saturday morning to get married in a chapel," she said.

Jack mashed his cigarette out in an ashtray and blew a trail of smoke. "Richard," he said, "it would do me a great honor if you will be my best man."

I realized then that I might be the closest thing to a male friend that Jack Roach had in the world.

"Sure," I said. "I'd be proud to stand up for you."

Jack jumped up and hugged me. He had tears in his eyes.

• • •

I returned to the Wizard Inn, took a shower, flopped onto the bed, and went to sleep. About two hours later the telephone woke me up. It was Paula calling from New York.

181

"Elrod and I are finished," she said. "He is such a jerk. Why didn't you warn me he's such a jerk?"

"Listen, Paula, I'm sorry, but I'm rushing off to an important meeting."

I was looking for my watch. I had left it on the basin in the bathroom. The digital clock on the alarm radio seemed to say it was 4:15. I lowered my head back onto the pillow and propped the phone against my ear.

"I walked out and left the son of a bitch," she said. "I'm back at home now."

"Home? What home?"

"My home at 86th and Madison."

Our apartment at 86th and Madison was a co-op. Ownership of it was one of the legal details so far left unsettled by our divorce court.

"You can't do that," I croaked. "I live there. You don't live there anymore."

"You haven't been here in three months. I could hardly get the door open for all the mail piled up. Jesus, don't you ever pay a bill anymore? I'm surprised they haven't turned off our lights."

"Utility and credit card bills go straight to the accountant. He also handles the—"

I caught myself and stopped. Paula already knew this arrangement with the accountant. She was provoking me.

"Come on, Richard, please. Don't you be a jerk, too."

Her voice was close to dissolving into weeping.

"All right. You can stay a few days," I said.

"I can stay here as long as I damned well please," she said.

"Then where am I supposed to live?"

"You're Mister Hollywood now. Use that stupid money they're paying you to write second class shit and buy yourself one of those Beverly Hills cottages with a statue in the courtyard of a naked Greek boy pissing in the fountain."

"Just a moment," I said. I covered the mouthpiece with my hand and counted to ten. "They're calling me into the meeting, Paula. I really have to go."

"How's it going for you out there?" she asked.

"It couldn't be better," I said.

"It's probably not too late for you to phone Roy and ask for your job back at the magazine."

"Paula, there's a roomful of people with clipboards waiting for me to make important decisions. I do have to run."

"All right, Richard. But if you do decide to come home, you can sleep on the couch in the den." She hung up on me. I rolled over and went back to sleep.

Twenty-nine

Sigal finished shooting Jack's part in the courtroom scenes at five o'clock on Friday afternoon and released his star for the weekend half a day sooner than expected. Jack and Katie had not told Oliver or Sigal or anyone except Dolly and me of the wedding plans. It was a four- or five-hour drive from the Wizard Inn to Las Vegas. Jack decided we should leave at once. We would arrive at the chapel in time for a midnight ceremony—and it was a full moon.

"I'll drive the Lamborghini," Jack told us when Katie, Dolly, and I joined him in his suite at the Wizard Inn. "Katie rides with me. Richard, you bring Dolly in your rental car."

"My Buick won't go much above ninety. Don't run off and leave us," I said.

"I'll keep you in the mirror, buddy."

In front of the hotel, I was loading Dolly's suitcase into the trunk of the Buick when Oliver Weintraub came out of the coffee shop.

"Hello, Dolly," Oliver said. "Saying hello to you always makes me smile."

"I am accustomed to it," Dolly said.

"What is going on here, Richard? Are you and Dolly running off together?"

"We're going to Vegas for two days. With Jack and Katie," I said.

"They're going in Katie's car," said Dolly.

"Why aren't the four of you riding in the same car?"

"Jack wants to drive the Lamborghini," said Dolly.

I slammed the trunk. Oliver wiggled a finger at me and jerked his head to indicate I should walk a few feet with him. Dolly didn't try to overhear us, anyway. She got into the Buick and began looking through her stack of music tapes.

"Keep an eye on him, Richard," Oliver said. "For God's sake, you know Jack is always at the edge of some cliff or other. You know how sick he is. Do not let him get drunk and get in a fight or do anything to screw us up now. We are so close to finishing."

"I know," I said. "I want to see this finished as bad as you do."

"You couldn't possibly," he said.

. . .

We headed northeast toward Bakersfield in lovely yellow sunlight. The hills were green and peaceful. The yellow Lamborghini set the pace, slowing just enough for the Buick to keep it in sight. After about a hundred miles, Dolly turned down the music. She was playing selections by Prince, Paul McCartney, Springsteen, Cyndi Lauper, and the Pointer Sisters. When Tina finished singing "What's Love Got to Do with It?" Dolly glanced at me and smiled. A smile for me from Dolly was a rare sight. But then she didn't say anything. Her silence gave that smile a whole different meaning.

I ignored her and kept my eyes on the taillights of the yellow Lamborghini in the fading sunlight.

"You're taking this whole thing rather well," she finally said.

"So are you," I said.

"I didn't expect you to be such a good sport."

The right turn signal of the Lamborghini began blinking. Jack was turning off Highway 5 onto a county road. We weren't going to Bakersfield after all. We were heading east into an area that I hadn't looked at on the map. I suddenly got the idea that Jack might be going to his place in the desert. The thought gave me a chill.

I turned the wheel of the Buick while we were still going faster than I was comfortable with. We skidded onto the county road. Dolly's smile froze into a grimace and she grabbed the armrest.

"Slow the fuck down!" she yelled.

I stomped on the brake pedal and turned on my headlights. I began flashing the lights. The Lamborghini flew on along the asphalt road.

"Jack knows this area," Dolly said. "He knows the roads and all that shit."

"Where is his desert place?" I asked.

"It's east of Barstow on the edge of the Mojave Preserve."

"Have you ever been there?"

I kept flashing my headlights. It wasn't dark yet, but the sky was turning gray and yellow and the fields alongside the road seemed striped with black.

"No."

"I know Katie has been there."

"She was there once, years and years ago. She never talked about it to me. She never went back."

Dolly clung to the armrest and checked her seat belt and tried to light a cigarette but her hand was shaking and she dropped the lighter.

"Why the hell are you blinking your lights?" she said.

"I want the asshole to stop. We're supposed to be driving to Las Vegas. Jack never said anything about stopping at his house in the desert."

She grabbed the lighter off the floor. "Why does that scare you?" she said.

"I don't know why, but it does," I said. "I want to get it understood with Jack that we are going straight to Las Vegas with no detours."

"You don't want him to take her to his house first?"

"No."

"Now you're acting like a jealous lover," she said.

"I'm responsible for Jack."

The yellow Lamborghini sped on. I quit flashing my lights and urged the Buick up to nearly a hundred, but Jack took my gaining on him as a challenge. The Lamborghini leaped forward another twenty or thirty miles faster than I was going in the Buick.

"Slow down," Dolly pleaded. "He's going to have to stop for gas in Barstow. You'll catch him that way."

"The son of a bitch is going to his place in the desert. I'm sure of it," I said.

"What difference does it make? So we spend a while at Jack's ranch? You're being crazy!"

I thought about the creepy feeling I'd got looking at Katie's photos on the wall in the Truth Room, but I didn't try to explain my alarm to Dolly. I couldn't really explain it to myself.

"You can talk to him in Barstow," Dolly said. "Straighten his ass out in Barstow."

But something got into me. I hit the gas pedal. Peering through Dolly's cigarette smoke, I saw the Buick's speedometer needle crawl up to 105.

Looking up, I saw the yellow Lamborghini pulling away from me again.

Then I saw Jack's right turn signal begin blinking. I jammed my foot on the brake. I knew I couldn't handle a turn at this speed, and I was going far slower than Jack. For an instant I felt we were going to flip over. The Buick screeched and fishtailed. Dolly's tapes bounced off the ceiling. I turned the wheel and scanned the intersection with the obscure county road that Jack had sped onto. I feared I would see the Lamborghini upside down. But in the dusk I saw the yellow car slowing, waiting for me. Jack had made that turn at more than a hundred miles an hour.

"Just creep up on him," Dolly said. "I want to get Katie out of that madman's car!"

Jack had slowed to about forty and I pulled up within ten yards of his rear bumper. I could see Katie through the rear window. Dolly zipped down her window and stuck her arm out and waved at Katie.

"Katie! Stop! Stop!" Dolly yelled.

Katie thrust an arm out her window and waved back at us. Then Jack kicked in that supercharged engine and the Lamborghini took off like a rocket.

I stomped on the accelerator and the Buick roared with a surge of surprising power, as if the speed of our pursuit had blown the rust out of its pipes.

"Don't chase him, you fool! He'll just go faster and faster!" Dolly yelled.

"I've got to catch him," I said.

The road our two cars sped along was a two-lane blacktop. The land on either side of the road spread into emptiness. Our engines growled and our tires whined like the eerie sounds of two powerful supernatural animals racing in the silence of the growing dusk.

Suddenly Jack's left turn signal began blinking.

"My God, he's doing it again!" Dolly yelled.

I couldn't see a road to the left. I thought Jack might be playing with me. But then the yellow Lamborghini slid sideways, gathered itself, and leaped ahead onto a narrow road that appeared suddenly in the shadows from high, drifting clouds.

I pumped the brakes and slowed the Buick way down. Jack had made another turn that would win at Le Mans.

Then I saw a dark object ahead of Jack. It was a truck of melons idling toward us with one broken headlight. The yellow Lamborghini was aimed like a bullet straight into the truck's grill.

Dolly screamed.

Somehow Jack forced the Lamborghini to spin sideways and scrape across the front of the truck before whipping around straight ahead again. With a blast from its mufflers the yellow car took off once more.

As I steered around the farm truck, Jack's headlights illuminated two cyclists in skin-tight uniforms pedaling down the middle of the road. Jack yanked the yellow Lamborghini to the left to avoid the bikers. His left front wheel hit a soft spot on the shoulder of the road. The yellow car left the ground in a shower of gravel. The car flew up several feet off the earth, rear end–first, and then slammed down on its nose to bounce and tumble across the field, slinging pieces of the car into the sky.

I slammed the Buick to a stop where the yellow car had left the road. Dolly and I jumped out and ran into the field. I noticed one of the bikers had a walky-talky radio at his ear. The other biker and the truck driver ran into the field behind us.

I reached the Lamborghini first. The car was crumpled and smoking. Jack looked out the window with his trademark grin, his face twisted at an impossible angle. The steering column had pierced all the way through his chest.

I ran to the other side of the mangled yellow car. The passenger door was gone. The windshield was blown out. But Katie was not there.

"What the hell happened?" a biker asked.

I shook my head, dazed, and looked around the field.

"Katie!" Dolly screamed.

I ran to where Dolly knelt beside the twisted body. Katie had been thrown through the windshield. Her blouse was torn off. Her arms were bent the wrong way. Dolly leaned over Katie's form. Dolly was crying, but she was calm as she felt for Katie's pulse. She put her cheek against Katie's broken mouth to feel for a breath.

Dolly looked up at me. "She's alive."

I saw Katie's wrecked face. You wouldn't have recognized her. I turned away. There was a siren in the distance.

Thirty

Dolly talked our way onto the medical rescue helicopter that landed in the field to pick up Katie. Dolly made sure the medics knew whom they were treating. All the chatter on the radio crackled sharply through the clatter of the rotors. I sat on an aluminum bench and looked at Katie covered with blankets. Bottles hung from tripods and fluids dripped through tubes into her struggling body. The medics crouched over her, busy with their instruments and dials. They covered her face with bandages.

We flew to Los Angeles, into Westwood, to the UCLA Medical Center that I had watched so often from my suite at the Westwood Marquis. This time the sad bundle that was unloaded on the hospital flight deck in the night was Katie.

I was pacing in the waiting room outside the intensive care unit when I saw Oliver Weintraub step off the elevator and come down the hall. He spoke to the security guard the hospital had posted to keep out fans and the press. The news was already on television that Jack Roach was dead and Katie Wynne was in critical condition after the smashup of her yellow Lamborghini.

Oliver made it past the guard and came to me. "How is she?" he asked.

"I don't know. She's in a coma and all beat to shit. Dolly is in there with her."

"Is there any point in me trying to go in and see her?"

"No. They won't let you in, anyhow."

"I heard on television that you and Jack were racing."

"Jack was showing off his driving skills. He made a mistake. That's all."

"You were not racing with him?"

"I was just trying to keep up."

"To Jack that's the same thing as racing," Oliver said.

Oliver lowered himself into a chair in the waiting room. He sighed and rubbed his beard. His eyes were swollen and he looked very tired. "Have you spoken to the press?" he asked.

"No, not yet."

"When you do, you and Jack were not racing."

"We were not racing."

I looked up as a nurse passed.

"I'm sorry. Katie is a sweet kid. I hope she doesn't die," Oliver said. He dug a cigar out of an alligator case and rolled it in his fingers and licked it, but didn't try to light it.

"There is a bright side to this. Now we don't have to fight with Jack about the ending. As Billy Wilder said, in this business you learn to take the bitter with the sour." Oliver's smile flashed but it was weak and quickly vanished.

"You're going to finish the picture?" I asked.

"Here is how I see it. Jack escapes from the jail in the middle of the night. It is very dark. We will use his double. He liberates his horse from the livery. He rides to the school marm's house in the darkness. He sweeps her up and they ride off together into the mountains. The end."

"How does he escape from jail?" I asked.

"He digs out. We will shoot some inserts of hands digging and scooping out dirt."

"He digs out of jail with his bare hands?"

"I know it doesn't make sense, but the audience wants Jack to escape and live. They don't care how he does it."

Dolly appeared in the doorway. Oliver stood up.

"Hello, Oliver. It's nice of you to come," she said.

"How is she?" he asked.

"She's going to live, but she's very badly hurt. She's sedated and will be out of it for hours. There's no use in you guys hanging around here. There's nothing at all you can do."

"Please give her my love," Oliver said. "I will be checking on her."

"I want to see her," I said.

"She is not seeing anyone," said Dolly.

"I must go back to work," Oliver said. He looked at me. "Are you satisfied with the ending?"

"Yeah," I said.

"Then George and I will take it from here," said Oliver. "It was nice to know you, Richard. I hope we can work together again sometime."

"I can write those inserts for you, the new ending," I said.

"No need for that. Your work is done here. Your contract is up. I will send your things back from Black Rock. I will also pay your hotel and per diem for three more days. Is that fair?"

"I guess so," I said.

Oliver stuck out his right hand. I shook it.

"Cheerio, kiddos," he said. He nodded to Dolly and went off down the hall. I watched him enter the elevator.

"I think I've been dismissed," I said.

"Could I have a cigarette?" Dolly asked.

I lit it for her. She took a drag and looked at me with sympathy and what appeared to be friendliness.

"It wasn't your fault. It was all Jack's fault," she said.

"Thanks."

"Seriously, Richard, you should go get some rest or have a drink or something. I will stay with her. It's my duty, and even more—she's like family. And I'm telling you it'd be best for you to give her some time. She's got a lot of healing to do. When she says she's ready to see you, I will let you know."

· · ·

It was midmorning when I left the hospital by a back door and walked through the neighborhood to the Westwood Marquis. I walked right past two mobile TV news units and a gathering of photographers and reporters. But they didn't recognize me.

The desk clerk at the hotel remembered me well. He let me register as Bim Gump. The suite that I had lived in for two months was available, but it was being cleaned. I said I would wait in the bar. I asked the concierge to send a razor and other toiletries to my suite. I went into the bar and took a table against the wall.

I ordered a Bloody Mary and lit a cigarette and leaned my elbows on the table and shut my eyes. I might have dozed for a few minutes. I sat up and noticed the bartender watching me. He was the morning bartender, a Frenchman. He didn't know me. I was his only customer.

"Are you all right, sir?" he called.

"Yeah. Bring me a phone, will you?"

"Isn't there one on the table?"

"Oh. Yeah. Here it is. Thanks. Bring me another Bloody Mary?"

I phoned my mother in Sag Harbor. I got her answering machine. I left a message that I was fine, don't worry, and I would phone her again soon. I phoned my father. He was playing golf. I left word for him at Kerrville Country Club. I thought about phoning Paula, but didn't do it. Anything I said to Paula I could expect to read in the next issue of *People* magazine.

Then I dialed the number of Roy Barker at his office at *Sports Illustrated* in New York. His secretary, Ann, answered.

"Richie!" she said. "Are you okay? I heard on TV that you were in a car wreck."

"I was just a witness. I'll tell you all about it someday. Is Roy available?"

"He's in a meeting on the fortieth floor with the big guys."

"I really need to speak to him," I said. "Please ask him to call me at the Westwood Marquis. Tell him to ask for Bim Gump."

"Bim Gump? Who is that?"

"I'm hiding from the press," I said. "Please, Ann. Tell Roy it's important."

"Take care of yourself, Richie."

"If Paula asks, you don't know where I am."

"I understand. Roy will get back to you, I promise."

I sat at the table drinking Bloody Marys, eating cashews, and reading the *Los Angeles Times*. The death of Jack Roach was at the top of page one, with another headline that said Katie Wynne was in critical condition. The front page was covered with photos of them and the crash scene and the mangled Lamborghini. The stories jumped inside the paper along with more photos of the two stars. Dolly and I made the third paragraph of the lead story and were mentioned several more times. I was identified as a failed novelist trying to break into films. A nameless source was quoted as hinting that Dolly was much closer to Katie than a personal assistant job would require.

After an hour or so I phoned Margie at the hotel switchboard and asked her to transfer Bim Gump's next call to the restaurant. I went to the buffet, where the chef tossed a ham, cheese, and onion omelet for me. I ate and read the *New York Times*. Now I was identified as a sports writer trying to break into films.

I drank coffee, smoked, and looked through *Variety*, the *Hollywood Reporter*, and the other large daily newspaper, the *Herald Examiner*. Eventually I signed the check, left a hefty tip in cash, and went back to the bar. Sitting at the table again I picked up the phone and told Margie that Bim Gump was at a new location.

I started planning my trip to the British Open at Troon in Scotland in July—if Roy would have me back. I remembered a round of golf I had played at Troon on a summer day when the wind blew forty miles an hour and it was so cold strings of mucus froze on our faces. At the edge of the one fairway we trudged past two Scotsmen sitting on aluminum lawn chairs in the howling wind. They had taken their shirts off, getting some sun while they watched the golfers.

Thinking about going to the open and seeing the regulars in the press hut made me smile and order another Bloody Mary. The bar was starting to get more crowded. The lunch drinkers were showing up. I thought about Jack wearing the silly fake beard in the bar at the Beverly Wilshire. I remembered the look of delight on Jack's face when he told me he had made a million dollars just by reading Claude Rimbaud's script and turning it down. I wondered what went through Jack's mind when the yellow Lamborghini took flight on that country road with Jack's hands on the wheel. Katie must have been screaming. Could Jack have realized at that moment that he was not immortal?

Or maybe Jack is immortal, I realized . . . or as close to immortal as we get in this world.

Finally I picked up the phone and called Margie at the switchboard and told her Bim Gump was going to his room. I entered the elevator in the lobby as Lee Marvin was getting off. He squinted at me.

"Tough night, huh, pal?" he growled.

"You don't know the half," I said.

I was starting to fade as I walked down the hall of my floor. Feeling exhausted and more than a little drunk, I opened the door to the living room of my suite. I closed the door behind me, leaned my back against the door, sighed, and looked up. Standing at the counter in my kitchen was the very tall, wide, and black figure of Erazmo Jones, aka X.

"You damned old daredevil," he said. "Racing with Jack Roach in the desert. I didn't know you had it in you, Richard."

"We weren't racing," I said.

"I told you that bastard Jack was big trouble," said a voice from the easy chair by the window. "I told you to ditch him."

The shutters were open and the sun shone onto the smooth, groomed face of Adam Wachinski. His skin was clear; his long hair was parted in the middle and combed hippie-style so that it covered his ears, but it looked carefully styled and almost beautiful. He was wearing a white silk shirt with the top two buttons undone, a pair of gray wool slacks, and soft black leather loafers. He looked rich and powerful.

"I'm glad I didn't listen to you," I said. "I would have missed a lot."

I looked at Bruno. He sat in the other easy chair. Bruno was wearing a dark suit with an open-collared shirt. His aviator sunglasses were pushed up onto his head. I noticed his skull was shaved totally bald. He crossed his legs and smiled at me.

"Hello, Richard."

Max Bloom came out of the bathroom, drying his hands on a towel. "Hey, champ, let's tee it up," Max said. "Have you ever played the Club de Golf in Rome?"

"No, I haven't. Why?"

"Nobody told him?" asked X.

"Wait a minute," I said. "I know this meeting is not to ask me how Katie Wynne is still alive in the hospital down the street, or to tell me how sorry everybody is that Jack Roach got killed yesterday. Before we go any further, let me tell you that I am going back to New York. I am not cut out to be a screenwriter. I can't make it out here."

Adam stood up. He crossed the room and stopped two feet in front of me. He stared into my eyes.

"Is Katie going to live?" he asked.

"Yeah."

"Are you sure?"

"I think so."

"I hear her face is all cut up."

I turned away and brushed past X and opened the refrigerator. I found a can of Dr Pepper and popped it open.

"I'm sorry," Adam said. "She was beautiful. I loved her, too, you know."

"Listen, guys, I'm waiting for a telephone call," I said. "Whatever you want with me, I am not going to do it. Now, please let yourselves out. I am going to lie down in the bedroom with the phone by my ear."

"Don't be crazy, Richard," said Max. "What Adam is talking about is $50,000 a week for twelve weeks with an option for eight more at $75,000 per. You get a suite at the Hassler in Rome. Everything first class, all expenses paid."

"No. I can't do it," I said.

"The story is all laid out," Adam said. "We have some small problems with the script that you and I can fix. Mainly I want you on location to punch up the dialogue, sharpen the characters, and add some color."

"You fix my dialogue, Richard. I want words to say that people will quote later," said X.

"Please, X, I wish you the best view above the smog line, but I don't want to do this anymore. I want to go back to New York. I want to write another novel that sells a handful of copies. I want to sit at Elaine's and bitch about money with the other writers. I don't want to get involved with a huge piece of movie shit unless it's of my own making," I said.

Bruno spoke up from his seat in the corner. "Adam, does he even know what *Giants* is about?"

The telephone began ringing. That would be Roy Barker at *Sports Illustrated*.

Thirty-one

The Aloha Airlines twin engine turboprop flight from Honolulu banked for a landing at the airport in Lihue on the island of Kauai. I felt my heart pounding as I looked out a cabin window at the deep blue water of the Pacific rushing onto the white sand beaches. We bumped and swooped and barely cleared the pineapple fields. The pilot put on the brakes just before we slid into the ocean at the end of the runway. I was heading to a meeting with Katie Wynne. After more than a year of not seeing or even hearing from Katie, I had received a brief handwritten letter from Dolly.

> Dear Richard:
>
> Katie wants to see you. Please come as soon as you can. Drop me a note c/o general delivery in Hanalei, Kauai, Hawaii, to say when we might expect you, and I will send you a map to our house. We have been reading about you. Nice going.
>
> Cheers,
> Dolly

I walked down the steps from the airplane and across the tarmac to the terminal. The warm air that struck my face smelled salty and oily. I was carrying only my small black Italian suitcase that had been all over the world with me. With no luggage to wait for, I went directly to the Hertz counter.

Dolly had reserved a car for me. I hadn't noticed what kind of car when I signed in. A dark-skinned boy in shorts brought it around to the front of the terminal for me—a brown-and-tan Volkswagen bus with a peace sign stuck to the rear window. I had to grin. This was Dolly's joke. There was no way I would be speeding or racing anyone in this Volkswagen bus.

I drove north for an hour on a road lined with palms and jungles of greenery and flowers. The north shore of Kauai is the most beautiful spot on earth. Mountains climb into the clouds and waterfalls stream down to splash into cold, clear pools, and there is color everywhere—reds, yellows, golds, and greens. Clear water flows in streams and ditches. Orchids bloom in the trees. Birds are everywhere you look. And always there is the great blue ocean thundering out there under the sun.

Following Dolly's map, I drove past Hanalei Town, past the Dolphin restaurant, past Ching Yung's general store and Louise's Tahiti Nui, where a bearded kid in an open shirt and board shorts sat in a chair on the porch drinking beer and playing his guitar. He was barefoot. A surfboard leaned against the wall next to him.

Beyond the little missionary church I turned onto a narrow road that led toward the end of the island. The VW bus purred across two tiny bridges, past tidal pools studded with lava rocks, into Polynesian jungle foliage that draped across the road.

The map told me to turn onto a one-lane path toward Hanalei Bay shortly before I reached the end of the island, where the Kalalau Trail climbed into the mountains. I followed the motor path through a stand of ironwood trees and came to a lawn and a driveway that led to the garage of a rambling, rustic house with shingled walls painted gray. Parked in front of the garage was a Jeep.

I climbed out of the bus. The view was of a beach a short walk away, and then the eyes took in Hanalei Bay and the spectacular Nā Pali cliffs. I breathed deeply. The air smelled like flowers. I looked out at the blue water under a cloudless sky. I had the feeling I could see all the way to Alaska.

"Welcome to paradise." Dolly seemed taller. She was slender and tanned in flip-flops, white shorts, and a yellow blouse knotted at the waist.

"You look terrific," I said.

"Katie would come out and greet you, but she doesn't walk very well. You'll see. Follow me," Dolly said.

"How is she?"

"She is in pain, always in pain. Keep that in mind."

I followed Dolly through the house to the large covered deck that over-looked the beach and the bay. There were whitecaps on the water. Half a dozen sailboats cruised the bay. The cliffs rose on the left. A figure in a big straw hat sat at a table on the deck, looking out at the water.

"Here he is, Katie." Dolly leaned close to me. "Remember—" She turned and walked away.

"Richard!" Her voice was the same as always. I felt relieved. I stepped onto the deck. "It is so good of you to come see me."

"I have missed you," I said.

"Please, sit with me."

The wide hat brim hid the top half of her face. She wore oversize sun-glasses. A blouse with a high collar covered her throat and neck. A sheet wrapped around her shoulders, covering her. She turned toward me with her head ducked so that I could hardly see her mouth.

I bent down to kiss her but she waved me off with a hand covered by a long glove. There was a chair placed not quite across from her at an angle that made it hard to look directly at her. A pitcher of pineapple juice sat on the table. I took the seat.

"What would you like to drink?" Katie asked.

"A beer would be nice."

Katie rang a small silver bell that she clutched with a hooked finger. A Polynesian girl in a red, sleeveless print dress padded barefoot down the deck. Katie ordered a Heineken for me and ice water for herself.

"It's all these damned medications, Richard. They keep me dizzy and confused and sometimes nauseous. But they keep me alive."

The girl brought Katie's ice water in a tall narrow glass with a long, bent straw. I took a swallow of the cold beer she sat in front of me.

"So, Richard, I read the reviews of *Giants*. Congratulations. It's a won-derful story—and right down your alley, wasn't it? A European professional basketball league with X as the star of the team in Rome? I'll bet it was fun to do. I wish I could have been on those locations with you."

"That would have made it perfect," I said.

"I was surprised to learn that *Giants* is about pro basketball. I thought it was to be an action movie with a superhero and a monster villain."

"Adam scrapped the action movie script while he was in rehab and wrote a new plot."

"That little girl who was naked in the pool that first night I met you? Her reviews are over the moon."

"She loved the idea of playing X's daughter with a Roman mother. It's a juicy character."

"Adam is so smart."

"Did you ever see our movie *Jack*?" I asked.

"Yes. I keep the tape beside my machine."

"They're disappointed in the grosses."

"It's a bad time for westerns."

I looked out at surfers paddling to catch a fresh set of waves.

"Did you go to Jack's memorial service?" she asked.

"I went to the big one. It was nice. Huge crowd, lots of speeches. I wasn't invited to the private service where his kids threw his ashes into the ocean."

I got up and walked over to the railing. At the far right I could see the bluff on which lay the Princeville resort. I idly wondered if Jack had played golf at Princeville when he came to Hanalei with Katie.

"Jack had one photo of you here at your Hanalei house, and one of you at his house in the desert. Most of the other forty-eight photos of you on his wall were at Aspen or Cannes or places like that."

"Jack and I traveled a lot at first."

"You look frightened in the desert photo. What happened to you at his house?"

"I told Jack I didn't want to see him any more. He had a tantrum. He scared me. I thought he would kill me." She made a low moan as she moved her legs beneath the sheet.

"I'm sorry," I said. "I know you're in pain. We don't need to be talking about Jack anyhow. We always get off on the subject of Jack."

"I want to tell you something," she said. "It's the reason I asked you to come. I have to tell you in person, face to face."

I sat down again and looked at her. She was a little less hidden now. I saw the creases of scars around her mouth that crawled up underneath the large sunglasses.

"Jack did this on purpose," she said.

"How do you mean?"

"Of course you know that Jack's autopsy showed he was eaten up with cancer. He was far worse than he told us. He had maybe three weeks to live and he knew it. He told me the truth that night while he was driving a hundred and thirty miles an hour. He said he was going to flip my car and kill himself and take me with him. He laughed like he was kidding, but I know he wasn't. When we came around that melon truck and saw the two bike riders, Jack shouted, 'Love me, babe! Love me!'"

We sat quietly. The Polynesian girl brought fresh drinks.

"I would hate him for doing that," I said.

"I can't hate him." Katie adjusted her hat brim as the breeze lifted it a bit. "Did you really ever love me, Richard?" she asked.

"I still do."

"Would you do something lovely for me? Would you write me a long, newsy letter once a month? Tell me what you're doing. Tell me the inside story on your new life. Dolly says you have an apartment in Santa Monica now. Tell me who your friends are now. Tell me gossip about Adam. Are you working for Adam again?"

"Yeah. Adam's not so bad. He's very honest."

"I wish he had hired me at least once. He'll never do it now." She smiled. Her upper lip twisted to reveal her gums. I looked away.

"I'm afraid I'm already getting very tired. It's a real bother. I never used to get tired," she said. "But it's the excitement of seeing you—"

"I'll be going then," I said. "I'll come back tomorrow."

"Wait." She picked up her glass of ice water in two gloved hands and turned the straw around to her mouth. I looked away again. "It makes me happy to think I will be receiving regular letters from you," she said. "It's very pleasant living way out here on this rock in the ocean, but I do get curious about what's going on in LA. I think about you, Richard. I want you to share pieces of your life with me. I will live vicariously through you."

"I'd like that," I said.

She turned and looked directly at me. "I'm sorry I won't be able to answer your letters," she said.

She set the water glass down. Slowly she peeled off a glove. She showed me her bare right hand. Surgeons had put the hand back together, but arthritis had taken over. Her fingers were knobby and twisted.

"I can't hold a pen, you see."

"I'll write you anyhow."

"Thank you," she said. "I will look forward to your letters, and when I get strong enough I will phone you wherever you are in the world. I want you to go to interesting places with interesting people and tell me the dirty scoop on all of them."

"I love your voice on the phone," I said.

"We'll carry on with our romance, only now it will all be long distance."

"I'll win you over someday," I said.

"This isn't fair, Richard. You have a right to see who you are writing to." She reached the crippled hand up toward her hat brim.

"There's no need to do that," I said.

But she removed her hat. She took off the dark glasses. Her eyes were lopsided. Her left cheek was swollen and misshapen. Her skin was patchworked onto her skull by many surgeries.

"Now do you still love me?" she asked.

I leaned across the table and kissed her on the lips.

She burst into tears. Weeping, she grabbed the hat and the dark glasses and put them back on. She pulled the sheet close around her shoulders. She was sobbing and shaking.

Dolly rushed onto the deck. "It's time to go," she said to me.

"I want to tell her goodbye."

Dolly clutched my arm. "Please, Richard. She needs to rest, can't you see?"

I followed Dolly back through the house. The rooms were large and comfortable. There was a collection of seashells on the mantle in the living room. Dolly walked with me to the Volkswagen bus.

"Please don't come back. It's too hard on her," Dolly said. "I'll let you know when you can visit again. I can always find you by phoning Max. Please tell Adam that Katie sends her love, and thank him for all the flowers and for sending us a tape of *Giants*."

"You wouldn't shortstop my letters to her, would you? You'll let her read them?"

"Why wouldn't I? I'm not the house Nazi. My job is to serve Katie. I do what's best for her. Making her as happy as she can be under any circumstances is my goal in life."

• • •

Driving south to Lihue to catch a flight back to Honolulu, I stopped at a roadside tavern that had a thatched roof and a beer garden with a view of the surf. Half a dozen surfers were sitting on a plank table drinking beer.

I took a pitcher of beer to a table and sat alone. The jukebox was playing rock and roll. Staring at the ocean and smoking cigarettes while I emptied the pitcher, I reflected on Jack wrecking the Lamborghini. Did he do it on purpose? I didn't know. But I believed that when Jack defied the curse by lying to me in the Truth Room that he already knew he would soon be dead.

I thought of the figure on the deck wrapped in a sheet. Jack had taken her with him all right, just not all of her and not all the way. I decided I would try to take the rest of her with me the rest of the way. And right there at the table in the beer garden, I opened my notebook and started writing the first of my Dear Katie letters and thinking about this memoir.

I promised Jack in the Truth Room that I wouldn't write about him for ten years, but Jack lied to me in the Truth Room. That should free me of my promise, shouldn't it?

Afterword

This novel should place my father up there with the other greats in LA fiction, like Nathanael West, Raymond Chandler, and James Ellroy. Having lived here thirty years, I can say he nails the place—in a celebratory way. Whenever he came to town, my wife and I would drive him to all the old places, listening to his funny stories and insight. This book gives you an exciting plot building up to a dramatic climax, then the sad dénouement, and a final emotional climax that rips your heart out. It is one of his most entertaining books. Hope you enjoyed it.

Peace,
Alan Shrake

Growing up, I didn't comprehend the "royalty" that seemed to gravitate to my father—the friends, celebrities, groupies, hangers-on, and other characters who were lucky enough to be around him at any given time. Was it because he was tall, dark, and handsome? Or that he always picked up the tab? Or perhaps that he was a captivating storyteller? Well, yes, but I believe it was also because they could see straight into his heart and soul. Yearning to have his same passion for life, they respected his eagerness and generosity to share all the incredible—and credible—things he had encountered and that were still swirling around in his mind.

—Ben Shrake

. . .

"Turning thirty hit me only in a romantic poet sort of way, since we were all supposed to die pretty soon or else publish a major literary sensation. Turning forty and fifty didn't hit me at all, because I was too drunk to notice. I was sober at sixty but couldn't really comprehend it. Turning sixty-five definitely caught my attention, though it was only days before I was suddenly sixty-six. I still don't believe the numbers. I think I am about forty now, though the mirror disagrees and my social life is certainly different from what it was at forty, when we stayed up all night and were incredibly charming."

—Edwin "Bud" Shrake